PENGUIN BOOKS

Lifting the Veil

Ismat Chughtai was Urdu's most courageous and controversial woman writer of the twentieth century. She was the first Indian Muslim woman to earn both a bachelor of arts and a bachelor's in education degree. She began writing in secret due to violent opposition from her family, and many of her works were banned for their fiercely feminist content. Her most celebrated short story, *The Quilt*, which is included in this publication, was brought to court on charges of obscenity for its suggestion of homosexuality. Ismat Chughtai refused the court's request to apologize for the story, and eventually won the case. She died in 1991.

Kamila Shamsie is the author of seven novels, which have been translated into over 20 languages, including *Home Fire* (longlisted for the Man Booker Prize), *Burnt Shadows* (shortlisted for the Orange Prize for Fiction) and *A God in Every Stone* (shortlisted for the Bailey's Women's Prize for Fiction). Three of her other novels (*In the City by the Sea*, *Kartography*, *Broken Verses*) have received awards from the Pakistan Academy of Letters. A Fellow of the Royal Society of Literature, and one of Granta's 'Best of Young British Novelists', she grew up in Karachi, and now lives in London.

M. Asaduddin translates Assamese, Bengali, Urdu, Hindi and English. He writes on the art of translation and fiction in Indian languages. He has recently edited *For Freedom's Sake: Stories and Sketches of Saadat Hasan Manto* (Karachi: Oxford University Press, 2001) and edited with Mushirul Hasan *Image and Representation: Studies of Muslim Lives in India* (Delhi: Oxford University Press, 2000). A former fellow at the British Centre for Literary Translation, University of East Anglia, UK, he currently teaches English literature and Translation Studies at Jamia Millia Islamia, New Delhi.

Lifting the Veil

ISMAT CHUGHTAI

Selected and translated by M. Asaduddin

With an introduction by Kamila Shamsie

PENGUIN BOOKS

PENGUIN BOOKS

UK | USA | Canada | Ireland | Australia
India | New Zealand | South Africa

Penguin Books is part of the Penguin Random House group of companies
whose addresses can be found at global.penguinrandomhouse.com.

First published in India by Penguin Books India 2001
First published with a new introduction in Great Britain by Penguin Books 2018
001

Set in 11/13 pt Bembo Book MT Std
Typeset by Jouve (UK), Milton Keynes
Printed in Great Britain by Clays Ltd, St Ives plc

A CIP catalogue record for this book is available from the British Library

ISBN: 978–0–241–34643–3

www.greenpenguin.co.uk

For Nasreen
who has crossed many barriers

Contents

Acknowledgements

It is a pleasure for me to acknowledge my debt to the following who helped me generously at different stages of the work: G. J. V. Prasad for agreeing to edit the manuscript despite his other pressing commitments; Karthika and Diya at Penguin for being very supportive; Moazzam Sheikh and S. M. Mirza for reading some of the translations; Ralph Russell for allowing me to use his translations; and, finally, to Zubin, for many distractions.

Introduction

'Perhaps my mind is not an artist's brush . . . but an ordinary camera that records reality as it is.' So the pioneering Urdu writer Ismat Chughtai wrote in the essay 'In the Name of Those Married Women', which is included in this gloriously provocative collection of short stories and non-fiction. It's possible to view that line as a modest utterance, or one that reveals the not uncommon discomfort among women to claim the mantle of 'artist' for themselves. But Chughtai's words often carry a sting, and so it is here – and not only because of that equivocating 'perhaps'. The essay was her response to the controversy ignited by her short story 'The Quilt', published in 1942, which landed her in court under obscenity charges for its depictions of lesbian sex. In claiming to be 'an ordinary camera that records reality' Chughtai was reminding both her readers, and the man with whom she was directly arguing, that everything she writes about is all around us – it's merely hypocritical to pretend otherwise. Elsewhere in the essay she went further to pinpoint people's discomfort with the story in order to reveal a further hypocrisy – the gender of the writer caused more scandal than the gender of the two lovers under the quilt.

Read today, 'The Quilt' raises eyebrows for different reasons. In it, the unhappily married Begum (unhappy because her husband is gay and has a string of lovers to entertain him while she is neglected) turns to another woman out of frustration rather than as a genuine expression of desire. But at the heart of the story is Chughtai's insistence that female sexuality is as potent and powerful as male desire. Female sexuality within a patriarchal world is Chughtai's central concern through many of her stories: in 'The Homemaker' a woman who enjoys the power of her sexuality tries to resist marriage to the man whom she really loves, knowing it will ruin their relationship; in 'The Net' two young girls find their friendship pulled apart when an awareness of sensuality enters their lives via a silken garment; in 'Kafir' a Hindu boy and Muslim girl grow up together with desire pulling them one way and social norms pulling them the other. But whether she is writing of women's sexuality, or of an Englishman who tries to make India his home after the end of empire, although neither the Indians nor the English want him to do it (in 'Quit India'), or of an ageing man who is tormented by his own diminishing potency (in 'The Invalid'), Chughtai always has the most acute eye for human psychology married to a refusal to shy away from any topic that interests her. 'I think the first word articulated by me after birth was "why",' she wrote in her memoir.

Perhaps the most moving piece in here is 'My Friend, My Enemy!', the non-fiction account of her relationship with the Urdu short-story writer Saadat Hasan Manto. Their shared friendship extended to sharing the dock in court – they were charged together for obscenity, she for 'The Quilt' and he for his story 'Bu' – and it made the bond between them very strong, though Partition physically moved them apart: Manto went to Pakistan, while Chughtai stayed in India. Here is Chughtai describing their first meeting: 'In a few moments we began to argue vociferously. It was as though we had suffered a great loss from not having met each other for a long time and were now impatient to make good the loss.' Let other writers write of like-mindedness; in the world of Ismat Chughtai, human nature is never so neat. People are drawn to each other simply because they are – and then begins the difficult, joyous, messy business of being human together.

Kamila Shamsie

Gainda

'This is our shack,' Gainda and I told ourselves as we crawled into the dense shrubbery. Sitting on our haunches, we began to tidy up the ground with both hands. In a little while we were squatting on the smooth floor of the shack without a care in the world. After a brief tête-à-tête we began to play our favourite game – dulhan-dulhan. Gainda drew her smelly red dupatta over her face and sat huddled like a real bride. I lifted the veil gently and had a glimpse of her. Gainda's round face turned crimson as a fresh wave of blood coursed through her veins. Her eyelids fluttered uncontrollably, and she could barely stop herself from bursting into laughter.

'It's my turn now, Gainda . . . my turn,' I said, seething with envy.

'Hey, what's going on here!' Bhaiya lifted the branches and growled. In panic Gainda flung away her dupatta and plonked herself on the ground. Our hearts were beating wildly.

Not just Bhaiya, if anyone else had seen us playing the bride we would have been soundly thrashed. We always played this fascinating game stealthily.

'Well . . . we're just playing,' I said nonchalantly.

Bhaiya was in a good mood. He bent over to come in and squatted there with us. But soon he got bored.

'You little devils – what do you mean, sitting here like this?' he snapped, shielding his nose from the spreading branch.

'And you, Gainda!' He pinched her chubby cheek. 'You're wasting your time here. I'm going to tell Natha.'

Gainda opened her big brown eyes and looked around. 'Arré baap re!' she exclaimed, and ran away gathering her short skirt.

'Oh Gainda, don't go!' I implored and tried to restrain her.

'Dada will bash me up.' She was scared of Bhaiya.

'No, he won't. You've already finished your chores.'

'Okay, you can sit here,' Bhaiya said gently, as he pulled her towards him. Then he turned to me. 'But bibi, I'll certainly get you thrashed. You're spoiling your clothes romping on the ground.'

'Do your worst. I don't care!' I was scared stiff and began to brush the dust off my clothes.

'Gainda . . . Hey, Gainda . . . Where on earth are you?' Bahu's voice rang out. Gainda snatched her hands from Bhaiya's grip and shot away like an arrow.

The game was ruined in a minute. I flew at Bhaiya and scratched him. 'Go away,' I screamed.

'Witch,' he hissed, grinding his teeth. He gave me a wallop and strode off.

'Who should a widow dress herself for?' Gainda asked philosophically.

'Widow!' I was grinding a piece of red brick on stone to make sindoor. Wiping it on my shirt, I asked in amazement, 'Widow?'

'Of course. I'm a widow.' There seemed to be a trace of pride in her voice.

'And I?' I was dying with envy.

'You?' she said with barely concealed contempt. 'You're a virgin! Hee, hee, hee.' She was making fun of me.

My heart sank. Gainda always slighted me. I could not compete with her in anything. She had been married off in the month of Baisakh the year before. All dressed up in red garments, she became the sole owner of a set of glittering silver jewellery. For days together she strutted around showing off her finery. I, a wretched creature, was of no importance. I was either gaping at her or following her around like a wistful kitten. I counted her bangles, tied up her anklets or ran solicitously to lift her tinsel-trimmed dupatta when it touched the ground. Just how unjust could Amma be! I was reprimanded even if I drew the quilt over my face. Why? Oh, why?

'Why are you fiddling with the quilt?' she would yell, as though I would spoil it by using it as a veil!

If ever I asked for a dupatta, she would brush me off. 'No. You'll trail it in the muck, I know.'

Granted that I was younger than Gainda, but I wasn't too young to be a bride. I was ready to spend my whole life with the bride's veil over my face without complaint. Gainda's husband had died during the rainy season. The whole household was drowned in lamentations. Gainda's glass bangles were smashed, and she cried her heart out. 'Poor Gainda' – everybody sympathized with her and cuddled her. No one paid any heed to me. They all said that I was still a mere child, too small.

To hell with it. How long would I remain 'too small'? I had grown taller, and my blue salwar now reached my knees. Even the pink kurta had been handed down to Niru. My one and only shiny kurta had become too short. I was considered 'too awkward' when it came to the good things of life; and when some real issues were decided I was dismissed as a child. I could not decide – was I big or small? It was so confusing.

'So you don't deck yourself up anymore?' I asked Gainda idly.

'When a girl's husband is dead, who will she deck herself up for?' Gainda said stoically. 'A wife wears sindoor or bangles for her husband only.' She mouthed the cliché as though she believed in it firmly.

'Look, Gainda, what a lot of sindoor we've made!' I said as I gathered up the brick powder in my hand. Like a widow longing for sindoor, Gainda gazed at it wistfully. But soon we were smiling.

'Don't tell Bhabi . . . please . . .' She drew closer, and we got ready to put on the make-up. With the deftness of an experienced woman, I arranged her dishevelled hair, dabbing it with water, and sprinkled sindoor in her parting.

Gainda's face flushed a deep red, and she hid her face shyly in her dupatta. Then she rolled over with laughter.

'What are you doing?' I chided her. 'It'll get messy.'

'Now it's your turn,' said Gainda as she dabbed my hair with water.

'And how about my bindi?' I asked, my eyes screwed up.

'Sure, I'll take care of it,' she reassured me.

Soon we had completed our make-up. Sindoor in our partings, bindis on our forehead and dupattas drawn over our faces we sat demurely in a corner. We stole glances at each other's face and were struck by our own beauty. This made us all the more bashful.

Seeing Bhaiya coming, Gainda blushed all over. We hurriedly rubbed off our bindis and started laughing sheepishly. Bhaiya brushed me aside and went up to Gainda. She felt terribly shy. Grinding his teeth, Bhaiya pinched her cheeks hard. 'Ah, ah' – she shrank within herself.

'What the hell is this?' Bhaiya kicked the mound of brick powder in disgust. His loose kurta got stained as he had tried to sit on it.

'This is sindoor. We made it,' I said proudly. Bhaiya poked his finger in it and pressed Gainda's leg with his own. 'Come on, let me put sindoor on you.' Bhaiya sprinkled sindoor in Gainda's parting.

'No!' She rubbed it off with her palm.

'Bhaiya, Gainda is a widow. She doesn't wear sindoor.' I tried to impress him with my knowledge.

'Doesn't she? . . . The witch. Let me . . . see . . .' He clasped both her hands and pushed her over. Gainda hid her face.

'Gainda, I won't talk to you ever again.' This made Gainda uncover her face after all.

'Gainda,' Bhaiya sidled up to her. 'Will you marry me?'

'Go away.' She looked even more beautiful.

I tried to be coy like her. For hours together we would talk about marriage and feel bashful. Bhaiya could not even dream of what Aapa and Nanhi talked about and which we overheard, hiding under the bed.

'Why go away?' Bhaiya nudged her with his elbow. 'Tell me, will you marry . . .'

The sound of Bahu's anklets startled us. She was coming to the well. 'Gainda!' she bellowed, and the next moment she was upon us. 'Hey raand, what are you doing here? Go, warm the iron,' she growled. Gainda tried to slink away quietly, but Bahu leapt and caught her by her plaits. 'And how dare you braid your hair and make the parting?' She gave her a whack. Gainda made good her escape. Bhaiya and I winced.

Bahu's tyranny left me seething in anger. Whenever she beat Gainda, I would pay her back some way or the other. That day, too, the moment she went out of sight, I threw a handful of ashes in her pure, transparent starch. In the evening, Bhaiya gave Natha two sharp blows for ironing the shirt collars clumsily.

'Smell it.' Gainda thrust her blouse-front into my nose.

'Arré wah! Where did you get attar?'

'Bhaiya!' She cackled. I suppressed my envy and smiled.

'Gainda!' Bhaiya called out from the veranda. 'Take this coat for ironing.' She gave me a knowing wink and left smiling.

How did Gainda walk? With a supple gait as though she had not a bone in her body. When I walked, it was like a galloping mare. I am . . . oh God! I began to feel unsettled. Burning with jealousy I made for the garden, and there engaged myself in riling the water in the tank with a stick. The red brick sindoor powder still lay where it had been. Bhaiya sprinkled attar on Gainda. Perhaps he had forgotten me. But why? Or did he do so deliberately? Come to think of it, I was his own sister. And Gainda? She was nothing to him. I detested Bhaiya at that moment and kept on churning the muck furiously.

'Stop! What are you doing, bibi?' Mewaram yelled from behind me. I gazed at Mewa. 'He's nothing to me,' I said to myself. His hands were filthy. He never cleaned them. He was always digging dirt. Well, never mind.

'Mewa. Come here for a minute,' I crooned softly and started gazing at the water trickling down from the stick drop by drop.

'What is it?' He turned nonchalantly. Sliding his cap over his eyes, he scratched his nape.

'Take this sindoor, and sprinkle it on my head,' I ordered him demurely.

'You call this sindoor?' He laughed heartily and turned away.

'Listen . . . I . . . a widow. Wait a minute.' I had a new idea.

'What is it, bibi?' He stopped and turned towards me.

'Mewa . . . will you marry . . . ?' I asked with a fluttering heart.

'Marry! But I'm already married.' He began to knock the handle of the khurpi on a tree trunk.

'When?' I asked in a deadpan voice.

'Oh God! It's been ages,' he said as though it was nothing.

'I see. So you're a widower?' I had decided for him.

'Oh no!' He laughed. 'My malin is sitting there in the hut.'

'Are you married to malin, then?' I asked in surprise.

'Hmm.' And he walked off.

'So, the crone who I thought was Mewaram's mother was actually his wife! What a strange world!' I thought to myself and began to stir the stick more vigorously . . . I bent down to smell my chemise to get a whiff of the perfume, but there was none. On the contrary, there was the stink of the gravy I had spilled that morning. I was piqued.

Gainda was going towards Bhaiya's room with silent steps, carrying a pile of dried clothes wrapped in a towel. I looked through a chink in the door, curious, and followed her quietly like a kitten. Gainda sat on the floor counting the clothes while Bhaiya stood in a corner scratching his head. 'Wrong! You can't count,' he said abruptly as he clasped both her hands. She lifted her eyes for a fleeting moment to look at Bhaiya, frowned, and then broke into a smile. When he tried to grab her, she ducked and threw herself on the carpet face down and would not get up. When Bhaiya tickled her on her waist she sprang up. Then, as Bhaiya moved closer, she gave him a sharp slap across his face.

It was a miracle that I did not faint from the shock. Slap Bhaiya! Bhaiya, who was feared by everyone in the house. How did she dare to slap him? I was ready to bolt as I thought Bhaiya would now strangle her to death. He grabbed her two hands and pulled her towards him. I held my breath . . . oh no! I ran away, overwhelmed by fear and wonder, and paused only when I reached the dense cluster of the kamarakhs. With my heart pounding like bellows, my ears buzzing, my tongue parched and my body shaking all over, I crouched there nervously for a long time.

I sat there lost in thought – first with eyes closed and then, with eyes wide open. But I could not make head or tail of it. Why didn't I understand such a lot of things? In the desolate, hot afternoon I waged a weary struggle to unravel strange riddles but could not. My eyes brimmed over with tears as though someone had beaten me severely.

I saw Gainda leap to the veranda. Only she could provide answers to my queries. Gainda always shared her secrets with me.

'What happened?' I asked anxiously.

'Nothing,' she said dismissively. But soon after, we sat in a quiet corner and talked of many 'strange' incidents. Gainda was a treasure-trove of such events.

'But . . . why all this?' I wondered as I listened to her. Gainda went off to prepare the starch, but I kept sitting there, lost in thought.

My mind rambled on – I thought of picking up little kamarakh beads and stringing them into a necklace, completing the canal that I had dug the previous day to water the plants, going to the shrubbery to have a look-in or, at least, ascertaining where the partridge had begun to lay eggs. But I wasn't interested in any of this that day. No game held any appeal for me. All I wanted was to sit quietly, eyes closed, and dream of a tiny little bride, and go on dreaming about her. What could I do, after all? Just look at Gainda! And me? The sound of Mewa's footsteps startled me. A sweet thought, a desire invaded my mind once again, and hiding my face with both hands I threw myself on the ground, face down.

'Tch . . . tch . . . bibi, why are you wallowing in the dirt? Get up! Quick!' he said.

I imagined someone was trying to lift me, and I wouldn't move. Someone was tickling me . . . but . . .

'Get up, or I'll tell Bhaiya that you're spoiling your dress,' he threatened, standing at a distance like a pole, not the way Bhaiya had stood, scratching his head. Totally indifferent to my feelings, he was paring a bamboo stick.

'Will you get up or . . .' He strode off to complain to Bhaiya. Just imagine how I fumed in anger.

'Pig! Who the hell are you? . . . Take this . . .' I screamed and hurled a pebble at his knee.

'Hey . . . just wait! I'll get you nicely whacked. She wanders all afternoon in the scorching sun and rolls in dirt. Try to stop her and . . . Wait!' He limped away, wincing.

'This Mewaram is a hopeless bloke. Never has a good word for me. As though he's the only man around!' I was so furious that I snapped off one by one all the branches of the jasmine trees that he had planted with great care. 'This is the right punishment for such a fellow!' I told myself and ran back into the house in tears.

Who was there to share my hurt? Bhaiya never spared a thought for me, Amma never cuddled me. The result – I became very obstinate. Because of this sense of deprivation, I made everyone my enemy. Throughout the day I wandered about aimlessly and fought with everyone. That is why, when Baaji came from her in-laws' place to visit us, she decided to take me along with her. I regretted having to leave Gainda, but the prospect of travel was exciting and made me forget everything.

Gainda, Bhaiya, Mewa and the memories associated with them receded into the back of my mind in two years. By the time I returned the world had changed. Bhaiya had been sent to Delhi, and his room was now used to put up guests. Mewa had died of pneumonia, obviously he had not given up his habit of messing with dirt and had caught a cold. It was surprising that I did not go delirious with joy and surprise when I got to know that Gainda had had a baby. But when I expressed my happiness, I was reprimanded. I couldn't see why. However, I heard snippets of conversation such as Shaikhani's: 'She tried hard . . . but . . .' I could not catch the rest.

'Oh my God! He was ready for murder and mayhem. What a lot of trouble it was!' Biwi said. 'I sent him off to Delhi immediately. A studious boy . . . these low-caste bitches! Trap . . . the nobles.' Though I listened to her with bated breath, I could not make any sense of it.

'Gainda's child!' I repeated to myself over and over again in my bed. 'But how?' My wonder did not cease.

'It would have been disastrous if Sarkar had got wind of it. That is why I turned her out without delay,' Biwi's voice rang out once again.

Slowly I began to understand. Past events flashed through my mind like images on a screen, and my heart sank. I was dying to see Gainda's child. I saw in my imagination a tiny baby, like the one we had met on the train to Lahore. We did not have children in the family, neither did they come with guests. My heart went out to Gainda's child. In the darkness I felt as though tiny hands were touching my neck and chin. I lay still lest the little, delicate fingers moved away.

That night, hundreds of children appeared in my dream. Some of them resembled us – me, Gainda, Bhaiya, even the dead Mewaram. Hundreds of frolicking children – bald heads, heads with hair, round heads, tiny hands. The whole universe teemed with children like countless grains of sand.

I quietly slipped away the following morning to see Gainda's baby. Gainda was busy with some chores. Startled by my footsteps, she quickly covered herself and looked at me with fear in her eyes. When I moved closer, I saw the tiny, half-naked human form on her knees, his mouth open in wonder.

'Ai, how tiny he is!' I squatted by her side. Gainda had become thin like a stick. She was nervous and turned her face away.

'What a little darling!' I crooned with joy and sat on the floor. I felt like holding Gainda and her child tight to my heart. I don't know why tears welled up in my eyes.

'Let me hold the baby . . .' I held out my hands. But Gainda sat quietly, wiping her tears.

'You're crying?' My voice choked. 'Such a darling of a baby, and you're crying! Give him to me.'

She kept wiping her tears and did not even touch the baby. I tried to pick him but he was like a slippery lump of flesh, and I could not lift him.

'Oh Gainda, please lift him for me.' I adopted the flattering tone with which I used to cajole her.

Gainda peered into my eyes searching for something. She seemed reassured; as though she had found whatever she was looking for. She effortlessly lifted the baby and put him in my arms. I was amazed by the practised way she did it. The baby was light as a wisp of cotton wool.

I sat on the gunny sack with the baby in my lap as Gainda recounted a hundred thousand 'strange' happenings. How she was beaten up for months together! Gainda, hardly fourteen or fifteen, did not herself understand many things. How could she explain them to me? We stopped invariably with, 'How?', 'Why?', 'How strange!'

When Bahu had had that coal-black baby who died a few days after birth, how they had sung and danced! Tons of ghee and jaggery had been forced down her gullet. And now when Gainda had had such a beautiful baby, what did they do? Nothing. She was beaten to a pulp and abandoned without food. She survived somehow.

Then, this tiny Lallu was born. He had just two shirts to beat the severe cold with, and cried all night long. Bahu cursed him, saying, why didn't he die and leave them in peace. Gainda had tied a black string around Lallu's ankle to ward off the evil eye. She expressed the view that in the entire world, Lallu was the most lovable creature – and Bhaiya and I too. At Bhaiya's name her eyes lit up with their old sparkle. And then she could not stop herself from talking about him.

'Now he doesn't come even during the holidays.'

'He'll come this time. Last year he had gone down to Mussoorie,' I said, counting Lallu's fingers.

'Bibi, will you write to him?' she asked wistfully.

'Sure,' I nodded vigorously.

'Will you tell him that Lallu sends his salaam and remembers him often?'

'Yes,' I said, though I knew that Lallu could not utter a syllable.

'Also write that he must bring a red vest for him like the one Basanti's son wears.'

'And . . . that . . .' her yearning gaze was fixed on the distant horizon, 'he must come this time, at least for a few days.' It was as though she were imploring someone. She broke into a smile and kept talking while I ran my fingers through Lallu's hair.

'Look, Gainda . . . how he nibbles . . .' I said as I felt his gums tickle my fingers.

'He's hungry.' Gainda became bashful.

'Feed him, or he'll start crying.'

Gainda lifted the baby in her frail arms and clasped him to her breast. Then she began to laugh, hiding her face in her sari.

I kept looking at Lallu's soft lips as he sucked his mother's milk, breathing noisily. The little mother took care of him, though rather clumsily.

The Quilt

In winter, when I put a quilt over myself, its shadows on the wall seem to sway like an elephant. That sends my mind racing into the labyrinth of times past. Memories come crowding in.

Sorry. I'm not going to regale you with a romantic tale about my quilt. It's hardly a subject for romance. It seems to me that the blanket, though less comfortable, does not cast shadows as terrifying as the quilt dancing on the wall.

I was then a small girl and fought all day with my brothers and their friends. Often I wondered why the hell I was so aggressive. At my age, my other sisters were busy drawing admirers, while I fought with any boy or girl I ran into.

That was why, when my mother went to Agra for about a week, she left me with an adopted sister of hers. She knew that there was no one in that house, not even a mouse, with whom I could get into a fight. It was a severe punishment for me! Amma left me with Begum Jaan, the same lady whose quilt is etched in my memory like the scar left by a blacksmith's brand. Her poor parents had agreed to marry her off to the nawab who was of 'ripe years' because he was very virtuous. No one had ever seen a nautch girl or prostitute in his house. He had performed hajj and helped several others undertake the holy pilgrimage.

He, however, had a strange hobby. Some people are crazy enough to cultivate interests like breeding pigeons or watching cockfights. Nawab Saheb had only contempt for such disgusting sports. He kept an open house for students – young, fair, slender-waisted boys whose expenses were borne by him.

Having married Begum Jaan, he tucked her away in the house with his other possessions and promptly forgot her. The frail, beautiful Begum wasted away in anguished loneliness.

One did not know when Begum Jaan's life began – whether it was when she committed the mistake of being born or when she came to the nawab's house as his bride, climbed the four-poster bed and started counting her days. Or was it when she watched through the drawing-room door the increasing number of firm-calved, supple-waisted boys and the delicacies that were sent for them from the kitchen! Begum Jaan would have glimpses of them in their perfumed, flimsy shirts and feel as though she was being hauled over burning embers!

Or did it start when she gave up on amulets, talismans, black magic and other ways of retaining the love of her straying husband? She arranged for night-long readings from the Quran, but in vain. One cannot draw blood from a stone. The nawab didn't budge an inch. Begum Jaan was heartbroken and turned to books. But she found no relief. Romantic novels and sentimental verse depressed her even more. She began to spend sleepless nights, yearning for a love that had never been.

She felt like throwing all her clothes into the fire. One dressed up to impress people. But the nawab didn't have a moment to spare for her. He was too busy chasing the gossamer shirts. Nor did he allow her to go out. Relatives, however, would come for visits and stay on for months while she remained a prisoner in the house. These relatives, freeloaders all, made her blood boil. They helped themselves to rich food and got warm clothes made for themselves while she stiffened with cold despite the new cotton stuffed in her quilt. As she tossed and turned, her quilt made newer shapes on the wall, but none of them held any promise of life for her. Then why must one live? Particularly, such a life as hers . . . But then, Begum Jaan started living, and lived her life to the full.

It was Rabbu who rescued her from the fall.

Soon her thin body began to fill out. Her cheeks began to glow, and she blossomed. It was a special oil massage that brought life back to the half-dead Begum Jaan. Sorry, you won't find the recipe for this oil even in the most exclusive magazines.

When I first saw Begum Jaan, she was around forty. Reclining on the couch, she looked a picture of grandeur. Rabbu sat behind her, massaging her waist. A purple shawl covered her feet as she sat in regal splendour, a veritable maharani. I was fascinated by her looks and felt like sitting by her for hours, just adoring her. Her complexion was marble white, without a speck of ruddiness. Her hair was black and always bathed in oil. I had never seen the parting of her hair crooked, nor a single hair out of place. Her eyes were black and the elegantly plucked eyebrows seemed like two bows spread over the demure eyes. Her eyelids were heavy and her eyelashes dense. The most fascinating feature of her face, however, was her lips – usually coloured with lipstick and with a mere trace of down on her upper lip. Long hair covered her temples. Sometimes her face seemed to change shape under my gaze and looked as though it were the face of a young boy . . .

Her skin was white and smooth, as though it had been stitched tightly over her body. When she stretched her legs for the massage, I stole a glance, enraptured by their sheen. She was very tall and the ample flesh on her body made her look stately and magnificent. Her hands were large and smooth, her waist exquisitely formed. Rabbu used to massage her back for hours together. It was as though the massage was one of the basic necessities of life. Rather, more important than life's necessities.

Rabbu had no other household duties. Perched on the couch she was always massaging some part or the other of Begum Jaan's body. At times I could hardly bear it – the sight of Rabbu massaging or rubbing at all hours. Speaking for myself, if anyone were to touch my body so often, I would certainly rot to death.

But even this daily massage wasn't enough. On the days when Begum Jaan took a bath, Rabbu would massage her body with a variety of oils and pastes for two hours. And she would massage with such vigour that even imagining it made me sick. The doors would be closed, the braziers would be lit, and then the session would begin. Usually Rabbu was the only person allowed to remain inside on such occasions. Other maids handed over the necessary things at the door, muttering disapproval.

In fact, Begum Jaan was afflicted with a persistent itch. Despite the oils and balms, the stubborn itch remained. Doctors and hakeems pronounced that nothing was wrong, the skin was unblemished. It could be an infection under the skin. 'These doctors are crazy . . . There's nothing wrong with you,' Rabbu would say, smiling while she gazed at Begum Jaan dreamily.

Rabbu. She was as dark as Begum Jaan was fair, as purple as the other was white. She seemed to glow like heated iron. Her face was scarred by smallpox. She was short, stocky and had a small paunch. Her hands were small but agile, and her large, swollen lips were always wet. A strange sickening stench exuded from her body. And her tiny, puffy hands moved dexterously over Begum Jaan's body – now at her waist, now at her thighs, and now dashing to her ankles. Whenever I sat by Begum Jaan, my eyes would remain glued to those roving hands.

All through the year Begum Jaan wore white and billowing Hyderabadi jaali karga kurtas and brightly coloured pyjamas. And even when it was warm and the fan was on, she would cover herself with a light shawl. She loved winter. I too liked to be in her house in that season. She rarely moved out. Lying on the carpet she would munch dry fruits as Rabbu rubbed her back. The other maids were jealous of Rabbu. The witch! She ate, sat and even slept with Begum Jaan! Rabbu and Begum Jaan were the subject of their gossip during leisure hours. Someone would mention their names, and the whole group would burst into loud guffaws. What juicy stories they made up about them! Begum Jaan was oblivious to all this, cut off as she was from the world outside. Her existence was centred on herself and her itch.

I have already mentioned that I was very young at that time and was in love with Begum Jaan. She, too, was fond of me. When Amma decided to go to Agra, she left me with Begum Jaan for a week. She knew that if left alone at home I would fight with my brothers or roam around. The arrangement pleased both Begum Jaan and me. After all, she was Amma's adopted sister. Now the question was . . . where would I sleep? In Begum Jaan's room, naturally. A small bed was placed alongside hers. Till ten or eleven at night, we chatted and played 'Chance'. Then I went to bed. Rabbu was still rubbing her back as I fell asleep. 'Ugly woman!' I thought to myself.

I woke up at night and was scared. It was pitch dark and Begum Jaan's quilt was shaking vigorously, as though an elephant was struggling inside.

'Begum Jaan . . .' I could barely form the words out of fear. The elephant stopped shaking, and the quilt came down.

'What is it? Get back to sleep.' Begum Jaan's voice seemed to come from somewhere else.

'I'm scared,' I whimpered.

'Get back to sleep. What's there to be scared of? Recite the Ayatul Kursi.'

'All right . . .' I began to recite the prayer, but each time I reached 'ya lamu ma bain . . .' I forgot the lines though I knew the entire Ayat by heart.

'May I come to you, Begum Jaan?'

'No, child . . . Get back to sleep.' Her tone was rather abrupt. Then I heard two people whispering. Oh God, who was this other person? I was really afraid.

'Begum Jaan . . . I think a thief has entered the room.'

'Go back to sleep, child . . . There's no thief.'

This was Rabbu's voice. I drew the quilt over my face and fell asleep.

By morning I had totally forgotten the terrifying scene enacted at night. I have always been superstitious – night fears, sleepwalking and talking in my sleep were daily occurrences in my childhood. Everyone used to say that I was possessed by evil spirits. So the incident slipped from my memory. The quilt looked perfectly innocent in the morning.

But the following night I woke up again and heard Begum Jaan and Rabbu arguing in subdued tones. I could not hear what the upshot of the tiff was, but I heard Rabbu crying. Then came the slurping sound of a cat licking a plate . . . I was scared and went back to sleep.

The next day Rabbu went to see her son, an irascible young man. Begum Jaan had done a lot to help him out – bought him a shop, got him a job in the village. But nothing really pleased him. He stayed with Nawab Saheb for some time. The nawab got him new clothes and other gifts, but he ran away for no good reason and never came back, even to see Rabbu . . .

Rabbu had gone to a relative's house to see her son. Begum Jaan was reluctant to let her go but realized that Rabbu was helpless. So she didn't prevent her from going.

All through the day Begum Jaan was out of sorts. Every joint ached, but she couldn't bear anyone's touch. She didn't eat anything and moped in bed all day.

'Shall I rub your back, Begum Jaan . . . ?' I asked zestfully as I shuffled the deck of cards. She peered at me.

'Shall I, really?' I put away the cards and began to rub her back while Begum Jaan lay there quietly.

Rabbu was due to return the next day . . . but she didn't. Begum Jaan grew more and more irritable. She drank cup after cup of tea, and her head began to ache.

I resumed rubbing her back, which was smooth as the top of a table. I rubbed gently and was happy to be of some use to her.

'A little harder . . . open the straps,' Begum Jaan said.

'Here . . . a little below the shoulder . . . that's right . . . Ah! What pleasure . . .' She expressed her satisfaction between sensuous breaths. 'A little further . . .' Begum Jaan instructed though her hands could easily reach that spot. But she wanted me to stroke it. How proud I felt! 'Here . . . oh, oh, you're tickling me . . . Ah!' She smiled. I chatted away as I continued to massage her.

'I'll send you to the market tomorrow . . . What do you want? . . . A doll that sleeps and wakes up at your will?'

'No, Begum Jaan . . . I don't want dolls . . . Do you think I'm still a child?'

'So, you're an old woman, then,' she laughed. 'If not a doll, I'll get you a babua . . . Dress it up yourself. I'll give you a lot of old clothes. Okay?'

'Okay,' I answered.

'Here.' She would take my hand and place it where it itched and I, lost in the thought of the babua, kept scratching her listlessly while she talked.

'Listen . . . you need some more frocks. I'll send for the tailor tomorrow and ask him to make new ones for you. Your mother has left some dress material.'

'I don't want that red material . . . It looks so cheap.' I was chattering, oblivious of where my hands travelled. Begum Jaan lay still . . . Oh God! I jerked my hand away.

'Hey girl, watch where your hands are . . . You hurt my ribs.' Begum Jaan smiled mischievously. I was embarrassed.

'Come here and lie down beside me . . .' She made me lie down with my head on her arm. 'How skinny you are . . . your ribs are showing.' She began counting my ribs.

I tried to protest.

'Come on, I'm not going to eat you up. How tight this sweater is! And you don't have a warm vest on.' I felt very uncomfortable.

'How many ribs does one have?' She changed the topic.

'Nine on one side, ten on the other.' I blurted out what I'd learnt in school, rather incoherently.

'Take away your hand . . . Let's see . . . one, two, three . . .'

I wanted to run away, but she held me tightly. I tried to wriggle away, and Begum Jaan began to laugh loudly. To this day, whenever I am reminded of her face at that moment, I feel jittery. Her eyelids had drooped, her upper lip showed a black shadow and tiny beads of sweat sparkled on her lips and nose despite the cold. Her hands were as cold as ice but clammy as though the skin had been stripped off. She wore a shawl, and in the fine karga kurta, her body shone like a ball of dough. The heavy gold buttons of the kurta were undone.

It was evening, and the room was getting enveloped in darkness. A strange fear overcame me. Begum Jaan's deep-set eyes focused on me and I felt like crying. She was pressing me as though I were a clay doll and the odour of her warm body made me want to throw up. But she was like a person possessed. I could neither scream nor cry.

After some time she stopped and lay back exhausted. She was breathing heavily, and her face looked pale and dull. I thought she was going to die and rushed out of the room . . .

Thank God Rabbu returned that night. Scared, I went to bed rather early and pulled the quilt over me. But sleep evaded me for hours.

Amma was taking so long to return from Agra! I was so terrified of Begum Jaan that I spent the whole day in the company of the maids. I felt too nervous to step into her room. What could I have said to anyone? That I was afraid of Begum Jaan? Begum Jaan who was so attached to me?

That day, Rabbu and Begum Jaan had another tiff. This did not augur well for me because Begum Jaan's thoughts were immediately directed towards me. She realized that I was wandering outdoors in the cold and might die of pneumonia. 'Child, do you want to put me to shame in public? If something happened to you, it would be a disaster.' She made me sit beside her as she washed her face and hands in the basin. Tea was set on a tripod next to her.

'Make tea, please . . . and give me a cup,' she said as she wiped her face with a towel. 'I'll change in the meantime.'

I drank tea while she dressed. During her body massage she sent for me repeatedly. I went in, keeping my face turned away, and ran out after doing the errand. When she changed her dress I began to feel jittery. Turning my face away from her I sipped my tea.

My heart yearned in anguish for Amma. This punishment was much more severe than I deserved for fighting with my brothers. Amma always disliked my playing with boys. Now tell me, were they man-eaters that they would eat up her darling? And who were the boys? My own brothers and their puny little friends! She was a believer in strict segregation for women. But Begum Jaan here was more terrifying than all the loafers of the world. Left to myself, I would have run out into the street – even further away! But I was helpless and had to stay there much against my wish.

Begum Jaan had decked herself up elaborately and perfumed herself with the warm scent of attar. Then she began to shower me with affection. 'I want to go home,' was my answer to all her suggestions. Then I started crying.

'There, there . . . come near me . . . I'll take you to the market today. Okay?'

But I kept up the refrain of wanting to go home. All the toys and sweets of the world held no interest for me.

'Your brothers will bash you up, you witch.' She tapped me affectionately on my cheek.

'Let them.'

'Raw mangoes are sour to the taste, Begum Jaan,' hissed Rabbu, burning with jealousy.

Then, Begum Jaan had a fit. The gold necklace she had offered me moments ago was flung to the ground. The muslin net dupatta was torn to shreds. And her hair-parting, which was never crooked, became a tangled mess.

'Oh! Oh! Oh!' she screamed between spasms. I ran out.

Begum Jaan regained her senses after a great deal of fuss and ministrations. When I peered into the room on tiptoe, I saw Rabbu rubbing her body, nestling against her waist.

'Take off your shoes,' Rabbu said while stroking Begum Jaan's ribs. Mouse-like, I snuggled into my quilt.

There was that peculiar noise again. In the dark Begum Jaan's quilt was once again swaying like an elephant. 'Allah! Ah! . . .' I moaned in a feeble voice. The elephant inside the quilt heaved up and then sat down. I was mute. The elephant started to sway again. I was scared stiff. But I had resolved to switch on the light that night, come what may. The elephant started shaking once again, and it seemed as though it was trying to squat. There was the sound of someone smacking her lips, as though savouring a tasty pickle. Now I understood! Begum Jaan had not eaten anything the whole day. And Rabbu, the witch, was a notorious glutton. She must be polishing off some goodies. Flaring my nostrils I inhaled deeply. There was only the scent of attar, sandalwood and henna, nothing else.

Once again the quilt started swinging. I tried to lie still, but the quilt began to assume such grotesque shapes that I was shaken. It seemed as though a large frog was inflating itself noisily and was about to leap on to me.

'Aa . . . Ammi . . .' I whimpered. No one paid any heed. The quilt crept into my brain and began to grow larger. I stretched my leg nervously to the other side of the bed, groped for the switch and turned the light on. The elephant somersaulted inside the quilt which deflated immediately. During the somersault, a corner of the quilt rose by almost a foot . . .

Good God! I gasped and sank deeper into my bed.

The Wedding Suit

A clean sheet was spread, once again, on the chauki, the wooden board, that day. Sunlight filtered in through the chinks of the tiled roof making odd patterns in the courtyard. The women of the neighbourhood were sitting around silently with awed anticipation as though a momentous event was going to unfold. Mothers clasped their babies to their breasts. Only some sickly, irritable infant was occasionally heard crying.

'No, no, my darling,' the scrawny mother would say, letting the baby lie on her knees and bouncing him as though she were shaking a winnowing tray. The baby, after a few hiccups, would fall silent.

That day many expectant eyes were riveted on the thoughtful face of Kubra's mother. The two short pieces of cloth had been strung together, but no one would dare to apply the scissors at this point. As far as cutting and measuring cloth was concerned, Kubra's mother's skill was undisputed. No one knew how many dowries she had prepared with her shrunken hands, how many suits she had stitched for new mothers and their babies, and how many shrouds she had measured and ripped. Whenever someone in the mohalla ran short of fabric while stitching and all her efforts at measuring and cutting bore no fruit, the case was brought to Kubra's mother. She would smoothen the edge of the fabric, break the starch in it, arrange the fabric sometimes in the form of a triangle, sometimes in the shape of a square. Then, her imagination fiercely at work with her scissors, she would measure the cloth in a final glance and break into a smile.

'Well, the sleeve and the hem will come out of this. For the lapels, take some snippets from my sewing box.' And thus the crisis would come to a resolution. She would cut the cloth and hand over the bundle of snippets to the woman.

But that day the piece of cloth was smaller than usual, and everyone was sure that Kubra's mother would fail to show her wizardry this time round. That is why they were all looking at her intently, holding their breath. Kubra's mother's face bore a resolute look without any trace of anxiety. She scrutinized the four-finger-long piece of fabric. The sunlight reflected on the red twill and lit up her bluish-yellow face, which suddenly brought to light the deep wrinkles on her face, like darkening clouds. It was as though a forest had caught fire. She smiled and picked up the scissors.

A deep sigh of relief rose from the crowd of women. Babies were separated from breasts and laid on the ground, eagle-eyed virgins leapt to thread the needles and newly wed brides put on their thimbles. By that time Kubra's mother's scissors were running along the fabric.

At the far end of the seh-dari, the veranda, Hamida sat thoughtfully on a couch, her chin resting on her palm, her feet dangling.

When lunch was over, Bi Amma would settle down on the chauki in the seh-dari, open her sewing box and spread out her a multicoloured array of snippets. Sitting on the stone mortar and scrubbing utensils, Kubra would observe the red-coloured snippets and a tinge of red would flush her pale, muddy complexion. As Bi Amma spread the network of design made of silver sequins on her knees with her delicate hands, her wilted face would suddenly brighten up with hope. Golden flowerets would glow like tiny candles against her deep, moat-like wrinkles. At every stitch, the golden embroidery sparkled and the candles fluttered.

No one knew when the sequins for the muslin dupatta were first made and put into the depths of the heavy, coffin-like wooden box. The edges of the sequinned network had faded, so had the gilt border; the spools of gold thread wore a forlorn look. But there was no sign of Kubra's wedding party yet.

When one suit of clothes meant to be worn on chauthi got old, it was set aside with the remark that the bride would wear it on her second or later visits to her parents and preparations on a new suit would start, raising new hopes. After a careful search, a new bride would be selected for the first snip and the sheet would be spread on the chauki in the seh-dari. The women of the mohalla gathered with babies at their breasts and paandaans in hands, their anklets tinkling.

'The border of the underwear can be taken off this, but there won't be enough for the bodice.'

'Well, sister! Just listen to her! Are you going to use the twill for the bodice, surely not?' Everyone looked worried. Like a silent alchemist, Kubra's mother measured the length and width with her eyes while the women whispered jokes among themselves about undergarments and broke into guffaws. While someone burst into a wedding song, another, now emboldened, lustily sang a number about wicked in-laws. This led to dirty jokes and giggles. At this juncture the unmarried girls were ordered to leave the scene, to cover their heads and sit somewhere near the tiling. As another burst of laughter rang out, the girls would heave deep sighs and long for the day when they would be allowed to join in the laughter.

Far away from this hustle and bustle, Kubra, overcome by shyness, sat in the mosquito-infested room, her head bent low. Meanwhile, the sartorial process would reach a delicate point. Some gusset would be cut against the grain and the women would be at their wits' end. Kubra would watch nervously from a chink in the door.

That was the problem! Not a damned suit could be stitched without some hassle or the other. If a gusset was cut on the reverse, there was sure to be some trouble arising out of the gossip of the naain, the barber woman. Either the groom would be found to have a mistress or his mother would provide a hurdle by demanding solid gold bracelets. If the hem got warped, it meant that the marriage would fall through due to disagreement on mehr, or there would be a scuffle over the bedstead with legs covered with silver work. The omens associated with the suit of chauthi were indeed portentous. In case of any mishap, all of Bi Amma's resourcefulness and practice would be in vain. No one knew why, at the critical moment, some trivial problem would crop up and hamper progress.

Kubra's mother had started to prepare her dowry at an early stage. Even if a small snippet was left, she would immediately stitch the cover of a bottle with it, decorating it with lace of gold thread, and then put it away. There's no telling about a girl – she grows up by leaps and bounds, as a cucumber grows. When the marriage took place, such farsightedness would pay off.

However, after Abba's death, even such foresight came to no avail. At that moment Hamida was reminded of her father. Abba was tall and frail, like Muharram's aalam. If he bent down once, it was difficult for him to straighten up. At the crack of dawn he would break a neem twig to brush his teeth, and seating Hamida on his knees, he would get lost in his world of thought. As he brushed absent-mindedly, sometimes a small splinter from the twig would find its way into his gullet, and he would start coughing. Hamida would get down from his knees in a huff. She didn't like her father shaking all over with the cough. Her father would laugh at her childish pique, and the phlegm would get stuck in his chest, making him writhe like a slaughtered pigeon. Then Bi Amma would come to his rescue and thump his back.

'God forbid! What sort of laughter is this?'

In the midst of the choking, Abba would lift his bloodshot eyes and smile helplessly. The coughing would stop after sometime, leaving him panting.

'Why don't you take some medicine? I've asked you time and again to do so.'

'The doctor at the main hospital says that I'll need injections. He also advises me to take a litre of milk and fifty grams of butter daily.'

'Shame on them, these doctors! The cough is already there, and on top of it he's advising you to take fat. Won't it create more phlegm? Show yourself to some hakeem.'

'I will.' Abba would draw on the hookah and choke once again.

'A curse on this hookah! It's because of this that you've got the cough. Do you ever think of your grown-up daughter?'

Abba would cast a pitiful look at Kubra's youth. Kubra had grown up to be a young woman. Whoever said that she had 'become' a young woman? It was as though right from the day of her bismillah ceremony she had heard intimations of her approaching youth and had been cowering back from it. What kind of youth was it that fairies never danced before her eyes, nor did curled ringlets play coquettishly with her cheeks? She did not experience any storm raging in her breast, neither did she impetuously ask the monsoon clouds the whereabouts of her beloved. Adolescence crept up on her unawares, with silent steps, as it were, and left her no one knew when! Sweet years gave way to sour ones, and finally they became bitter.

One day Abba stumbled on the threshold and fell on his face. Neither a hakeem's prescription nor a doctor's could get him on his feet again.

After that, Hamida gave up making demands for sweet roti, and Kubra's marriage proposals somehow lost their way. It was as if no one ever knew that behind the sack-cloth curtain someone's youth was at its last gasp. And there was another whose youth was raising its head like a serpent's hood.

But Bi Amma's routine did not change. She would spread the colourful snippets in the same way on the seh-dari and continue her doll game.

During the month of Shab-e-baraat, scrounging and economizing, she somehow managed to buy a crêpe dupatta that cost her seven and a half rupees. She just had to buy it. A telegram had arrived from Kubra's maternal uncle saying that his eldest son Rahat was coming to stay with them during his police training. Bi Amma began to drive herself mad with worry. It seemed as though it was not Rahat but a veritable baraat that had arrived on the threshold. And she had not yet chipped the gold leaf for the bride's hair-parting! Too nervous to do anything by herself, she sent for Bundu's mother, who was her moohboli behn, her adopted sister. The message was: 'Sister, may you find me dead if you don't come immediately.'

Then the two women began their hushed whispers. Once in a while they would glance at Kubra, who, sitting on the veranda, would be winnowing rice. She knew well what these whispers were about.

Bi Amma pulled out the clove-shaped earrings weighing four massas from her ears and handed them over to her adopted sister so that she could buy a tola of fettered gold, six massas of gold leaf and stars, and a quarter yard of twill. The room in the front was swept and dusted clean. A little lime was brought, and Kubra painted the walls with her own hands. The walls became sparkling white but the skin of her palm came off because of the lime, and that is why when she sat down to grind spices that evening, her head began to spin and she fell. She kept tossing and turning all night long, partly because of her palms, and partly because Rahat was to arrive by the morning train.

'Oh God, dear God! Let Aapa be blessed with good fortune this time. Oh God, I shall say a hundred voluntary prayers in Your exalted presence,' Hamida prayed after her fajr namaaz, the dawn prayers.

By the time Rahat arrived, Kubra had already hidden herself in the mosquito-infested room. Rahat helped himself to the breakfast of sewaiyaan and parantha and retired to the sitting room. Then Kubra came out from the room with halting steps like a newly wedded bride and picked up the used dishes.

'Bi Aapa, let me wash them for you,' Hamida said mischievously.

'No.' Kubra became bashful and lowered her head.

Hamida kept teasing while Bi Amma smiled and stitched the gold lace on the dupatta. The gold flowerets, the cockades and the silver anklets went the way of the clove-shaped earrings. And finally the bangles, too, which Manjhle Maamu had given her on the day marking the end of her mourning after Abba's death. Eating simple food herself, she would fry paranthas, kofta and meat pulao for Rahat every other day. The aroma of kofta and meat pulao filled the air. She would swallow her dry morsels with water but feed her would-be son-in-law rich meat dishes.

'These are hard times, my child,' she would try to pacify Hamida, who would go into a sulk seeing her mother's behaviour. 'So we have to starve to feed the "son-in-law",' Hamida thought. Bi Aapa would get up at the crack of dawn and begin doing her chores like a machine. Taking just a glass of water herself, she would fry paranthas for Rahat and keep the milk on the boil until a thick layer of cream formed over it. If she could, she would have cut some fat out of her own body and stuffed it in the parantha. And why not? After all, one day he was going to be her very own. Whatever he earned, he would pass on to her. Who does not water a plant that gives fruit? And, when flowers would blossom and the fruit-laden branch would bend low, then all the backbiting women would be shamed. This thought made my Bi Aapa's face glow with bridal anticipation. The sound of the shehnai rang in her ears as she swept Rahat's room to keep it spotless. She would arrange his clothes lovingly, as though they talked to her. She washed his dirty socks, his stinking vests and handkerchiefs filled with mucous. And on his oil-smeared pillow cover she embroidered 'Sweet Dreams'. But things did not progress quite as expected. Rahat stuffed himself with eggs and paranthas at breakfast and went out. On his return he ate kofta and went to sleep. Bi Amma's adopted sister whispered her disappointment.

'Poor boy! He's very shy,' Bi Amma offered the alibi.

'That's all right. But we should get some hints from his gestures or looks.'

'God forbid that my daughters exchange glances with anyone! No one has ever seen as much as her pallu,' said Bi Amma with pride.

'Oh dear, no one's asking her to come out of purdah.' Considering Bi Aapa's swollen pimples, she had to admire Bi Amma's foresight. 'Dear sister, you're really a simpleton. I'm not suggesting that at all. This wretched younger one – when will she be of use, if not now?' She would look at me and break into a laugh.

'You good-for-nothing girl! You must chat and share jokes with your brother-in-law, you crazy child.'

'But what do you want me to do, Khala?'

'Why don't you chat with Rahat Mian?'

'I feel shy.'

'Just look at her! He won't eat you up, will he?' Bi Amma said angrily.

'Oh no . . . but . . .' I could not say anything. They pondered over the issue. After much thinking, kababs were made with mustard seeds. That day, Bi Aapa also smiled quite a few times. She whispered to me, 'Look, don't start laughing. That'll ruin the whole game.'

'I won't,' I promised.

'Do take your meal, please,' I said as I lowered the tray of food on the stool. Rahat took out the water-tumbler from under his bed and while washing his hands he looked at me from top to toe. I immediately took to my heels. My heart was beating wildly. Oh my God, what piercing eyes he had!

'You wretched girl, just go and see how he reacts. You're going to spoil the fun.'

Aapa looked at me. There was pleading in her eyes. One could see there images of departing wedding parties and the sadness of old wedding clothes. I lowered my head, returned to Rahat's room and stood there leaning against the pillar.

Rahat ate quietly without looking at me. Seeing him eating those mustard-seed kababs I should have laughed and made fun of him. 'Are you enjoying these mustard-seed kababs, dear brother-in-law?' I should have teased, but it was as though someone had clutched at my throat.

Bi Amma got angry and called me back, cursing me under her breath. How could I tell her that the wretched fellow, far from telling the difference, seemed to be enjoying the food!

'Rahat Bhai, how did you like the kofta?' I asked, tutored by Bi Amma.

There was no reply.

'Hey, girl, go and ask him properly,' Bi Amma nudged me.

'Please say something.'

'You brought them and I ate. They must be good.'

'What a stupid boy!' Bi Amma could not restrain herself. 'Why, you couldn't make out that the kababs you ate were made of mustard seeds.'

'Mustard seeds? But I eat the same stuff everyday. I've got used to eating mustard seeds and hay.'

Bi Amma's face fell. Bi Aapa could not lift her eyes. The following day she sewed twice her normal measure.

In the evening when I took his meal to him, Rahat said, 'Tell me what you have brought today? Paranthas made of sawdust?'

'Don't you like the food here?' I asked, stung by his remark.

'Not exactly. It seems somewhat strange. If it is mustard-seed kababs someday, on other days it is curry that tastes like hay!'

I boiled with rage. We ate dry rotis so as to provide him with plentiful food and stuff him with paranthas dripping with ghee. My Bi Aapa could not buy jushanda for herself while she must get him milk and cream. I walked away in a huff.

Bi Amma's adopted sister's scheme worked, and Rahat began to spend a greater part of the day at home. Bi Aapa was always busy at the hearth, Bi Amma occupied herself with stitching the jora for chauthi, and Rahat's filthy eyes stung my heart like arrows. He would tease me for nothing while eating, saying that he wanted some water or a pinch of salt. And he would make suggestive remarks. Embarrassed, I would go and sit beside Bi Aapa. I felt like asking her point blank whose goat he was and who would supply him with fodder! Dear sister, I won't be able to noose this bull for you. But Bi Aapa's tangled hair was covered with flying ash from the hearth . . . Oh no! My heart missed a beat. I picked up a strand of her hair that had become grey and tucked it into her plait. A curse on this cold! The poor girl's hair had begun to turn grey.

Rahat called me once again on some pretext.

'Hunh!' I was stung. But Bi Aapa looked at me with the gaze of a slaughtered chicken and I had to go.

'Are you angry with me?' Rahat grabbed my wrist as he took

the water-tumbler. I was scared out of my wits. I snatched my hands away and ran from there.

'What was he saying?' Bi Aapa asked in a voice smothered with modesty. I stared at her mutely.

'He was saying – "Who cooked the food? Simply delicious! I could go on eating . . . devouring the hand that cooked the food . . . Oh no! What I mean is . . . kissing the hand,"' I blurted out hurriedly and clasped Bi Aapa's rough hand reeking of turmeric and coriander. I was in tears. 'These hands,' I thought, 'that remain busy, like bonded slaves, from morning till night grounding spices, drawing water, chopping onions, laying the bed, cleaning shoes. When will their slavery end? Will there be no buyers for them? Will no one ever kiss them lovingly? Will henna never adorn them? Will they never be perfumed with the bridal attar?' I wanted to scream out.

'What else was he saying?' Bi Aapa's hands were rough, but she had such a sweet and lilting voice that if Rahat had ears . . . but he had neither ears nor nose . . . only the hell of a stomach.

'Well, he was saying – "Tell your Bi Aapa not to work so hard . . . and to take jushanda for her cough."'

'You're lying!'

'Not me. It's he who is a liar. Your . . .'

'Silly girl!' she shut me up.

'Look, I've completed knitting the sweater. Please take it to him. But you must promise that you won't mention my name.'

'No, Bi Aapa, no. Don't give him the sweater. Your body which is just a bag of bones needs it badly,' I wanted to tell her, but couldn't bring myself to do so.

'Aapa Bi, what will *you* wear?'

'Come on, I don't need it really. It's always scorching hot near the hearth.'

Seeing the sweater, Rahat puckered up one of his eyebrows mischievously and said, 'Did *you* knit it?'

'No!'

'Then I can't wear it.'

I felt like scratching his face. 'Villain! A lump of clay! This sweater was knitted by hands that are living slaves. Woven in each of its stitches are the longings of an ill-fated woman. The hands that knitted it are meant to rock the cradle. Clasp these hands, you ass! They will serve as oars and save your lifeboat from the tumultuous storms. They may not play musical notes on the sitar, may not show the Manipuri or Bharatnatyam mudras; they have not been trained to dance on the keyboard of a piano, nor have they learnt how to arrange flowers, but these are the hands that toil from morning to evening to provide you sumptuous food, and mend your clothes; they remain soaked in soap and soda water, bear the flames of the hearth. They wash your filth so that you can maintain your dazzling image of a hypocrite. Hard work has bruised them. Glass bangles have never tinkled on them. No one has ever held them lovingly!'

But I stayed mute. Bi Amma says that my friends have vitiated my mind with their new-fangled ideas – frightening thoughts about death, hunger and famine, about throbbing hearts being silenced forever.

'Why don't *you* wear this sweater? Your shirt looks so flimsy.'

Like a wild cat I scratched his face, nose and shirt-front and pulled his hair. Then I ran back to my room and fell on the bed. Bi Aapa put the last roti on the tawa, washed her hands hurriedly, wiped them on her pallu and then came to sit by me.

'What did he say?' she could not resist asking, her heart beating fast.

'Bi Aapa, Rahat Bhai is not a good person.' I resolved to tell her everything today.

'Why?' she smiled.

'I don't like him. Look, all my bangles have been smashed to bits,' I said tremulously.

'He's so mischievous!' she said, blushing coyly.

'Bi Aapa . . . Please listen to me. Rahat is not a good person,' I said angrily. 'I'll tell Bi Amma today.'

'What is it?' asked Bi Amma as she was spreading the prayer mat.

'Just look at my bangles, Bi Amma!'

'Rahat has smashed them?' Bi Amma chirped joyfully.

'Yes.'

'Good! You pester him endlessly! And why are you complaining so much? As though you're made of wax and would melt at his touch!' Then she comforted me: 'Take your revenge on the chauthi ceremony. Tease him as much as you can so that he doesn't forget it, ever.' Saying this, she began her prayers.

Once again, there was a conference between Bi Amma and her adopted sister, and seeing that the matter was proceeding fruitfully towards the desired goal, they smiled happily.

'Silly girl, you're no use at all! I tell you, we used to make life miserable for our brothers-in-law.'

And then she proceeded to describe how to tease brothers-in-law. She recounted how two of her maternal uncle's daughters for whom there was no prospect of marriage at all were married merely by the inventiveness of teasing and mischief.

'One of the grooms was Hakeemji. When young girls teased him he would become bashful and have nervous fits. Eventually he sent word to the uncle saying that he would consider it an honour to become his son-in-law. The second one was a clerk in the viceroy's secretariat. The moment girls came to know that he had arrived in the house they would begin to play pranks on him. Sometimes they stuffed hot chillies in the paan; sometimes they fed him sewaiyaan with salt rather than sugar . . . But, can you believe it, he began to come everyday. Rain or thunderstorm, he would arrive unfailingly. Eventually, he approached an acquaintance to arrange his marriage in the family. When asked, "Which girl?" he said, "With either one." God is my witness that I am telling no lies – if you looked at the elder sister, you would think of an approaching banshee. About the younger one, the less said the better. If her one eye faced east, the other one faced west. Her father gave fifteen tolas of gold in dowry and arranged a job for the groom in the Burra Saheb's office.'

'Well, if one can afford to give fifteen tolas of gold as dowry and a job in the Burra Saheb's office thrown in, there should be no dearth of suitable boys.'

'That is not the point, sister. Nowadays, the hearts of marriageable boys are like eggplants on a plate – you can tilt them anyway you like.'

Rahat was not an eggplant, but a mountain. I could be crushed under his weight, I thought. Then I looked towards Aapa. Sitting quietly in the veranda, she was kneading dough and listening to everything. Had it been in her power, she would have split the bosom of the earth and vanished underneath along with her curse of spinsterhood.

Did my sister hunger after men? No. She had already shrivelled up at the mere thought of such a hunger. The thought of a man did not come to her as a longing, but as an answer to her need for food and clothing. She was a widow's burden and must not continue to remain so.

However, even after all the hints and innuendoes, Rahat Mian did not spill the beans, nor did any marriage proposal come from his family. Overcome by despair, Bi Amma pawned her anklets and arranged a niyaaz dedicated to Pir Mushkil Kusha, the patron saint. Through the afternoon, girls of the mohalla made a racket in the courtyard. Bi Aapa retired to the mosquito-infested room where mosquitoes sucked up the last drops of her blood. Exhausted, Bi Amma was putting the last stitches on the suit of the chauthi, sitting on the chauki. Today, her face bore the marks of destinations. It was the last stage, the impasse would soon come to an end. Today, her wrinkles once again shimmered like lit-up candles. Bi Aapa's friends were teasing her, and she was trying hard to make a blush appear on her face with her last drops of blood. For the past several days her fever had not remitted. Like a candle in its last gasp, her face would light up for a moment and then fade out. She beckoned me to her side, removed her pallu and handed over to me the plate which contained the sweets consecrated by the niyaaz.

'Maulvi Saheb has said a special incantation over it.' The hot, feverish air breathed out by her touched my ear.

I took the plate and wondered – Maulvi Saheb has read a special incantation over it. Now the malida will be offered to Rahat's stomach, which was like a furnace, a furnace that had been kept warm with our blood for the last six months. The sanctified malida would fulfil the wish. Wedding trumpets rang in my ears. I rushed out to the roof to see the baraat. The groom's face was adorned with a billowing flower wreath which touched the horse's mane. Wearing the shahabi jora and laden with flowers, Bi Aapa stepped slowly and gingerly. The gold-embroidered suit shimmered. Bi Amma's face bloomed like a flower. Bi Aapa lifted her bashful eyes for a moment and a tear of gratitude trickled down and got entangled like a star amidst golden sequins.

'All this is the result of your efforts,' Bi Aapa's silence seemed to say. Hamida felt a lump in her throat.

'Go, my dear sister.' Bi Aapa woke her up from her reverie. She got up with a start, wiped her eyes with the corner of her dupatta and made for the veranda.

'This . . . this malida,' Bi Aapa said, controlling her leaping heart. Her feet were trembling, as though she had entered a snake hole . . . And then the mountain moved . . . Rahat opened his mouth. Hamida stepped back. At a distance the shehnai of some wedding party screamed out as though it were being stifled. With shaking hands, she made a lump of the sacred malida and held it towards Rahat's mouth.

Her hands were pulled by the mountain where they got drowned in the bottomless, putrid abyss. A big rock stifled her scream. The plate of sanctified malida tumbled from her hands and hit the lantern. The lantern fell on the ground, gasped a few times and gave out. In the courtyard, the women of the mohalla were singing songs praising the saint Mushkil Kusha.

In the morning Rahat left by train, after thanking them for their hospitality. His marriage had been fixed, and he was impatient to reach home.

After that, no one fried eggs, made paranthas or knitted a sweater in that household. Tuberculosis, which had been haunting

Bi Aapa for a long time, now pounced on her. And she quietly surrendered her futile existence to its fatal embrace.

Then, once again, a clean sheet was spread on the couch in the seh-dari. The women of the mohalla gathered there. The white expanse of the shroud spread before Bi Amma like death's mantle. She was shaking all over in the effort to control herself. Her eyebrow was twitching. The desolate wrinkles were howling, as though a thousand pythons were hissing in them.

Bi Amma straightened the fabric, then folded it in the shape of a square. And a thousand scissors ran through her heart. Today her face bore the marks of a terrible peace, a fatal contentment. Unlike the other suits of chauthi, this one would not have to be stitched.

All of a sudden, the young girls gathered in the seh-dari began to twitter like so many mynas. Flinging the past aside, Hamida went over to join them. The mark of the white cotton on the red twill. How many young girls would have merged their longings in its red, and how many unfortunate virgins would have mingled its white in the whiteness of their shrouds. And then, everyone became quiet. Bi Amma put in the last stitch and snapped the thread. Two large tears trickled slowly down her cotton-soft cheeks. The wrinkles on her face glowed, and she smiled. It was as though today she felt sure that Kubra's wedding suit was finally complete and the trumpets would ring out any moment.

Kafir

'Eh! your mahadevji looks like a monster. One is sure to get a temperature if one sees him at night,' I told Pushkar, looking at him contemptuously.

'And your Mastanshahji, the giant-like pir who comes to bless you every Thursday, looks like a highwayman. The very sight of him makes me lose my tongue,' said Pushkar.

'Pushkar, you're a kafir,' I told him in the manner of a maulvi. 'You'll go to hell. Angels will pierce your body with iron rods and lash you with whips of fire. Blood and pus will be your diet.'

'You dirty girl! Your talk will make me throw up. I'll beat up your angels. If I'm a kafir then you're a kafirni. You told Babuji the other day that you'd marry me. Then you, too, will get a sound thrashing in hell.'

'Eh – I'm a Muslim, and you're a Hindu. Dear sir, all Muslims will go to paradise. We, too, will just saunter in. You'll be left behind, just see for yourself.'

'Left behind? I'll go to a better place than yours. You're a Musalmanti, you'll go to hell and burn there!'

'Pig! You dare call me Musalmanti! You're a sweeper – you . . . you . . .'

'Then you're a sweepress and a kafirni.'

I slapped him hard. But he was not to be cowed down. He whacked me twice. I pressed my nails on his wrist so fiercely that they pierced his flesh. Chachi ran to us when she heard the thuds of shoes and slippers and separated us.

'You brat, let Babuji come. He'll thrash you soundly,' Chachi said, aiming her fist at Pushkar. Pushkar was sitting on the parapet, making faces.

'Chachi, I can't marry this pig,' I said, sobbing.

'Who's going to marry a blackie like you! Ma, she wants me to drink blood and pus. Barf!' He made a face as though he would throw up.

'Hai Ram, you've become a mlechch. Shut up.'

'I'm telling the truth. She says all Hindus will go to hell, and she is the one to go to paradise!'

'No, no. Chachi won't go to hell, nor will Bhaiya nor Babuji. But this owl will certainly be flung there,' I said with confidence.

'If I have to go, then I'll drag you there by your legs!'

'That's some cheek! I'll bite you so fiercely that you won't survive.'

Chachi laughed so much that her face became red. 'Will your bickering continue in hell? Munni, if you kill him, he won't go to hell.'

'He'll still go to hell, you just see, Chachi. He is so mean.'

'Look, Ma, if she continues like this, I'll throw stones at her.'

'What's happening?' asked Babuji, as he entered the house.

'Hindu–Muslim riots,' Chachi replied, laughing.

Pushkar, coward that he was, ran away. Chachi led me away tenderly and gave me some tasty daalmut. Chachi was a Muslim, only this Pushkar was a kafir.

Diwali came, and Pushkar's house was lit up with diyas. I made up with him instantly. We made wicks for lamps and ate toy-shaped sweets throughout the day. Chachi yelled, 'Ai, Munni, you're rubbing the cotton into knots and spoiling it!' But I wasn't about to listen. In the evening Pushkar dressed up for the occasion – white billowing dhoti and purple malina kurta. He parted his hair with great care and put a red teeka on his forehead. Chachi was wearing a Benarasi sari, and her anklets rang out as she wandered about holding diyas in both hands. Pushkar was guarding every object in the house. That day he had turned into a rabid Hindu and was trying to escape my touch. He was the same Pushkar who had shared my half-eaten plums so many times. Today he was holding a kachauri out to me with an outstretched hand. I was fuming inside.

'Pushkar, please draw the sandal paste teeka on my forehead,' I implored him, trying to revive old feelings.

'No,' he shook his head arrogantly, 'you are not a Hindu.'

'No, Pushkar. I'm a Hindu now. Don't tell Amma, okay?'

He was moved and put the paste on my forehead.

However, I took my revenge on Id. I called him a kafir and fought with him. But when my hands and feet were decorated with henna, I began to wait for him eagerly. He came, but I sat listlessly with my hands resting on my lap.

'Aha, Munni's palms have turned crimson, show me, Munni!'

I pushed away his hands. 'Just be off. Id is ours, not yours. Do you fast all day? The Muslims fast, that is why Id comes to them.'

'And do you fast?'

'Sure. I did for a few hours.'

'Don't you brag. You keep on munching things throughout the day. If this is fasting, then I can also fast.'

'Eh! You're a Hindu.' I played the trump card.

'What difference does it make?' He was angry.

'I'll wear new clothes tomorrow,' I said with a swagger.

'I'll also wear my new jacket.'

'Eh! You're a Hindu. Why should you wear new clothes on Id? I won't give you our sewaiyaan either.'

'Then why did you cram so many sweets on our Diwali? I put sandal paste on your forehead. You also wangled some toys from Babuji. And now you're talking like this! What a mean liar you are!'

I quarrelled with him and compelled him to leave. But as I changed my dress, I had to go to him to show it off.

When I went to Pushkar, dressed up in brocades like a doll, all his anger vanished. Instead, he began to flatter me. But I explained to him time and again that he was a Hindu and he had no right to be happy on our Id.

He was filled with despair and said, 'Well, I'll become a Muslim. Don't tell anyone.'

But he turned out to be a cheat. On Holi, he again became a

kafir. It was his day, and despite my coaxing and cajoling, he flatly refused to allow me to play with colours.

'You're a Musalmanti,' he said.

'Okay, let Id come. I'll give you such a thrashing that you'll remember it for a long time,' I said, shaking my head.

'Then you become a Hindu,' said Panditji, turning his head away recklessly.

'Okay. Give me the mica-mixed colour-powder.'

'You were telling me the other day that each part of the body where the colour falls goes to hell. Now why do you ask for colours?'

'Now I've become a Hindu,' I said without artifice.

'Oh, what a cheat she is! She becomes a Hindu when it suits her and then turns Muslim. First you promise that you won't be a Muslim again.'

'Okay.'

'And you'll marry me, won't you?'

I agreed to this last condition as well. However, long before Id, I became a follower of Islam during Muharram and called him Yezid. He was, after all, a kafir and hell-bound.

The Pandits are by nature simple-minded people, especially the Kashmiri Pandits, who are like angels. I used to beat up Pushkar, but he would make up with me. He was such a coward that once when he saw a goat being slaughtered, he started crying. 'Why does your family kill so many goats?' asked he, opening his eyes wide in anguish.

'You fool! This is a virtuous act,' I replied wisely.

'Virtuous act! Is the killing of goats an act of virtue?'

'And why not? When we go to paradise we'll cross Pulsirat on these goats. We'll cross the bridge between the worlds with ease, but Pushkar, you'll be left behind.'

'I'll cross it on my bicycle!'

I was incensed. 'My dear sir, Pulsirat is finer than hair and sharper than a sword. You'll tumble down to hell and we'll go trot-trotting on our goats.'

'I'll ride on your goat, then.'

'Eh! I'll throw you off.'

'I'll push you down.'

'How dare you?' I slapped him. Before I could react, he whacked me twice and ran away.

My heart bled at the sight of my broken bangles, and I let out such wild screams that Babuji was compelled to take me to the market that very instant and buy me bangles.

God knows how many Ids and Holis have gone by since then. Times changed, so did attitudes. It was as though we had perfectly understood the philosophy of religion. Pushkar continued to come on Holi to drench me in colours.

On the occasion of Janmashtami, he gifted me a marble statue of Krishna. Below its feet there was a photograph of Pushkar in a little frame. I kept both the statue and the photograph on my table and quite often got lost in them.

Pushkar left for Benaras for his studies, while I went to Aligarh. Our school holidays fell at different times, so we could hardly meet, even on Id or Holi. May God shower His blessings on the month of December which always brings good tidings for everybody! I was lying down on the veranda and reading something when the call of 'Musalmanti' declared Pushkar's arrival. I greeted him by yelling back, 'Kafir!' He rubbed colour on my face.

'Do you want to play Holi in December?' I asked, pushing him away.

'Yes, I saved this colour for you from Holi. Won't you give me sewaiyaan?'

'No, because you're a kafir.'

'And you're a kafirni. Do you remember the promise made on Holi?'

'Which one?'

'Again! Didn't you promise to marry me?'

'Shut up, you scoundrel.'

'How phoney you are!'

Both of us broke into laughter.

'I hear that Mussolini is causing you great trouble.' Pushkar misses no chance to make a dig at my dark colour.

'You White Mouse, be on your guard. I've heard there's a reward of one anna per mouse.' I made a dig at his fair complexion.

As we began discussing communal riots between Hindus and Muslims, I told him, 'Run away from here. You're a Hindu. What can I do if you decide to stab me with a knife or something?'

'It is you who are the butcher. I'm a coward. You've crammed hundreds of goats in your tummy.'

'But Pushkar, you're a bull, not a goat.'

He gripped my arms so hard that I writhed.

'If you weren't as dark as soot, I'd certainly have married you!'

'Pushkar, you're unfair. I'm not so dark.'

'So, I should marry you!' exclaimed he, his eyes shining.

'Shut up, kafir!'

'Do you know in what sense poets have used the word "kafir"?'

'That kafir is different, you Hindu donkey!'

'Are Hindu donkeys different from Muslim donkeys? And how about Jewish donkeys?'

We had great fun debating how to classify donkeys on the basis of religion.

Time wore on. Pushkar became a deputy collector in our neighbouring district. On Sundays he would come in his car. Several times he reminded me of my promise made on Holi. But I told him it was sheer nonsense and asked him never to mention it.

'Will you keep threatening me like this? I'll broach it with Ma today. Let there be a battle, I don't care. You coward!'

'Pushkar, you'll be thrashed with shoes. Abba will rip apart your tummy.'

'I'm not scared at all. How long should we wait in the hope that someone will descend from the heavens and help us?'

'Pushkar, we're talking rubbish. There's a gulf separating us – religion.'

'To hell with such religions. Are they meant to help us or make martyrs of us?'

'Think of the long-lasting friendship between Abbu and Chacha. Think of the disgrace they will face if we get married. Newspapers, starved of interesting subjects, will publish the chronicle of our love along with photographs and put the whole blame on the modern education system. They'll make our life hell. An inter-religious marriage is not a crime, but it is an open invitation to trouble. Boys of our community are allowed to marry Hindu or Christian girls, but we are not allowed to marry boys from other religions. They declare proudly that Muslim girls should not marry Christian boys. I don't know how far that pride is valid.'

'Well, I'm ready to become a Muslim.'

'What difference does it make? Moreover, I don't approve of it. As for me, your becoming a Muslim does not change anything because you'll continue to be as mischievous as you are. Religion has nothing to do with like or dislike.'

'Then you become a Hindu.'

'Take care what you say. If I tell the people of the mohalla that you're trying to make me an infidel, they'll make mincemeat of you. If I become a Hindu, my nose won't be safe even if I get one made of rubber. Pushkar, we are slaves. We've no control over our lives. Society dictates it. It can do with us whatever it wants. We can't do anything about it.'

'This is nonsense. I can't understand it. Your brother brought a European mem even though he had a wife at home. She's Christian. I've seen her going to church regularly. Your brother, too.'

'Pushkar, she's a mem, and you're a Pandit. I am, as you call me, a Musalmanti. Do you see the difference?'

Pushkar began to pace up and down restlessly. 'I'll rip apart this society into pieces. Listen, let's have a civil marriage, today.'

'What's the use of all this fuss? You know Abba will get a severe shock. And your community will make you an outcast.'

'What should I do, then? Tell me honestly – are you going to get married to that bloke Hamid and ditch me? I'll get him thrashed so severely that he'll forget everything. Look, if we continue to remain afraid of society, we cannot live our own lives.'

'You're really crazy, Let me think over it. Maybe God will show us some way.'

'God has done that already, I'm telling you. Let's get out by the kotwali to the right. There's a straight road from there.'

'And on return, there's the shoe-beating by Abba!'

'Why return? From there we'll proceed on a journey.'

'Then people will say that I've eloped.'

'No, they will say I've eloped with you. Get up, quick. And yes, do you want to be paid mehr or whatever you call it? I'll get the registration done.'

'I'll give you mehr! My salary is only slightly less than yours.'

'Okay, get up and let me have it.'

'But whenever we want, we can get a divorce!'

'That won't be wise. You pick up a quarrel every minute. You'll divorce me seven times in an hour. Hurry up. Change your sari.'

'And the rubber nose?'

'Okay, I'll fetch you a sharp one. Yours is very flat, as it is.'

'I'm not going,' I said, clutching at the door.

'You can't have it your way.' So saying, he dragged me along.

Soon we were walking down the big, straight road to the right of the police station.

'Let's go back. There's still time,' I whispered into Pushkar's ear.

'Really?' he asked in a serious tone.

I nodded – God knows whether to say 'yes' or 'no'. Pushkar shook me thoroughly by my shoulders.

'Kafir!' I exclaimed and dug my nails into his wrist.

'Of the poets.'

I nodded – this time, to say 'yes'.

Childhood

The other day when I was tidying up the library, I chanced upon some old issues of *Asmat*. I glanced at one of the titles, and my mind raced back in time. The write-up was by Hijab Ismail, and the title was 'Childhood'.

Miss Hijab Ismail (rather, when she was still Miss Hijab Ismail) was the queen of newspapers. It was a romantic name that evoked novelty, grace and a glimpse of melancholic beauty. Her writings like 'Oh God!', 'An Unending Procession of Words', 'The Casement', 'Feeble Figure', 'Naval Coat', 'Candle-like Fingers', 'Doctor Ghaar', 'Old Buffalo', 'Chuhiya zu Naash' were beyond ordinary ken and made one feel stupid.

To come to the point – the essay mentioned above was on her happy childhood. I could not help a faint smile. Childhood! Everyone you meet is singing paeans to childhood. It is usually described as 'carefree days filled with joy', 'days of fun and frolic', and so on. When I see others talking zestfully about the interesting stories of their childhood, about how they were pampered, etc., I join the bandwagon as well and twist the realities a bit to regale them: 'We played like this!', 'Ammijan took me in her arms with such affection!', 'Such toys we used to have as gifts from our parents!', and so on. Tell me, what else can I do? Shall I tell everyone that I thank God for sheer survival? That I'm glad childhood was temporary, and that it's over and done with? If it were not so, then life would have been unbearable for those of us who didn't have an Uncle Ghaar, a Captain Harley or who never had qahwa to drink or bundles of chocolate to eat. As for us, as long as childhood lasted, we were like a juggler's monkeys. Come dawn and Aapa would install herself with a lota and a packet of tooth powder to get the morning ablutions done for the whole horde. You told her a hundred times that you'd washed your face just the day before, still she would give you a sharp reprimand and say, 'Then don't eat food today; you ate just yesterday!' Now who could counter her and her philosophy? While brushing our teeth her fingers often missed the target and entered our nostrils. Sometimes her fingers would descend on our cheek and smear the skin with the grainy powder. With the five fingers of the other hand, she would hold our neck in a firm grip – the way one does to an overcharging cart driver, ready to give him a shove. In the general cacophony, no one could hear anything. Just think about it – if your complexion had remained a little dark, what could be the problem? We weren't going to view a groom – as Aapa would say when she had to make us wear untidy clothes and we protested. Every day we had to subject ourselves to rigorous soap-rubbing. If we protested, we were told, 'If you cry, I'll rub the soap into your eyes!' As though she was not doing that already!

Even if your eyes burned, you didn't have the right to cry. Having crossed all these hurdles, if one asked for food, one was greeted with jibes. 'Shame! Don't you have any patience? Come morning and she begins cribbing for roti. Even the birds wouldn't have pecked at anything yet. If you get so hungry then tie some rotis to your stomach when you go to sleep at night.' Now tell me, why were we made to wash our face then? Do birds wash their faces? One washes one's face before sitting down to one's meal. Fed up with getting her face washed every day, one day Shaukat Aapa had said, 'I'm not going to wash my face today as I won't be eating anything.' They make fun of her even today.

Then began the breakfast. Aapa's breakfast consisted of the leftover kofta and rotis from the previous night. She warmed the kofta and sprinkled ghee and water on the rotis. We were given only tea. Aapa didn't drink tea as it dehydrated her. If she forgot to mix sugar in the tea, there would be another hassle. When I asked for sugar she would snap, 'Damn! How much can I do with just a pair of hands? I can hardly breathe. Dying for sugar, ant that she is.' Well, that was it. When after complaining feebly for a while, I would drink the tea without sugar, and she would exclaim: 'Oh God, how greedy can you be! Couldn't you wait a minute? Drank it just like that! Such greed – that, too, in a girl – that you didn't feel the difference!'

Being a girl seems to have been my undoing!

Breakfast over, I would barely have taken two, three rounds of the house when someone would cry out – 'Master Saheb is here.' My spirits would immediately flag. I wouldn't have a clue what to do. I could never find the book even after a thorough search. The inkwell would have turned over on the table on its own. I would have forgotten to wipe the slate clean. Baaji surely had stood with her full weight on the pen, breaking it to pieces. From one corner of the house to the other, I would keep looking for one thing or another. Eventually they would be taken care of and then, sitting on the chabutara, Master Saheb would begin my instruction, which was seen as a solution to the problem of female education.

One book stuck to us like a curse. Abba's frequent transfers meant that we couldn't have a permanent teacher. As and when we went to a new place I had to start with the *Muhammad Ismail Reader* all over again. Looking at the shape and colour of the book, I could recognize it as my own though I remained largely a stranger to its contents. I didn't know what the method of instruction was; the teacher would cling tenaciously to it for months together, but the light of knowledge would still elude us.

My feckless mind would wander far away from the book. I would look around and feel pity for myself. Naseema, having finished scrubbing the utensils, could be seen playing kabaddi and my gaze would irresistibly turn towards her antics. Mungia, having finished with the cow-dung cakes, would be eating jamuns right before me. Even Dhalu and Balka – mere puppies – would run around in total freedom while I had to chant sentences like 'Go to the bridge', 'He is her brother-in-law', 'Ganga is bigger than Yamuna', and so on. My condition was really pitiable.

When Master Saheb was satisfied that I had had enough of a dressing down and my arms and thighs had enough blue blobs (as I was a member of the female species, Master Saheb wouldn't hit me but only gave me sweet pinches. Further, he would threaten to kill me if I told the elders about it. When Aapa saw the blue marks while bathing me, she would add one more mark to them saying: 'Why on earth do you go to places where you fall and bruise your body?'), then came the turn for dictation. The problem here was the ink. I did not know what scientific method was applied to prepare ink; I could never master its exact thickness. So when I dipped the pen in the inkwell and drew it up, congealed ink would dangle from its nib; at other times I would shake the pen hard, but the ink would just refuse to come.

What a relief it was when the class was over! Satchel under the arm, fingers drenched in smelly ink, I returned dispiritedly, dragging the slate along. If someone showed the slightest sympathy, I would break into tears. After all this, when I asked for food, I would get the reply, 'Eat me, oh yes!' The food would be rotten – either too hot or too cold. If I asked for a piece of meat, I would be told, 'Tear out a piece from my body.' If I said, 'Give me egg as you've given to Chunnu,' pat would come the reply, 'Yes, I've brought the egg cage, so I have to dole out eggs – as though my father is . . .' Poor Aapa would be left with a meatless bone. Those who served food usually had the worst fare. Curry would often run short, and they would have to get a few eggs fried to make do.

At noon, we would be made to lie down in a row. The khus matting and the punkah would fight off the heat and curfew would be imposed upon us.

'Don't move.'

'Don't turn on your side.'

'Don't roll on the floor.'

'Don't keep counting the water melons and musk melons kept by the door. And don't dare touch them.'

'Don't hang by the hem of the punkah.'

'Don't lie upside down.'

'Don't do this.'

'Don't do that.'

Now just think over this –

As we came out of the khus room, Chunnu and Shamim would run to play games, but, being a girl, I would play with dolls. They say playing with dolls teaches one good conduct. My aversion to dolls was infinite. How could one play with them? They were just lumps of rags in the shape of children and stood nowhere in comparison with the English dolls, which did not get spoilt even if you washed them. Our dolls, on the other hand, turned into dead mice in two days.

The game usually consisted of the marriage of dolls. I had many dolls, but only one filthy gudda. By turns, he would become the divine lover of all the dolls. If I asked the elders to get me some more guddas, they, for some psychological reasons, would instruct me to play with dolls and say that there was no need for guddas.

Hardly would the session with the Master Saheb be over when Maulvi Saheb would arrive, unnerving me. I would feel like lying down and resting, but no. I would be given a jerk and made to stand up. Eventually I would grab the first book of the Arabic *Reader* and proceed towards the study. If I stopped to drink water on the way, Chunnu would also stop, insisting that he must go with me. Even if I drained several glasses, he would continue to stand and wait for me there, and not go on by himself despite my chiding.

The practice of verb conjugation would start with the usual gusto – aank, oonk, eenk; thaank, thoonk, theenk. But gradually the pages of the *Reader* grew less and less interesting. Black, ugly-looking alphabets made faces at me. My eyes wandered. It seemed that every object was vying for my attention: Chunnu's ball dangling by the drain, Aapa's dupatta fluttering on the clothes line, leaves of trees, Maulvi Saheb's cap leaping up, even Shamim's twisted reddish ear began to seem interesting and beautiful.

Aapa's status in the house was comparable to that of Mussolini or Hitler. From time to time, she would issue commands regarding the improvement of our morals. As I finished the first sipara, or chapter, she got worried about my welfare and ordered that I should be taught recitation of the Quran, which would ensure a smooth passage through this world and the world hereafter. Heaven's windows would open up to me. However, this sinner was not destined to learn recitation. Either a cacophony of voices came out of my throat or it seemed as though someone was tightening a noose around my neck, and it got tighter as it reached the letter 'qaf' while I tried to resolve mystical issues. Chunnu would smile at my pitiable fate. Shamim, smiling derisively, would follow each gesture of mine so that he could mimic it later before others and drive me to tears. Meanwhile, if any wedding party or some exciting pageant passed by, we would involuntarily exclaim, 'Maulvi Saheb, there's a wedding party.' Immediately Maulvi Saheb's hands would descend on our cheeks in a torrent of slaps, and we would start sobbing. Ostensibly, Maulvi Saheb only shook me by the shoulders, but he very deftly joined his thumb and forefinger and pinched me so severely that it would make me writhe in pain.

Maulvi Saheb had warned us, the infidels, that we must chant 'la hawla vala' as soon as we heard the beat of drums, because, on the day of Judgement, Dajjal would arrive to the accompaniment of drums. Music lovers would be drawn by his music and led to hell by him. A hush would descend on us as we contemplated the virtues to be cultivated for the hereafter.

The lesson being over, we would run to the kitchen to see Aapa frying something. But she wouldn't allow us so much as a peep. 'Get lost, or I'll hit you with the ladle. If you touch the lagni, I'll pour the boiling oil on your hand; and if you ask for atta once more, I'll put a live ember on your palm.'

Chunnu, after all, was a boy. His faults were no faults. However, the girls must be perfect; otherwise, they would ruin their husbands' families. But Aapa would remember this only during a game when it was my turn to play, and then she would order me to go stitch a waistband or break my head over some such detestable task.

There was no place where we could play. 'Don't play on the bed, it'll sag!', 'Don't jump on the boards, the noise will burst the eardrums!' There was no space on the chabutara; we weren't allowed to play in the courtyard, which contained Aapa's fancy flowerbeds. Inside the house we stumbled on the stone slab, the lota toppled over; sometimes we stepped on the brass plate or our feet got entangled in children's cribs. If not these, then the bamboo pole leaning at the corner would choose to slide down on our head and the soap case would leap from its place, dangle by the drain precariously before finally landing on the sleeping dog. That would invite a torrent of curses from the elders: 'What a miserable life! O God, take these children away or send death to me. Do such children exist anywhere in the world? If they did, then why should anyone live?' After such relentless chiding, we would be made to sit down quietly. 'If you move, I'll break your bones.'

At night we would be sent to bed with the pious wish – 'Off to hell.' Well, before going there we would laugh our heads off. The laughter simply wouldn't stop. 'If you even breathe now I'll stifle you to death,' came the last threat. Now when sleep finally came, in the place of sweet dreams we would dream of bulls, dogs, monkeys or owls coming in droves . . . The one-anna coins were littered everywhere. We gathered them up happily. But the moment we woke up and opened our eyes, we would find our fists still clenched with no coins inside. We burst into tears. 'No peace even at night. Hush! If you don't shut up, I'll hand you to the dog.' Then came morning, and there would be Aapa with the tooth powder and us standing before her.

And now . . . By God's grace, everything has changed. I am my own boss – free and independent. I drink tea lying in bed, then I get up to take breakfast. After that, I deck myself up and go to the office. If the servant delays serving a meal even by a minute, he gets bashed up. I eat plenty of meat – well-cooked and soft. I can have as many eggs as I want. I laugh and enjoy myself as much as I want, and no one complains about the noise. I can jump as much as I want on the bed, it does not sag and if it does, Hamid will be roughed up. I can caper on the board with no one complaining that his eardrums might burst. Even if I throw all the atta in the pan, no one threatens me with the ladle. Yes, Aapa still gets the tooth powder prepared, and I still get the rubbing, but with butter.

For me, it's now a soft brush and a scented paste. No teacher is ever allowed to come except for the music teacher, and even he is sometimes shown the door if I feel lazy. The fact is, we aren't children anymore without a care in the world! Carefree life, innocence, simple talk, sound sleep. Alas! if only childhood could . . . once more . . . oh, well –

The Net

'Attan, Safiya . . . where on earth are you?'

'Ji, ji, . . .' Attan's voice came from a distance.

'Coming, Bi,' yelled Safiya from the dark room at the extreme corner of the veranda. Both the girls rushed out like two kittens. Attan's shirt ripped noisily as it caught the nail, Safiya's shoes got stuck in the doorway, and she fell on her knees near the spittoon. The spittoon had not been emptied for several days, and as it toppled over, Safiya's knees got stained with patches of thickened paan spit.

'Why don't you take care? Have you no shame? . . . Even on a Sunday you're acting crazy!'

'Look at the dupatta . . . it's never on their head!'

Safiya wiped off the paan spit and rushed into the bathroom.

'Did you recite the Quran this morning?'

'Well . . .' Attan was nervous.

'I asked – did you read the Quran this morning?'

'Unh . . . Safiya . . . ah . . .' Attan was wringing her fingers.

'I'm not asking about Safiya, but you. You didn't care to perform the isha namaz last night either. Your mother tried to wake you up, but you just slept like a log.'

'In fact she . . .' Attan wished she could disappear under the bed. Khala Bi looked her up from top to toe, nudged Bi meaningfully, and whispered something into her ear. She nodded, waving the nutcracker, and both seemed to arrive at some suitable conclusion.

'Now get lost.' Then she addressed Khala Bi: 'Well, how do I know? They're still so small – wretched girls.'

Attan bent over and walked zigzag to the store room. Noon, they sat with their heads close together and chatted away for several hours in semi-articulate sentences. Sitting in that dark room smelling of rat piss, they stitched two odd-shaped vests out of an old pair of pyjamas. They felt suffocated as they wore them. It was as though a roadroller had passed over them. Yet they felt satisfied. Oh, what a great time Bhaiya had! He would take off his shirt and go about only with his pyjamas on. Attan had prickly heat all over her back which stung her like needles.

Attan wished she were dead, and so did Safiya. They would read sentimental stories in the dark room, get worked up on them and fall into each other's arms.

'Bajju, I feel my heart is going to burst.'

'Suun . . .' Attan sobbed. The heroines of those stories were lucky that they died. If only these two could die like them! Then Bi, Khala and Mullani would beat their breasts and cry their heart out. 'Hai, I couldn't see the sehra on Attan', 'Hai, I couldn't see Safiya a dulhan.' The desire to die before becoming a dulhan brought tears to their eyes, and they felt a lump in their throat. In the mohalla when Bhori's daughter died as a spinster her funeral was a sight to behold. Long, scented sehras were put from one end of the bier to the other. The red brocade dupatta that she longed to touch while alive was spread over her. Bhori, who used to reprimand her all the time, was dying for her. Instead of the usual filthy abuses she now used the most endearing terms for her. If Attan and Safiya died, Bi would groan and wail like Bhori: Khala Bi would curse herself. Mullani Ma would tear her hair, the thought of which inevitably made them grin with pleasure. How she pulled their locks! They would get immense pleasure imagining her covering them in their shrouds and leaping into their grave to chide them.

On Sundays they were given a bath which was no less than the ritual bath before burial. Then a bowlful of khali would be ground and soaked in water. This khali was made of linseed and pepper, which killed lice. When chickens got infected, people applied paraffin oil, and though it made their skin peel off, it killed the lice. The khali was used as a substitute for paraffin oil. When the khali, soaked in water, swelled up, Mullani Ma rubbed it on the heads of Attan and Safiya so vigorously that their heads almost touched the ground, their buttocks leapt into the air and the stools fell over. And . . .

'Why are you tottering down? Don't you have any strength in your shoulders?' Mullani Ma would growl, and their tears, mixed with khali grains, would hurt their eyes and sting their noses. Their temples would almost burst. Why did God, in His infinite wisdom, think of growing hair on the head, and then why did he bestow such strength to Mullani Ma's hands? Those who were bald did not have to worry about either oil or comb, nor did they have to put up with such deadly rubbing. Once when Attan was afflicted with pox, her hair was shaved off, and she roamed about with a lightness of spirit. Of course she had to forgo the teeka jhumar in the bargain. Safiya and Aapa would wear the teeka with gusto, but she looked silly with her shaven head.

'Pour four lotas of water on the right shoulder, four on the left' – this was Mullani Ma's recipe to purify oneself. In winter it was painful to pour four cupfuls on one's body, not to speak of four lotas. But in summer they would sit under the tap and let the cool water cascade down their body. The gurgling stream of water would flow down their shoulders, run between their thighs and into the drain. It was as though someone was pouring down wine . . . and they would begin to doze off. Also, the bathroom was a place that gave them swaraj, as it were. Liberation! Liberation from all inhibitions. They ran about uninhibitedly from the stool to the tap, from there to the heap of dirty clothes and then to the almirah to look for the soap or besan in its upper shelf. They would frolic and gambol. The air would beat against their bodies. All their limbs would feel light. As they rubbed the soap, their smooth hands turned slippery as though someone had covered them in silk cloth. They would rub the besan and savour the light, pleasant sting and inhale the sweet smell of half-ground gram. They liked to go on stroking slowly with their fingers and longed for some abrasive object to rub against their body to cure the continuous tickle . . .

'Hey, haven't you finished your death-bath yet?' This growl would startle them out of their reverie, and they would try to embrace the current of water one last time and look balefully at the grotesque vests which acted like a roadroller on their bodies.

Being the only ones used, they were always soaked in sweat and emitted a hideous burning-ghat stink. The girls were not orderly enough to wash the vests quietly at night, hang them to dry and pick them up early morning. One day when Bhaiya laid his hand on one of the wretched things, he went around showing it to everybody. No one could guess as to what it actually was. Eventually, Bhaiya decided that it belonged to Nanwa, and that he used it to apply filthy medical potions.

'Saheb, may worms eat my body if it's mine. It must be Deen Mohammad's.' But Deen Mohammad disowned the object right away and began to curse its owner.

Lowering their heads, Attan and Safiya kept reciting the Quran. Sometimes their eyes met, and their lips fluttered. After this incident it became a norm . . . when the vests began to rot and disintegrate like old paper, the accumulated dirt on them began to hurt, and they no longer served the purpose for which they were made, the girls rolled them up into a ball, threw them into the lavatory and buried them under a heap of ash.

Attan and Safiya were not born as twins, but circumstances had thrown them into the same pot. In the world they were each other's only friend and support. When Attan had a searing waist pain and she writhed like a slaughtered chicken, it was Safiya who fetched her the hot water bottle and massaged her waist for hours together. And when Safiya's shins throbbed in pain, Attan would tie her dupatta tightly around them and stop the convulsions. Thus they were each other's mainstay on this earthly journey.

However, this partnership would break at school as they attended different classes. So, according to the code agreed upon, Attan had to have a crush on Miss Charan and Safiya on Miss Hyder. Even by mistake Safiya wouldn't comment on Miss Charan's rough, snake-dark complexion and her flat nose, nor would Attan taunt Safiya about Miss Hyder's artificial locks and her sari worn awkwardly above the ankle. They were like sisters and on the whole friendly with each other. Whenever Bhaiya had a chance encounter with those much-suffering teachers, he would raise a storm. One day Attan and Safiya took Bhaiya's camera with great difficulty, loaded the film and then took several photographs of Miss Charan and Miss Hyder in different poses. When Bhaiya got the film developed and brought the photographs home, he made such fun of their features before everyone that Attan and Safiya once again longed to die like the heroines of sentimental stories. That would make Bhaiya feel sorry. He would bang his head against the wall while their corpses would smile nonchalantly.

These were not all. They had a million other aches that made them miserable. Life had spread itself like a net – Khala was its warp, and Mullani the weft. Every step was a snare, every breath a gasp. What of the others – Anwar Bhai, Rasheed Bhai, Qutab Bhaiya – and one does not know how many other 'Bhais' came, but all of them came to gaze at the Aapas and Baajis!

'Attan, girl, take this to Sarwari. Quick . . .'

'Saffu darling, we'll give you a nice gift . . . Go and hand it over to Kubra. And mind, give it to her secretly. Khala Bi should not see it, you understand.'

'What gift will you give?' she asked.

'Whatever you like – a doll, a net covering for the pillow. Now, run . . .'

And she would run. Every other day she had to carry bundles and envelopes across to the enemy camp, hiding them from the eyes of Khala Bi and others. But she would burn inside . . . Everyone was ready to give her dolls.

'I hate these wretches . . . I'll pass them over to Bannu.' Attan would flare her nostrils. As if she needed only dolls! Why don't they give dolls to their admirers? But that was just an act. The girls would talk in the closed room for hours. They wished they also had someone to tease them in the stairways and galleries. Envelopes and packets should also come for them which would bring a flush on their face and make them run inside and throw themselves, face down, on the bed. Well, that was all wishful thinking. Their lot was confined to carrying the messages across and to soiling their hands as happens in the business of coal.

But their worst moment arrived when they betrayed the trust and opened a bundle. They turned it upside down for sometime but could not make head or tail of it. It was an intricate web of delicate silk laces. Fine pink netting border and thin silk and elastic threads. Oh! Embarrassed, they quickly hid it in the almirah where they kept old clothes, and rushed out of the room. Their hearts were beating wildly. They were out of breath as they came out and engaged themselves in sifting wheat grains like maids devoted to housework. But their minds were constantly working on the bundle. Heads lowered, they ostensibly sifted the grains while a pink web would spread itself wide and then disintegrate in their mind's eye. They would look at each other meaningfully and break into a smile. This tiny, harmless secret was burning in their hearts like a flame that made their faces flush. As though they had brought back something from the land of fairies and jinns, and no one knew what treasure was hidden amidst those old rag skeins. After their meal when they passed by the almirah, Attan broke into a guffaw, so did Safiya. Unable to suppress laughter they ran towards the dark room.

'God's fury on you! Grown-up girls hopping like mares!' Mullani Ma muttered because while running Attan had stumbled on her bedpost. Trying to suppress laughter they fell on each other. This tickled them further, and they began to roll on the floor.

'Bajju . . . ho, ho . . .'

'Ha, ha . . .' Attan responded.

Now wherever they sat the pink netting would begin to spread itself. Lace would begin to flutter all around. Fine elastic silk threads would tighten round them from all sides, and they would be panting so much that their tattered, smelly and grotesque vests would nearly burst at the seams.

When everyone else slept they would take out the booty stealthily and gaze at it in the pleasurable darkness of the room. They felt shy to take a close look at it in each other's presence. So one day Attan took it out when alone, but Safiya immediately landed on the spot and pounced on her like an eagle. It was a breach of trust!

'Shall we go and hand it over to Aapaji?'

'Yes, let's. Anwar Bhai . . .' And both were choked with emotion.

They began to lose trust in one another. They feared leaving each other alone and guarded each other like snakes. If Attan attempted to go somewhere Safiya would immediately start putting on her shoes to accompany her. That love and attachment was gone. Now when Attan's shins throbbed Safiya turned away her face, pretended to be asleep and did not tie her dupatta around the spot. And when Safiya had shooting pain in her waist, Attan did not fetch the hot-water bottle. Rather she prayed that the pain might be so severe that she would become unconscious and would not come back to life again. Let people mourn and lament her death, cover her body in a red brocade dupatta and take her to her grave. Meanwhile, she would take out that silk web from the last shelf of the almirah and . . . But that was a vain hope. Safiya got fatter by the day, and her cheekbones acquired a light crimson glow. And Attan's shoes had begun to pinch her. Afraid, they would tremble at each other's growing strength. Both wanted to show that they did not care much for those silk snares and that those flimsy clothes were not at all like nooses around their necks.

The saying goes, when God bestows His gifts He does so on a silver platter. Kubra's dowry clothes were being stitched and Khala Abbasi had called Aapa Bi to cut the dress material for a jumper.

'Who's going with me?' she asked, looking at Attan and Safiya. They pretended not to hear. Attan was stitching the flares on Bi's pyjama like a docile girl. The feckless Safiya was pulling out stitches with scissors.

'Safiya, you come along. You're fiddling with the scissors. Come.'

'Where?'

'To Abbasi Khala's. Where else? Hurry up.'

'And Bajju . . . ?' She dilated her eyes in apprehension.

'Bajju's working,' Bi growled. Attan went on stitching with bowed head. She did not even break the thread for fear of attracting attention. Safiya gave her a murderous look. But it was in vain.

Attan's hands began to shake. Her heart began to strike against her ribs.

'Hey girl, put two stitches on this string.' Mullani Ma handed over an object that looked like a check drawstring juggler's bag.

Though Attan's heart was pounding like a railway engine in full steam, she got up nonchalantly as if she was in no haste!

'Here you are, daughter . . . This button . . .' Taya Abba landed there, his sandals creaking like the wheels of a bullock cart.

'Daughter, wash the paan leaves and put them in the box . . . Sprinkle water on them. Today Bi's taking a keen interest in stitching. And Taya Abba – may God afflict him with colic pain that sends him to his grave.'

If Attan had to endure the tension a minute longer her veins would have burst or she would have been struck by paralysis. With trembling hands she lifted the silk skein as one lifts a nestling, and then she moved ahead gingerly as though she were a new bride proceeding towards the bridal chamber on the wedding night taking care that her anklets and sandals did not make any noise. That day she realized how ugly she was. She stood silent in the twilight glow of the room biting her lips . . . As she went to pull up the bolt the window made such a noise that she began to cough vigorously to muffle that noise. Then as she moved ahead the tiny silk strings began to play with her fingers. She felt as though a current of cool water flowed over her body caressing every vein. She clasped the strings in her hands and then let go. They fell sideways as when a snake sloughs off its skin. The next moment she felt she was totally free – free from her surroundings – covered in flowers moist with cool dewdrops. She felt she was flying upwards – higher and higher – like feathery, soft-hued butterflies. Her breathing became heavy . . . Through the screen of tears she saw the pink flower swing swaying gently . . . Pleasurable sensations made her fingers tingle . . . Fine needles began to prick her all over.

'Creak . . . creak . . . bang!' The loose bolt came off. Aapa stood right there, and Safiya's mischievous eyes were gleaming.

Attan's arms fell . . . her shoulders went limp . . . and her head went down, lower and lower. And finally she covered her face inside the smelly, hideous vest.

The Mole

'Choudhry . . . O Choudhry . . . Listen to me . . .'

Ganeshchand Choudhry was silent.

'Sh . . . sh . . .'

'Why are you chirping like a cricket?'

'I'm tired.'

'Sit quietly, or else . . .'

'I can't sit anymore! Look, my back has become stiff as a board. Hai Ram!'

'Chh, chh . . .'

'I feel such a chill . . .'

Choudhry didn't say a word.

'Here . . . right here in the buttocks, ants are biting me.'

'Look here, Rani, it's not yet ten minutes, and you're already tired.'

'So? Am I made of clay? Wah . . .' Rani pouted her thick lips and slid off the white marble stool she was sitting on.

'Witch! Sit still, I'm telling you. Bastard!' Choudhry tossed the palette on the stool and shook her hard by the shoulders.

'Well, then . . . Here you are!' She lay down on the floor. Choudhry was beside himself with rage. He felt like whiplashing her delicate, dark cheeks, but he knew that would only make her wilder and provide her with a chance to yell and cry. And the portrait for which he was taking so much pain would remain incomplete.

'Look, sit quietly for a little while and then –' said Choudhry in a conciliatory tone.

'I'm dead tired.' She rolled over on the floor.

'Dead tired! And, didn't you get tired when you wandered about collecting cow dung throughout the day? Bitch!' Choudhry was again angry.

'Who collected cow dung? You? What a mean fellow you are to taunt me like a cantankerous mother-in-law!' She began to sulk, and Choudhry knew that another precious day was lost.

'All right, here's the watch. Sit quietly just for half an hour.'

'Oh no, not half an hour. Only six minutes,' she said as she climbed on the stool.

The fact was, she could count only up to six or seven. Choudhry knew very well that he could keep her sitting for half an hour while she would think it was just six minutes. Rani straightened her waist, adjusted the heavy, floral pitcher on her shoulder and sat down. No one could say for how long.

'Is it all right now?'

'Yes.' Choudhry quickly bent over the canvas.

'Look at me . . .'

'Yes, yes, it's all right.'

'Look at me . . .'

'Yes, yes, it's all right.'

His brush moved in silence for a while, and colours merged into one another rapidly. However, hardly a minute had gone by when she lost her patience and heaved a deep sigh.

'Ahh . . . That's all, Choudhry. Your six minutes are over.'

'Hunh . . . hunh.' His glance moved back and forth from the half-formed patches on the canvas to her.

'It's so chilly. Can I wear the shawl?'

'No.'

'Ohh . . . ahh . . . It's so cold.' She started whining like a dog.

'Shut up,' growled Choudhry.

'My waist, oh my stiff waist, Choudhryji.' She was in a roguish mood that day. 'Shawl . . . shawl . . . Where's my shawl?'

'Shut up,' growled Choudhry again.

'Hunh! Don't you hear me say how tired I am! I'll throw away the pitcher . . .'

Choudhry quickly turned to look at her. He had borrowed the pitcher from the museum for his painting. If she broke it, he would smash her skull.

'What can I do if I feel tired? And there are lice crawling in my hair.' She rested the floral pitcher on the floor and began fiddling with the luxuriant crop of hair on her head.

Choudhry spread his legs apart, his eyes glowered, and extreme anger made the muscles in his face twitch. His grizzled beard began to flutter like the white sails of a boat caught in a wild storm. Beads of perspiration appeared on his smooth, bald pate.

'My lower back hurts.' But Choudhry's demeanour scared her, and she took position again. Then suddenly she burst into tears.

'Oho . . . ho . . . brrr . . .' she blubbered. 'Oho . . . ho . . . no one cares if I die . . . brrr . . .'

Choudhry glared at her. Whenever she started crying, the muscles in his cheeks twitched, the bridge of his nose went askew, and the brush in his hand danced like firecrackers. The colours in his palette flowed into one another, making a puddle. He didn't know what to do. This agonizing state would persist until the thorn pricking his brain was dislodged. Right now, Rani's gestures seemed to pierce him like a spear and not a thorn, through his soul.

No one could have escaped the impact of Choudhry's histrionics. Rani was no exception. She sucked in her stomach once again, made a whining sound with her lips and sat down.

For a few moments the world continued to revolve on its axis, and Choudhry's brush made quick strokes. The palette now looked ugly and untidy. Then –

'Choudhry,' Rani cooed softly. Choudhry felt a strange sensation in his armpit. The world's axis swayed just a bit. No one knows whether the world sways on its axis. But to be sure, something did happen.

'Choudhry, have you seen this?'

Choudhry's shoulders quivered. The beads of perspiration on his smooth skull grew larger. Rani spoke again.

'Look at this – this black mole just below my neck. Over here, a little below, on the left.' She held the floral pitcher with one hand as she peered down her cleavage, parting her lips wide.

'Did you see it? And . . . So you're looking, Choudhry.' She pretended to be coy. 'Oh, I feel so embarrassed.'

'Sit still,' Choudhry growled.

'Hunh! What airs! Does any decent man peer at another's mole, especially when it is in such a bad spot!' She grinned shamelessly. 'Yes, in a bad spot, and now you've seen it, haven't you?'

'I haven't seen any mole, nor do I want to.' Choudhry's exasperation mounted.

'Hunh! Liar! You're looking at it from the corner of your eye. And . . .' She continued to snicker immodestly.

'Rani!'

Rani merely turned her nose up at him. Defeated, he slumped on the wooden box near the canvas.

'Do you know how old I am?'

'Hai Ram! How old?' Resting the pitcher, she leaned towards him.

'I'm old enough to be your father, nay, grandfather. And you? Tell me how old are you? . . . Hardly fifteen. And you've become an expert in obscene talk!' Choudhry was not old enough to be her father, let alone her grandfather. He had said that just to shut her up.

'Hunh! You're the one who talks obscene. Peering down at my mole! And it's in such a bad spot, too.' She began to grope for it with her hands.

'You're such a little girl –'

'A little girl! Who says I'm a little girl? Had I been so, then –'

'Then? Then what?'

'Ratna says that whoever has a mole on the breast is . . .'

'Ratna? How does Ratna know where you have moles?'

'I showed it to him.' She began to stroke the mole.

'You did? You . . . you showed the mole to Ratna?'

Choudhry's blood began to boil again. There was a twitching in his armpits, and the muscles in his cheeks quivered. Then his brush began to make frantic strokes and colours mingled with one another.

'Ah . . . well . . . wah! What could I do if he saw it?'

'How . . . how could he see the mole when you, you . . .' Choudhry's teeth clattered like a door loose on its hinges.

'I was bathing when he . . .' She held the pitcher and climbed on the stool again.

'You were bathing, and he landed there – bastard!'

'Yes, I was bathing in the pond. I was scared to go alone, so I took him along lest someone came there without warning. Yes, I was bathing. I also washed my blouse.'

'You took him along because you were scared that someone would come there?'

'Yes,' she said with naivety.

'Rani!' Choudhry edged forward.

'I told him to turn his face the other way, but . . .'

'But?'

'He was sitting far off. Then I said, "Ratna, I have a mole, but in a very bad spot." As he didn't show any interest, I said to him, "Well, don't look if you don't want to. I don't care." Right, Choudhry?'

'Then how could you say that he saw it?'

'That's true. I was going to drown – the water was this deep, you know,' she said, placing a finger a little below the mole.

'Whore!' Choudhry threw away the brush and was going to pick up the stick lying nearby.

'Hai Ram! But . . . but listen, Choudhry. Would you rather that I had drowned?'

'Bitch, don't you know how to swim? You've been bathing in the pond all your life. Why didn't you drown, then?'

'Oho! I wasn't going to drown really. I . . . I was just going to show him the mole.'

'So you faked the whole thing so that you could show him the mole?' Choudhry flung the thin stick in the air. He was smiling now.

'Hai Ram! Let me at least wear the dhoti, Choudhryji.' She leapt monkey-like and landed on the steps. 'If you hit me, I'll go out on the road. That will embarrass me, and I'll tell people that Choudhry, Choudhry . . .'

The man stopped dead in his tracks. 'What will you tell them?'

'I'll tell them, "Choudhry says that my mole . . . h'm . . . h'm." '

'Whore!' Choudhry sprang up like a mad fox. Rani knew that the arrow had hit its mark.

'I'll tell everyone, Choudhry. Did you hear? Come on, hit me if you dare. Why are you staring at me like that? . . . I'm so young. Just a little girl . . . You're very naughty.' She edged towards the door slowly.

Choudhry sat there dumbfounded. For a moment, he felt like setting fire to the painting and beating Rani to a pulp. But then he was reminded of the exhibition where he aspired to receive an award of five thousand rupees.

His head was in a swirl. He had painted thousands of pictures in his career – pictures of blooming roses, of undulating verdure, of dancing, leaping cataracts. He had even successfully represented sighs and fragrance in colour. And women from far-off countries had had the honour of posing for him – both in the nude as well as dressed up. But this restless, illiterate chit of a girl he had picked up from the filth in the gutters to serve as a model for his masterpiece was completely unmanageable. The most disturbing fact was that despite all known permutations and combinations, he could not make the tint that would replicate the exact shade of her skin. He mixed sandalwood colour with black and then added a little blue, but the tint of her skin was a mixture of alabaster, sandal, blue and a touch of ochre. It wasn't just that. If her complexion looked oyster one day, the next day he could see early morning vermilion bursting from it . . . And then suddenly it would acquire the tint of lilac clouds at dawn, while at other times he could see the blue of a serpent's poison shining through.

Her eyes, too, changed colour constantly. On the first day, he confidently prepared a tar-black tint. But suddenly he saw red lines around her pupils, and then the space around them seemed to fill up with the blue of clouds. He lost all patience and a lot of paint was wasted. But his exasperation crossed all limits when, in a few moments, the tar-black pupils began to turn green and dance like two emeralds. The space around the pupils turned milky-white and the red lines became redder. Hell! He clasped his head in desperation. That was, however, not the end of his troubles.

'Mosquitoes are biting me,' she whimpered like a child. Choudhry had resolved that he would remain calm that day whatever the provocation.

'They are biting me like hell – these mosquitoes.' Choudhry was mute.

'Ohh . . . how hard they bite – these mosquitoes.'

Choudhry sprang to his feet. Rani had blurted out an obscene invective that left Choudhry aghast. How could she utter this, being a girl? He was not familiar with such words, and the ones he knew were rather mild. He had never pondered this issue, but he felt that even the police inspector would not mouth such obscenities. At the most, he would use a few terms as metaphors just as a matter of necessity.

'Where did you learn such odious swear words?'

'Which one? You mean this?' She repeated the obscenity with calm relish.

'Rani!' he howled.

'I heard it from Chunnan when he cursed mosquitoes. There are swarms of mosquitoes in his shack.' She tried to skirt the issue.

'In Chunnan's shack? You were there in his shack?'

'Yes. He took me there to give me some gurdhani.'

'So, you ate the gurdhani?'

'Oh no! There was no gurdhani there. He lied. But now he fetches it for me.'

'So, Chunnan brings you gurdhani now?'

'Yes. Kheel too.' She was now stroking the patterns on the pitcher.

'Kheel too!' Choudhry knew that his shock was unwarranted. Rani was just crazy about gurdhani. Why Chunnan's shack, she would be prepared to snatch it from the jaws of a dog in the gutter to swallow some!

'I've given you money, but you're still taking gurdhani from Chunnan?'

'Hunh! I don't beg him. He brings it to me and asks me to go to his shack. I don't like him at all – he has such a big moustache, it makes me sneeze. Phun . . . phun! . . .' She sniffled as though someone had thrust a wick up her nose.

'Choudhry, can I scratch my back a little?'

Choudhry began to experience the fits all over again. He seemed to hear the sound of clapping in his brain, his cheeks fluttered, and five thousand tinkling coins took the shape of tiny stars that hopped and receded further and further from him. Brown, black, grey and yellow – all the shades collided with one another, and he felt as though a mushroom was sprouting on his skull.

The question now was whether he should endeavour to paint or surrender to the madness that was going to envelop him. At this rate, he would soon be seen in tatters rolling in the dirt in the street like a mad dog, his thin, haggard body bruised and scratched. Or he would be compelled to drown his burning head in the waters of the small pond.

His steps led him automatically towards the pond, which was not far. It was his usual haunt. Sitting on the bank he would gaze for hours together at the shimmering and swaying reflection of the setting sun on water. He was a poet – a natural one. He lived in the world but was distanced from it. He was not old, but one couldn't call him young either. He was too careless to trim his beard, which grew unwieldy and dishevelled and had now become grizzled.

'Ohh! . . .' Something quivered in his armpit again. He seemed to hear Rani's voice along with the croaking of a frog. Was it a frog? But the rainy season was yet to come. So it mustn't be a frog but a cat purring. Well, if not a cat, it must be something else.

But when his pious eyes saw Rani and Ratna romping in the water, he thought for a moment it must be some delusion. His fancy tormented him by imagining such scenes. And today it had crossed all limits.

However, as he advanced, the tumultuous laughter stopped and the two images, transfixed as a marble statue, had their eyes pop out in surprise. How vivid that illusion was! Every feature stood out loud and clear – the bulge of Ratna's thighs, his wet tuft of hair, his two deep-set eyes. And Rani's tousled locks and her body, the tint of which was a mixture of ashen-grey, pink, brown, camphor-white and blue. And the mole? The protuberant mole seemed to strike Choudhry like a bullet.

Ratna edged sideways and somehow made good his escape picking up his dhoti, but Rani stood there undeterred, flapping the water with her hand. It seemed to Choudhry that someone had put him in a swing and given it a mighty push so that he was swinging higher and higher.

'So you're looking at my mole? How naughty!' she said coquettishly to pacify Choudhry.

Choudhry could barely hold himself back at the edge of the precipice.

'Come out of the water,' he said, pushing away the new Choudhry, who was sinking slowly.

'Oonh, you'll hit me.' She raised her head above the water.

'I'll flay you alive today.' Choudhry had to convince himself that it was the same girl who had grown up like a frog in the gutter.

'Won't you feel ashamed, raising your hand to beat a woman?'

Choudhry flared up.

'Do you beat naked women? . . . What a thing to do!' She was half above the water. She was afraid, so her tone was belligerent.

'Go away . . . you.' Now she was coy.

The swinging stick dropped from Choudhry's hand and his height increased by a few inches. His arms swelled and ants seemed to crawl inside his brain. A gust of cool, vapour-laden, black wind swept away everything. The sparks were ignited in full force and flames began to leap up. His hungry eyes landed on the black, protruding mole, which seemed to transform itself into a black stone and strike him on the forehead. He turned and ran like a vanquished dog to his room and lay down on the bed. The same day Choudhry turned Ratna out. He kept on pleading that he had had the loincloth on all the time, but Choudhry was like a man possessed. He fought with a veritable army of ogres the whole night. It was as though someone was trying to bore a hole through his body with a drill but could not do so because a massive rock stood in the way.

That day he had a host of colours at his disposal. He mixed ochre with a little blue that produced a shade that was alive and deep and soggy like the bottom of the ocean. And for the eyes he mixed light green with black – no, just a hint of grey with pink at the edge of the eyes. He wanted to look at himself in the mirror, something he had not done for a long time. Does an artist have to look at his face in the mirror? What can the mirror show him? The myriad paintings by him were the mirror in which he could see not only his face but also view every nook and crevice of his soul. His heart and mind, created and recreated in varying shades, were right there before him.

Nevertheless, he wanted to see the reflection of his face. He took a tin box, which had brought paints from far-off cities, and turned it upside down. Two crickets jumped out, brushed against his nose and flew away. He wiped off the spider's web with his elbow and looked at his face. At first he could not see much. Whatever he could discern looked like some fine tassel-like undergrowth at the bottom of the ocean. Or like when the eyelashes get stuck and everything looks blurred and foamy. Then he could see a grotesque beard and eyes burning with hunger. Oh! Was it he? His own face? But he never looked like this. Did he? He turned the box upside down and tried to look at his face again. His beard was still visible, and when he closed one eye, he could also see his smudged nose and unkempt moustache. The moustache. If he had had a pair of scissors, he would have trimmed the moustache – trimmed it just a bit so it would look decent.

Rani had said Chunnan's moustache made her sneeze – phun . . . phun . . . He made sniffling noises with his nose. He knew that Ratna had been wearing the loincloth. Or maybe he had worn a dhoti . . . or was going to wear it when he appeared on the scene.

But what about Chunnan and his gurdhani? Choudhry had a curious feeling that the walls of his house were made of gurdhani and he was being squeezed between them. Then he got stuck on a heap of gurdhani like a half-crushed fly and was fluttering in the wind. When he got tired of pacing up and down and his legs almost gave way, he sat down on the stool. He lifted the screen from his half-finished work, and in a few moments the spots and dabs began to fly around and then became still. The shoulders glinted like polished leather, and the eyes sparkled with blue, black and green lights. And the mole? How did the mole come here? Protruding and coiled like a snake! Oh the mole! Tick! Tick! Tick! His heart beat like a clock.

He got up in a moment, and his feet led him towards Rani's hut. It was a dirty, dingy and suffocating shack with a narrow door. He thought he would have its roof raised the next day. Oh no, that won't do. The room where he stored his empty boxes would serve the purpose. He advanced in the darkness. His heart still beat like a clock while the darkness inside it clung to him like wet charcoal. His hands got stuck in the strings of the charpoy. He groped frantically in the darkness, but Rani was not there. Mosquitoes swarmed on his entire body and began sucking his blood. Large, whining mosquitoes. Then slab after slab of gurdhani fell over him.

The next morning he felt like holding Rani by her locks and asking – 'Bastard, where have you been last night?' But she was sure to ask why he was in her hut and groping in her bed. He worked in silence. Rani, too, was quiet that day. He wanted her to speak so he would know where she had been the previous night. But she made a face and continued to sulk.

'Are you tired?' he asked gently as he saw her resting the pitcher on the floor. He didn't want to fight with her that day.

'Of course. Do you think I'm made of clay?' She was massaging her waist with both hands.

Choudhry wanted to say something tender, but he felt shy of changing his tone.

'Come on, that's enough rest for now.' He expected her to fight, but she quietly lifted the pitcher and struck the pose.

That day his colours turned belligerent and seemed to ridicule him. He had expected to paint the mole that day. Just like that. Couldn't paintings have moles in them? But seeing how rebellious his colours were he dropped the idea.

As Rani got up to leave, a piece of gurdhani fell from her dhoti. She was not at all aware of it, but Choudhry felt as though the roof had collapsed over his head.

'This – this gurdhani?' He was foaming at the mouth in anger. She stopped in her tracks to pick it up but seeing Choudhry's mood, she changed her mind.

'You can have it,' she said, shrugging insolently.

A death-like stillness paralysed Choudhry. He stared at Rani's receding figure and then suddenly ground to smithereens the piece of gurdhani with his heels.

The next day Rani disappeared without a trace. She didn't bother to take any clothes with her and left as she had come, to wallow in squalor and dirt again, no doubt.

Choudhry's painting remained incomplete. Five thousand rupees got frozen in his mind like a black mark – a mark that looked like a tiny, protuberant mole. What a bad place for a black, singed mark! Right in his heart.

After this Choudhry lived in a state of mental agitation. He could not tell people about Rani's disappearance lest they suspect him of some foul play. Days went by, and he continued painting. But no one was ready to pay even six annas for his paintings. This was because he started filling his flowers and twilight with such bizarre and frightening shades of brown and grey that people thought he was out of his mind. All his colours got mixed up and were reduced to a puddle.

More unpleasant developments followed. People started asking him about Rani. He replied that he didn't know where she had gone. But such straightforward answers did not satisfy people.

'Choudhry has sold Rani to someone.'

'To a trader for several thousand rupees.'

'He had illicit relations with her . . . Must have got rid of her somehow.'

The conjectures were endless. Choudhry's life was reduced to a dark dungeon. It seemed that people wanted to roast him alive and devour him. That was not all. What a stir it created when the police caught Rani while she was leaving a blood-soaked bundle on the road! Immediately the village was raided, and Choudhry lost whatever sanity was left in him. The riddle concerning Rani's disappearance was solved easily. Choudhry was dumbfounded. What injustice! A lifetime of piety and goodwill was destroyed by this unfounded accusation. But God knew that he had not sinned, and he hoped he would be saved as all innocents are saved. Truth always triumphs. But . . . how he wished he were guilty! Well, he was guilty anyway – of being born into this world.

Yes, he wished he were an accomplice! Imprisonment, pain, suffering, calamity, public disgrace – he would have taken it all upon himself, smiling. If he had known that he would be acquitted in that manner, he would not have pleaded innocence to God and prayed to Him. True, there was that mole. Well, yes. But wasn't God aware of the weaknesses of human beings? It is He who has burdened them with these weaknesses. But little did Choudhry know that when Rani would be interrogated by the police and he would be trapped in the net of logic by lawyers, she would use this strategy to free, or in other words, destroy him completely!

'It was not Choudhry's,' she swore before a crowded court. 'Choudhry is impotent,' she blurted out carelessly. 'Ask Rama or Chunnan. How do I know which one it is? Hunh!'

A black mountain crashed over Choudhry's existence. It was accompanied by lightning and a quiet peal of thunder. And far away, quite far, a deep black, round, protruding dot gyrated like a top.

To this day, sitting by the road, Choudhry traces lines with a piece of charcoal – long, conical, round lines – like a singed mark.

The Homemaker

The day Mirza's new maid Lajo entered his house there was a great commotion in the mohalla. The sweeper who was in the habit of running away after a few swipes of the broom now stayed on and scrubbed the floor vigorously. The milkman who adulterated his ware with water now brought milk thick with cream.

No one knew who gave her the name Lajo, the coy one. She was a stranger to bashfulness or the sense of shame. No one knew who begot her and left her on the street to fend for herself. She grew up on the leftovers of others and reached an age when she could snatch away things from others. When she grew up, her body proved to be her only asset. Soon she learnt the secrets of life from the village louts of her age and became a freewheeling mare.

She didn't haggle. It was wonderful if it was a cash-down proposition; if not, it was sex on credit. And if someone could not pay even on credit, it was sex on charity.

'Hey, don't you have any shame?'

'I have!' She would blush with impudence.

'You'll burn your fingers some day.'

Lajo could not care less. She could take the rough with the smooth in her stride. She was a picture of innocence – with her deep black eyes, evenly set small teeth and pale complexion. Her swinging gait was so provocative that the onlookers lost their tongue and stopped in their tracks, staring at her.

Mirza was a bachelor. Kneading dough and flattening rotis had made his life miserable. He had a small grocery shop which he pompously called 'General Store'. It kept him so busy that he didn't find time to go home and get married. Sometimes the business would be dull, taking him to the brink of bankruptcy, while at other times, the ceaseless rush of customers would not allow him a moment's rest.

Bakshi, Mirza's friend, had picked up Lajo from a bus stop. His wife was at an advanced stage of pregnancy and a maid was needed. After the child was born, Lajo was turned out. She didn't mind, accustomed as she was to being beaten and turned out. However, Bakshi had grown fond of her, but as he got a job overseas, he thought of making a gift of her to Mirza. 'He wastes money at brothels, why not savour this dish for free?'

'La hawla wala quwwat! . . . I'm not going to keep a whore in the house,' Mirza said nervously.

'Come on, Mian, she'll do small chores for you,' Bakshi tried to persuade him.

'No, brother. Don't foist her on me. Why don't you take her along?'

'They've sent tickets only for me, not for the whole family.'

But Lajo had already invaded Mirza's kitchen. Her lehnga tucked up like a diaper, she had tied the broom at one end of a bamboo pole and was stomping around the house. When Bakshi told her of Mirza's response, she did not pay any heed. She just asked him to arrange the pans on the shelf and went out to collect water from the tap.

'I'll take you home if you so wish.'

'Are you my husband that you want to leave me at my mother's? Get lost. I'll tackle the situation here.'

Bakshi upbraided her, saying that a bastard like her should not take on airs. In reply, Lajo began to hurl such filthy abuses at him that even Bakshi, lecher that he was, broke into a cold sweat.

Bakshi's departure took the wind out of Mirza's sails. He ran out to take refuge in a mosque and kept thinking of the additional expenses. She might be a pilferer, for all he knew! He was really in the soup.

When Mirza returned home after the evening prayer, he had to hold his breath for some moments! As though Bi Amma, his late mother, was back! Every object in the house – the earthen pitcher, the newly scrubbed bowl, the lantern – was sparkling.

'Mian, shall I fetch your meal?'

'Meal?'

'It's ready. Please sit down. I'm fetching rotis – fresh and hot.' She left for the kitchen without waiting for his response.

Spinach mixed with potato, moong daal laced with onion and cumin seeds – just the way Amma prepared it! He felt a lump in his throat.

'Where did you get the money to buy these?' he asked.

'Got them on credit from the bania.'

'I'll pay you the return fare.'

'Return?'

'Oh yes. I can't afford a servant.'

'Who wants wages?'

'But . . .'

'I hope the food is not too hot?' asked Lajo as she slipped a fresh roti onto his plate. It was as though the issue was resolved once and for all! Mirza wanted to say that he was hot all over. But Lajo engaged herself in bringing rotis one after another. She was so quick that it seemed there was someone else helping her in the kitchen. 'Well, we'll see about it in the morning,' thought Mirza as he went to bed. He had a strange feeling because it was the first time he was going to sleep under the same roof as a woman. However, being tired, he fell asleep soon enough.

'No, Mian. I'm here to stay,' Lajo said firmly when Mirza raised the question the next morning.

'But . . .'

'Didn't you like my cooking?'

'It's not that.'

'Didn't I tidy up the house well?'

'You certainly did. But . . .'

'Then, what's the problem?' Lajo flared up.

For Lajo it was love at first sight. She was in love – not with Mirza but with the house. Without a mistress, it was as good as hers. A house does not belong to a man. He is more like a guest. Bakshi, the bastard, was a stale morsel. He had kept her in a separate room that had earlier been occupied by a buffalo. The buffalo had died long ago, but it had left a deadly stench that got into her system. On top of it, Bakshi would often throw tantrums.

Here at Mirza's house, she was the queen. She knew the moment she set eyes on him that Mirza was a simpleton. He would come quietly, much like a guest, and eat whatever was laid before him. He would leave money with Lajo for household expenses; he checked the accounts a couple of times and felt satisfied that she did not cheat.

Mirza left the house in the morning and returned in the evening. Lajo kept herself busy throughout the day fixing up things in the house and bathing in the courtyard. Sometimes she went across to Ramu's grandma for a chat. The pimple-faced, dissolute Ramu was Mirza's teenaged help at the store. He had a crush on Lajo at very first sight and told her that Mirza often visited courtesans.

Lajo felt a stab in her heart. Those courtesans were witches. For Mirza, it was just a waste of money. After all, what was she for? Till now, wherever employed, she gave full satisfaction to her masters in every way. But here, a full chaste week had passed! Nowhere had she felt so slighted before. She had a very large-hearted concept of the man–woman relationship. For her, love was the most beautiful experience in life. After attaining a certain age she was initiated into it, and since then, her interest had only grown. She had no mother or grandmother to teach her what was right and what was wrong. Now, she received overtures from other quarters as well, but she did not heed them. She was Mirza's maid and could not allow others to make fun of him.

Mirza seemed like an iceberg, but a veritable volcano was burning within him. His heart was in a tumult. The carefree lads of the mohalla further added to his agony. Lajo's name was on everyone's lips. One day she clawed the milkman's face, the next day she hit the paan-seller's face with a dung cake, and so on. People offered her their hearts on a platter wherever she went. The schoolteacher would start giving her instruction if he met her on the street. The sound of her bangles would make Mullahji, coming out of the mosque, mutter 'Ayat-ul kursi', to ward off evil.

That day, Mirza entered the house in a foul mood. Lajo had just had her bath. Her wet hair nestled against her shoulders. Blowing into the fire had flushed her cheeks and filled her eyes with water. Lajo grinned as she saw Mirza enter, making him almost topple over. He ate his meal in silence, then went out and sat in the mosque. But he did not find peace. He was constantly reminded of the house. Unable to bear it any longer, he returned home and found that Lajo was quarrelling with a man at the door. Seeing him, the man slunk away.

'Who was that?' Mirza asked like a suspicious husband.

'Raghua.'

'Raghua . . . ?' Mirza did not know his name even though he had been buying milk from him for years.

'The milkman!'

'Shall I prepare the hookah for you?' Lajo changed the topic.

'No. What was he saying?'

'He was asking how much milk he should bring from now on.'

'What did you tell him . . . ?'

'I said, "Go to hell. Bring the usual measure." '

'Then?' Mirza was stung by jealousy.

'Then I said, "Bastard, feed the milk to your mother." '

'Scoundrel! He's a rogue, this Raghua! Don't take milk from him. I'll bring it on my way home from the store.'

After dinner, Mirza put on a starched kurta with great flourish, stuck a scented cottonwool ball in his ear, grabbed his walking stick and went out. Lajo burnt with jealousy as she watched him mutely and cursed the courtesans. Didn't Mirza fancy her? How could that be?

The courtesan was busy with another customer. This annoyed Mirza, who left her and sat in Lala's shop. There he passed time talking about the rise in prices and politics. By the time he returned home, weary and peevish, it was past eleven. The water pitcher was kept near his cot, but he didn't see it. He went to the kitchen and drank a lot of cold water, but the flame within him would not be quenched.

Mirza could glimpse Lajo's lissom, golden legs through the door, which was ajar. Her anklets tinkled as she turned clumsily in sleep. Her legs stretched further. Mirza drained one more glass of water and, chanting 'La hawla wala quwwat', fell on his bed.

His body turned to a blister, tossing and turning on the bed. Constant drinking of water bloated his stomach. The thought of the enticing legs made him restless. A strange fear stifled his throat. He knew that the bitch could kick up a row, but the devil egged him on. From his cot to the kitchen he had already walked many miles. Now he had no strength to go on.

Then a harmless thought entered his mind: If her legs were not bare, he would not feel such thirst for water. This thought made him bold. If she woke up, what would she think? But Mirza had to do it for his own safety.

He left the slippers under his cot and tiptoed ahead, holding his breath. He held the hem of her lehnga and pulled it down. The next moment he felt a touch of regret thinking that she might feel uncomfortable in the heat. Unable to reach any decision, he stood for a while shaking all over. Then he seemed to harden his heart and turned back.

He could not have reached the door when there was an explosion. Lajo turned on her side and grabbed him. Mirza was dumbfounded. He had never encountered anything like this before. He went on pleading as Lajo seduced him thoroughly.

When they met the next morning, Mirza felt shy, as though Lajo was his newly wedded bride! Lajo, with the pride of a victor, was humming a tune as she smeared the parantha with layers of ghee. Her eyes did not reflect any memory of the night. She sat on the threshold as usual and kept on swatting flies. Mirza was apprehensive about whether she would now demand more of him.

There was a new lilt in her gait when she came with Mirza's lunch to the store at noon. Seeing Lajo, people would stop by and ask the price of groceries. Some of them would end up buying something or the other. Lajo, without any cue from Mirza, would begin to weigh things and would wear a smile of coquetry as she wrapped them up. She sold in a short time what Mirza couldn't through the entire day! However, he did not like it that day.

Now Mirza was richer than a king. He put on weight, and his looks improved. People knew the reason and felt jealous. Mirza, in turn, grew jittery. The more Lajo took care of him, the more crazy he got about her, and the more scared he grew of his neighbours. They knew of her uninhibited ways that turned one crazy. She was utterly shameless. When she brought Mirza's lunch, she would get the entire bazaar crashing down on her. She would make fun of someone, snapping her fingers at him, challenge someone else with her raised thumb. As she reached the shop swinging her buttocks and abusing people fulsomely, Mirza's blood would begin to boil.

He would say, 'Don't come with lunch anymore.'

'Why?' Lajo's face would fall. She would go mad sitting at home all day long. The bazaar, with its laughter and banter, was a pleasant diversion.

The day she didn't bring lunch to the shop, Mirza's mind would be assailed by suspicions. He would wonder what she was up to. He began to drop in at odd hours to spy on her, and she immediately got busy looking after his comforts. Her endearing ways made him more suspicious.

One day when he reached home at an odd hour, he found that Lajo was haranguing the junk vendor, and the chap was grinning all over. Seeing Mirza, he sneaked away. Mirza leapt up, caught Lajo by the throat and gave her a few slaps and kicks.

'What was it?' His nostrils flared.

'The cursed fellow would give only ten annas per seer. I said, "Bastard, give the money to your mother."'

The going rate for junk *was* ten annas per seer.

'Who asked you to sell junk?' Mirza thundered.

But the day he found her playing kabaddi with the lads of the mohalla, he was beside himself with rage. Her lehnga was fluttering in the wind. The lads were busy in their game, but their fathers were engrossed in her lehnga. By turn, each of them had already offered to make her his mistress, but she had spurned them all.

Lowering his head in shame, Mirza passed by silently. People were laughing at him: 'Just look at him, as though she's really his real wife!'

Mirza had got deeply attached to her. The thought of separation from her drove him mad. He could not stay in the shop for long now. The thought that someone could take her away with a better offer made him restless.

'Why don't you marry her?' Miran Mian suggested, seeing his plight.

'La hawla wala quwwat . . . How can I form such a sacred bond with this whore?' After warming the bed of so many, she had made herself unfit to become his bride.

However, the same evening when he didn't find her home on his return, he felt that the ground under his feet was receding. The wily Lala had been on her trail for a long time. It was no secret – he said publicly that he would offer her a bungalow. Even Miran Mian, his close friend, had made an offer to Lajo on the sly.

Mirza was sitting confused when Lajo returned. She had gone to give a massage to Ramu's grandma. That evening, Mirza decided that he would marry Lajo, and to hell with family honour.

'Where's the need?' Lajo asked, puzzled.

'Why? Want to have flings with others?' Mirza was annoyed.

'Shame on you! Why should I go for flings?'

'That Raoji says he would put you up in a bungalow.'

'I won't spit on his bungalow. I flung my shoe at his face.'

'Then – ?'

But the need for marriage totally escaped Lajo. She would remain his forever. And, what crime had she committed that the mian felt the need to marry her? It was a matter of luck to come by such a master. He was like an angel. Lajo had suffered at the hands of many. All her masters would fall for her, and when they had had their fill, they would throw her out after a good thrashing.

Mirza, on the contrary, was very tender and loving. He had bought her two new sets of clothes and gold bangles. None of her ancestors would have ever had the chance to wear gold jewellery.

When Mirza spoke with Ramu's grandma, she, too, was surprised.

'Mian, why do you want to put the bell around your neck? Is she throwing tantrums? Give her a good thrashing, and she'll be all right. Why think of marriage when a shoe-beating would do?'

But Mirza was insistent – he must marry her.

'Hey, girl, do you have any objection to his religion?' Ramu's grandma asked her.

'Not at all. I've always looked upon him as my man.'

Lajo was gentleness personified. She would regard even a passing customer as her husband and serve him accordingly. She was never miserly with her lovers. She didn't have wealth. But she gave herself entirely – body and soul – to her lovers. She also extracted as much. But Mirza was a class apart. She had an entirely different experience of give and take with him that sent her heart soaring. Compared with him, the others looked like pigs. She had no illusion about herself: only virgins got married, and she could not remember when she had lost her virginity. She was not fit to be anyone's bride.

Lajo cried and pleaded, but Mirza was obsessed with the idea of marriage. So, one night, an auspicious hour was chosen after the isha prayer, and they were married. The whole mohalla was bursting with excitement. Nubile girls broke into espousal song – one group sang for the groom, the other group, for the bride.

Mirza gave his formal consent to the marriage with a smile, and Lajo, alias Kaneez Fatima, and Mirza Irfan Beg became man and wife.

Mirza put a ban on the lehnga and instructed her to wear tight-fitting churidar pyjamas. Lajo was used to open space between her legs. Two separate legs joined by a strip of cloth were truly bothersome. She kept pulling at the strip and then, at the first opportunity, took off the pyjamas and was going to slip into the lehnga when

Mirza appeared on the scene. She got so nervous that she forgot to hold the lehnga around her waist and let it fall.

'La hawla wala quwwat . . .', Mirza cried out in agony, pulled up a sheet and threw it over her. Then he broke into a lengthy oration that went over her head.

What was her fault? Previously, the same act would have made Mirza swoon over her. Now he got so incensed that he picked up the lehnga and flung it into the fire.

Mirza left, muttering to himself as Lajo sat there, crestfallen. Throwing off her sheet she began to scrutinize her body. Could it be that she had contracted leprosy? She kept wiping her tears as she bathed under the tap. The mason's son, Mithwa, on the pretext of flying kites from the roof, used to watch her stealthily as she took her bath. She was so depressed today that she neither stuck out her thumb nor threatened to hurl her shoe at him, nor went running into the house, but just wrapped the shawl around her.

With a heavy heart she got into the pyjamas, long as the devil's intestines. To make matters worse, the drawstring slipped into the waistband. Her frantic yells for help brought Billo running over, and the string was extracted.

'Which sadist invented this contraption? One has to tie and untie it each time one goes to the lavatory!' Lajo gave vent to her spleen.

The string again gave the slip when Mirza returned home in the evening. She was trying desperately to hold it between her fingers. Seeing this, Mirza felt a sudden fondness for her and took her into his arms. After a long chase, the string was located, and Lajo felt somewhat reconciled to her new attire.

But there was a fresh problem. Lajo's coquetry that had seemed enchanting before marriage now seemed objectionable in a wife. Such sluttish ways did not become decent women. She could not become Mirza's dream bride – one whom Mirza would beg for love, one who would blush at his advances, one who would feign anger and one he would coax into submission. She was like a stone slab on the road; she could not become a flower for offering on the altar. Mirza's constant chastisement had put restrictions on her freewheeling ways, and eventually she was tamed and reformed.

Mirza felt contented that he was able to make a decent woman of her. Now he didn't feel any urge to get back home in a hurry. Like other husbands, he spent time with his friends so that no one could call him henpecked! A man can do anything to please his mistress, but the wife is altogether a different kettle of fish.

To make up for his absence, he suggested employing a maid. Lajo glared at him. She knew that the mian visited courtesans; all Mirza's male neighbours did. But she could not share the house with another woman. If anyone dared to enter her kitchen or touch her sparkling vessels, she would break her legs. She could share Mirza with another woman, but as far as her home was concerned, she was the undisputed mistress.

Having installed her in the house, Mirza seemed to have forgotten about her existence. For weeks he would speak only in monosyllables. As long as she had been his mistress, everyone had had an eye for her. Now that she was married to a decent person, she became 'mother', 'sister' and 'daughter'. No one cared to throw a glance at the jute curtain. Except Mithwa, the mason's son. He was still loyal to her, flying kites on the roof. After Mirza left in the morning, Lajo would finish the daily chores and then go for her bath under the tap. The tap was fixed to facilitate observance of purdah, and Lajo would not even look at the terrace now.

One night Mirza stayed out, celebrating the festival of Dussehra with friends. He returned in the morning, took a quick bath and left for the shop. Lajo was left fuming. That day Lajo's eyes went up the terrace once again. She saw that Mithwa's eyes were piercing her wet body like spears. The lad's kite snapped, and the broken cord brushed against Lajo's bare back. She gasped and, either unconsciously or deliberately, ran for the house without wrapping the towel around her. It was as though a lightning flashed and thunder fell on Mirza's house. Then she remembered that she had left the tap running and returned there hurriedly.

After that day, whenever Lajo drew aside the jute curtain and looked for someone to be sent to the halwai's, she always found Mithwa loitering around Mirza's house.

'Hey, Mithwa, don't stay put like a dunghill all day! Get me some kachauris. Ask the fellow to put enough pepper in the pickle.'

Mithwa was now more drawn towards her. If he forgot to appear on the terrace while she was taking her bath, she would rattle the bucket loud enough to wake up corpses in their graves. The love of which she had always been generous was now available to Mithwa. If Mirza skipped a meal, Lajo would not throw away the food but give it to a needy person. And who was more deserving of her generosity than Mithwa?

Having bound her in the fetters of wedlock, Mirza felt confident that he had made her a housewife. So he would not have believed it if he had not seen it with his own eyes. Seeing Mirza at such an odd hour, she could not help breaking into a smile. She could not imagine that he would be so incensed by what he saw. But Mithwa knew. Picking up his dhoti, he ran for his life and paused only after he had crossed three villages.

Mirza beat Lajo so severely that she would have died had she not been made of sterner stuff. The news spread like wildfire through the village that Mirza had caught his wife with Mithwa and that he had beaten them to death. Mirza was humiliated. His family honour had bitten the dust. People came in droves to see the fun, but they felt sorely disappointed when they found that Mithwa had bolted and Lajo was beaten up but alive. 'She'll live. Ramu's grandma will bring her round,' they said.

One would have thought that Lajo would begin to hate Mirza after such a severe beating. Far from it. Rather, it made the bond stronger. The moment she came to, she asked after Mirza. All her masters would, sooner or later, turn into her lovers. After that there was no question of wages. On top of it, they would give her a thrashing now and then. They would even lend her to their friends. Mirza had always been so gentle. He had come to regard her as his own – and asserted his right over her. For her, this was an honour. Though he didn't make use of her anymore, she was still dear to him. Even in that condition, her heart yearned for Mirza. All advised her to run away to save her life, but she didn't listen to them.

The least Mirza could do now to save his family honour was to kill Lajo. But Miran Mian restrained him. Lajo had survived, and he had lost face. How could he face the world now?

'Come on, do you want to stick your head in the noose for a bastard?'

'I don't care.'

'Divorce the whore, and get rid of her,' Miran Mian advised him. 'Had she been from a decent family, it would be different.'

Mirza divorced her right there. He sent the thirty-two rupees mehr money and her other belongings over to Ramu's grandmother's.

Lajo heaved a sigh of relief as she heard about the divorce. It was as though a heavy load was off her shoulders. Marriage did not suit her. All this happened because of it. Good that it was over and done with.

'I hope Mian is not angry?' she asked Ramu's grandma.

'I don't want to see your face. You've disgraced us; now leave this place.'

The news of Mirza's divorce spread through the village. Immediately, Lala sent a feeler –

'The bungalow is ready.'

'Put up your mother there,' Lajo sent her reply.

Out of the thirty-two rupees of mehr money, she gave ten to Ramu's grandma for providing her food and lodging. She sold the tight-fitting pyjamas to Shakur's mother for a small sum. In a fortnight she was on her feet again. It was as though she had been spring cleaned after the beating, which left her complexion glowing more than ever before. There was a new magic in the swing of her hips. When she made forays into the market to buy paan or kachauri, she took the whole place by storm. Mirza's heart would ache.

One day she was quarrelling with the paan-seller over cardamom. The paan-seller was drooling. Mirza passed by quietly, trying to avoid the scene.

'Mian, you're crazy. Let her do what she wants. Why give a damn? You've divorced her. What's she to you now?' Miran Mian argued with him.

'She has been my wife. How can I overlook that?' Mirza fumed.

'So what? She's no longer your wife. And if you ask me, she never was your wife.'

'How about the nikah?'

'Absolutely impermissible.'

'What do you mean?'

'The nikah was not valid, brother. No one knows whose illegitimate brat she was. Nikah with a bastard is haram – strictly forbidden.' Miran Mian declared the verdict.

'You mean, the marriage didn't come into effect?'

'Absolutely not.'

Later, Mullahji also confirmed that marriage with a bastard was not valid.

'So, I haven't lost my honour?' Mirza smiled. A heavy load was off his head.

'Not at all,' Miran Mian reassured him.

'Great! So, there was no divorce?'

'My dear brother, there was no nikah, so there's no question of divorce.'

'So, my thirty-two rupees of mehr went down the drain,' said Mirza with a note of regret.

This news also spread soon throughout the village, that Mirza's marriage with Lajo was not valid, and there was no divorce, though Mirza had lost thirty-two rupees in the bargain.

Lajo began to dance when she came to know of it. The nikah and the divorce were nightmares that were now over. She felt greatly relieved. However, what made her the happiest was that Mirza had not lost his face after all! She would have felt very bad if he had. Being a bastard served her in good stead! God forbid, if she had been the legitimate child of her parents, she would have faced the music now!

Lajo felt suffocated at Ramu's grandmother's. Never before in her life had she got the opportunity to become the mistress of a household. She missed the house. Mirza would not get anyone to sweep it for fear of pilferage. The place must be in a mess.

Mirza was going to the shop. Lajo stopped him on the way.

'Mian, shall I come along tomorrow to resume work?' Lajo said with coquetry.

'La hawla wala quwwat . . .' Mirza lowered his head and passed her quickly taking long strides. 'I must employ a maid. If the bitch wants to come, let her.' So ran his thought.

Lajo didn't wait till the next day. She ran over the roofs and jumped down into the house. She tucked up her lehnga and began to work.

When Mirza returned in the evening, he felt as though his late mother was back! The house was spic and span. The smell of incense filled the air. The water pitcher was new, and a well-scrubbed bowl had been placed over it . . . Mirza's heart brimmed with emotion. He began to eat the stewed meat and the roti quietly. As usual, Lajo sat on the door sill, fanning away.

At night when she spread two curtains on the kitchen floor and lay down, Mirza once again felt severe bouts of thirst. He kept on tossing and turning on the bed as he heard Lajo's anklets tinkling.

A nagging feeling that he did not value her worth overwhelmed him.

'La hawla wala quwwat . . .' He got up from his bed abruptly and gathered the homemaker in his arms.

Touch-me-not

'Illahi khair! O Ghulam Dastgir! Obeisance to the twelve imams! . . . Make a move dear . . . carefully . . . steady, steady . . . pull up the salwar . . . easy, easy,' Bi Mughlani bellowed like a herald. I pulled Bhabijan up, Bhaijan pushed from the other side and thus she, a veritable advertisement for amulets and talismans, took the small step and rolled over to the chair like an inflated balloon.

'Praise be to Allah, the Almighty!' Bi Mughlani sighed with relief, and we felt a great load lift from our minds.

Bhabijan was not exactly born with a silver spoon in her mouth, nor had she had ayahs and other ladies-in-waiting at her disposal. Yet, before long, the frail slip of a girl had become as tender as a swollen wound. The fact is, the moment her mother stopped feeding her, she came to adorn Bhaijan's bed. Here she had pretty little to do and blossomed like a flower, fresh and fragrant, without any sense of life's harshness. Bi Mughlani took charge of her from the day of her marriage. She woke up from sleep at a leisurely hour, but remained in bed while Bi Mughlani flurried around attending to her person. Later she would be given a choice breakfast. Having washed it all down, she would keep sitting – her cheeks resting on her hands and lips parted in a smile.

The smile began to fade in the second year of her marriage as nausea made her throw up all the time. Finding his beautiful, doll-like bride turning into a permanently sick woman, Bhaijan began to lose interest in her. But Bi Mughlani and Ammijan were bursting with excitement. From the first month of pregnancy they threw themselves into the baby project wholeheartedly – stitching diapers, etc. with such enthusiasm as though the delivery was imminent. So covered was she with amulets that even a mole could not have peeped through. Constant application of witchcraft and charms wore her down. As it is, Bhabijan was never a great one for walks and sprints, but now even if she turned on her side herself, Bi Mughlani would raise such a racket that the whole house would come rushing in. Even a half-baked clay pot was not handled with greater care. Pirs and fakirs became permanent fixtures in the house, ever ready to mutter prayers and ward off evil spirits.

In spite of Bi Mughlani's rigorous vigil, however, the shell cracked before time and expectations drew a blank. The blossoms withered away and the branch remained bare. But a thousand thanks to Allah that her life was saved. Allah is bountiful. If the mother survived, more could come. And did. The vigil was intensified. Yet hopes again drew a blank. The third time round, matters took a grave turn. The poor thing was choked with pills and syrups. A sick pallor gave her the look of a sweet potato turned bulbous. Her evenings stretched to the early hours of dawn. Ammi Begum and Bi Mughlani were not too pleased. Lying in her bed, Bhabijan seemed to hear the shehnai of Bhaijan's second marriage.

However, by the grace of Allah, the pregnancy advanced quite a bit without any mishap. This time, besides pirs and fakirs, Delhi doctors also descended in their full armour. From the second month, she was treated as delicately as a soap bubble and provided with all comforts. No one was allowed to sneeze or blow their nose in her vicinity lest the bubble should burst once again. When the doctors declared her out of danger, Ammi Begum decided that the delivery should take place at Aligarh. It was hardly a two-hour journey. Bhabijan was reluctant to leave Delhi even though the doctors had given the go-ahead. Her horizon was darkening. She knew that another miscarriage would be her husband's ticket to a second marriage. Now Bhaijan could do anything in the name of progeny. Only Allah knew why the fellow was so keen on keeping his name alive. As it is, he didn't have a name to speak of. If she failed in this one conjugal duty, she would have to forgo all bridal comforts. She had reigned so long on the strength of her beauty and charm. Now she was perched on a boat her husband was prepared to topple. Where could the poor thing go? She didn't learn needlework because of lack of interest in it, and the little she had studied was long forgotten. In the absence of a provider, she could resort to one thing only – that is, to render the same service to everybody which was, so far, exclusive to her husband. That was why she was desperately looking forward to the delivery which would make her life secure. If the father of the newborn lacked interest, the grandfather would certainly provide for her maintenance.

As if she did not have enough on her mind already, there came Ammi Begum's imperial command to start for Aligarh, and we were thrown aflutter. A bunch of new amulets would see her through.

'Illahi khair!' Caught unawares by a particularly strong jolt of the speeding train, Bi Mughlani crashed down and Bhabijan clutched at the vessel by her. 'Is this a train or a transport to hell! O Pir Murshid, help us . . . O Hazrat Ali . . .' Holding Bhabijan's tummy, Bi Mughlani started muttering prayers and verses from the holy Quran. Somehow, we reached Ghaziabad.

The Toofan Mail, true to its name, tore along without stopping. The entire couch was reserved for us. Hence the threat of jostling crowds was out. I was intently watching the crowd in front of the window and Bi Mughlani shielded her ears against the train's shrieking whistle. Bhabijan nearly fainted at the sight of the crowd from afar.

As the train chugged off, the couch door opened and a peasant woman moved in. The coolie tried to pull her away but she stuck to the handle like a lizard and would not budge. Slowly she dragged herself to the bathroom door, despite Bi Mughlani's constant chiding, and leaned against it, panting.

'May Allah forgive our sins!' Bi Mughlani murmured. 'Hey, you! Are you pregnant for the full term?' The panting woman just managed to spread her parched lips in a strained smile and nodded assent.

'By Allah, this girl has some cheek!' The shock was too much for Bi Mughlani, and she began to slap her face repeatedly. The woman stood mute. The intensity of pain made her restless, and she clutched at the bathroom door with both hands. Her breath came in gasps and perspiration appeared on her forehead like dew-drops on cool ground.

'Is it your first pregnancy?' Bi Mughlani asked angrily, piqued by her lack of experience. The woman could not reply as fits of pain swept over her. Her face turned pale and tears trickled down her dilated eyes. Bi Mughlani kept up her litany of lament as the woman continued to writhe in tearing pain.

'What do you think you're doing, looking on like that? No dear, look the other way; you're still a virgin maid.' I turned away. But the heart-rending cry of the woman made me turn back involuntarily. Bi Mughlani was incensed – 'Allah's curse! As though she'd achieve salvation if she sees a child being born!' Bhabijan, her face wrapped in her dupatta, kept on staring. Bi Mughlani's burkha dropped to her nose and she badly smeared the floor of the couch with her constant spitting.

All of a sudden it seemed that the world shrank on its axis and twisted itself. So intense was my reaction that my ears began to burn and tears welled up automatically. 'This is the end,' I thought. But the tension in the atmosphere melted abruptly. The burkha slipped from Bi Mughlani's nose as a lump of red flesh dropped near Bhabijan's royal shoes, the Salimshahis. I cried out in surprise and joy and bent down to look at the tiny wonder that broke all hell loose by letting out a full-throated yell.

Bi Mughlani raged on. Bhabijan clung to my pallu as I handed over a pair of nail-cutting scissors to the woman. She was my age, maybe a few months older. I was reminded of field animals like sheep and goats who bring forth their offspring as they graze along, without any fuss and not caring for the help of lady doctors, and then tidy up by licking them with their tongue.

Elderly people prevent young girls from watching a delivery, saying that when Zebunnisa saw her sister giving birth to a baby, she was so shocked that she never got married. So much for old folks and their old wives' tales! Zebunnisa's sister must have been as fragile as my Bhabijan. If she had witnessed this woman's delivery, she would have been convinced, like me, that people make a lot of fuss for nothing. Giving birth is as easy a job for women as getting on or off the train is for Bhaijan. After all, this is not something to be ashamed of. Far more revolting is the gossip between Bi Mughlani and Amma about fellow women, which falls like hot embers on my ears day in and day out making them burn.

For some time the woman tried to breastfeed the child in her clumsy way. Her tears had dried up, and she broke into occasional fits of laughter as though someone was tickling her. Bi Mughlani's chiding subdued her somewhat. She wrapped the baby in a rag, put it under the seat and stood up. Bhabijan let out a scream. Bi Mughlani soothed her. The woman fetched water from the bathroom and began to clean the couch. Rubbing off the stains from Bhabijan's brocaded shoes, she left them standing in a corner. Then she picked up her child and sat leaning against the bathroom door with the air of one who, having finished the day's chores, sits down to relax. As the train drew to a halt, she stepped down.

'Where's your ticket?' asked the ticket collector. She held out her dupatta with a flourish as though she was exhibiting jamuns that she had plucked stealthily. Too shocked to speak, the ticket collector stood transfixed while she turned away and vanished in the crowd.

'Allah's wrath on all these harlots! They go on breeding bastards . . . the witches!' Bi Mughlani muttered to herself. The train gave a lurch and chugged off.

Bhabijan's smouldering sobs abruptly turned into a searing scream. 'Oh Allah! What's wrong, Begum Dulhan?' Bi Mughlani's heart came to her mouth as she looked at the Begum's terror-stricken face. Writ large on it was the vision of her husband's second marriage:

Thus does fate play with us
Shows the shore and capsizes the boat.

The unborn child got cold feet and wilted away before its entry into the world. My flower-like Bhabijan felt so unnerved after witnessing the bizarre delivery in the train that she had a miscarriage once again.

Quit India

'The saab is dead,' announced Jinat Ram as he returned from the market with groceries.

'Saheb who?'

'That blind Saheb.'

'Oh, you mean Jackson, the one-eyed Englishman. Ah! Poor fellow!'

I looked out of the window. Beyond the mossy ruined walls was a crumbling chabutara. Sakku Bai mourned volubly in Marathi as she sat stretching her legs on the crumbling chabutara on the other side of the wall, moss covered and partly demolished, like a set of bed teeth. Pattu sat on his haunches beside her, crying spasmodically. Pattu, that is Peter, was a unique blend of the white and the black commingling. His eyes were black and hair brown like Jackson Saheb's, his wheatish complexion had become brassy because of excessive exposure to the sun.

I have been watching this strange family for years through this window. It was right here, sitting by the window, that I had struck up a conversation with Jackson for the first time.

Those were the heady days of the Quit India Movement in 1942. A trip from Grant Road to Dadar provided a brief but exciting vista of the ferment the country was in. At the blocked end of Mangton Road a bonfire was lit where the ties, hats and trousers of the passers-by were being thrown zestfully. The scene, though a trifle childish, was interesting nonetheless. Fluttering ties, stately hats and newly ironed trousers were being ruthlessly thrown into the flames. The fire-setters, mostly dressed in tatters, were flinging in the new clothes without any qualms. It didn't occur to them even for a moment that they should cover their bare, black shins with the new gabardine trousers rather than make a bonfire of them.

Meanwhile, a military truck had arrived, and the ruddy-faced, machine gun-wielding tommies hopped down one by one. The crowd vanished in no time. I watched this spectacle from the secure enclosure of the municipal office. Seeing the machine guns I quickly crept back into the office.

A similar scene took place in a railway compartment as well. When the train had pulled out of Bombay Central, only three out of the six seats were intact. By the time the train reached Lower Parel, those three seats were also wrenched from their place and flung out of the window. I had to stand up all the way to Dadar. Yet I didn't feel angry with those lads. It seemed as though the railway, the ties, the trousers, etc., did not belong to us but to our enemies. Setting those on fire was like setting the enemy on fire, uprooting them from here and throwing them out of the country. Close to my house they had put the long stump of a tree on the road, and by heaping garbage on it built a barricade to block traffic. I had crossed it with great difficulty and reached the doorstep of my flat when the military lorry came. The tommy who climbed down first was none other than Jackson. The youths who were putting up the road block ran away and took refuge in the nearby buildings.

As I lived on the ground floor, many boys sought shelter in my flat. While some hid themselves in the kitchen, others stole into the bathroom and the lavatory. Since my front door was open, Jackson entered along with two armed tommies and began to interrogate me.

'The scoundrels are hiding in your house. Surrender them to us.'

'There's no one in the house except my servants,' I answered nonchalantly.

'Who's your servant?'

'These three.' I gestured towards the three men who were scraping utensils.

'Who's there in the bathroom?'

'My mother-in-law is taking a bath.' Only God knew where my mother-in-law was at that moment.

'And in the lavatory?' There was a mischievous glint in his eyes.

'Maybe my mother or sister. How do I know? I've just come.'

'Then how did you know that it's your mother-in-law in the bathroom?'

'As I entered a while ago she had called out for the towel.'

'I see. All right, tell your mother-in-law that blocking road traffic is an offence,' he said in a subdued tone and asked his companions, who waited outside, to go back to the lorry.

'Hunh – hunh, hunh!' He shook his head, and smiled, as he left. His eyes sparkled as though they had fireflies in them.

Jackson's bungalow stood on the plot adjacent to my house, with the sea on the western side. Those days, his wife, the Memsaheb, had come to India with their children. The elder daughter was a grown-up lady while the younger one was twelve or thirteen. Memsaheb used to come to India for a short stay during the holidays. With her arrival, the bungalow would undergo a dramatic transformation. The servants would be seen scurrying about, tripods would be laid at different places inside and outside the bungalow, and to embellish the garden, new flower pots were brought, which were stolen by the neighbours the moment Memsaheb left. On the eve of Memsaheb's next visit Saheb would get another supply of pots from the Victoria Garden. As long as the Memsaheb stayed, the servants would be seen in livery. Dressed in uniform or an excellent gown, Jackson would be seen walking smart dogs in the garden as though he were a Pucca Saheb.

With the Memsaheb gone, Saheb would breathe a sigh of relief and go to his office at leisure. After work, he would slip into shorts and sit in a chair on the chabutara and enjoy his drink. There would be no trace of the gown. The bearer would have stolen it. The dogs would accompany Memsaheb on her return trip. Seeing the abandoned look of the bungalow, pie dogs would make the compound their home.

Throughout Memsaheb's stay, dinner parties were thrown every other day. She would call out to her ayah in a shrill voice first thing in the morning – 'Hey, Sakku . . . u . . . u . . .'

'Yes, Memsaheb.' The ayah would run to do her errands. But it was said that as soon as Memsaheb left she would take her place in the house, playing her substitute. Philómina and Pattu were living proof of her liaison with the master during Memsaheb's absence.

Memsaheb had got fed up with this dirty, soggy land and its people. The convulsions of the Quit India Movement further upset her, and she left for 'home' in a hurry. I saw Jackson again during that period through the self-same window.

'Has your mother-in-law finished her bath yet?' he asked mischievously in the Bombay lingo.

'Yes, Saheb. A bloodbath!' I said curtly. Several young men, all of them about fourteen years old, had died in the firing at Hari Nivas only a couple of days ago. I am sure some of them were the same youths who had taken refuge in my house when the military lorry had arrived. I was repulsed by the sight of Saheb. A living tool of British imperialism stood before me and made fun of the innocent martyrs who had died at his hands. I felt like scratching his face with my nails. It was difficult for me to know which one of his eyes was made of glass because it was the best specimen of Europe's surgical excellence. It smacked of the duplicity of the white race to which Jackson belonged. His sense of superiority, which was like poison, glimmered equally forcefully in both his eyes. I slammed the window shut.

I used to feel a growing fury against Sakku Bai. The bitch was like an easy morsel for the shameless white cur. Was there any dearth of lepers and bastards in this land that she was bent upon besmirching the self-respect of the country? Everyday Jackson would get drunk and give her a thrashing. The country was in the throes of convulsive changes. The days of the white rulers were numbered.

'This is the fag end of their rule,' some would say.

'It's just a daydream. To drive them out of the country is no joke,' countered others. I listened to the long, interminable speeches of the leaders of the country and wondered why no one ever mentioned the one-eyed Jackson. He felt free to beat Sakku

Bai to pulp. Pattu and Philomina also. Why didn't the slogan-shouting freedom fighters do something about this scoundrel?

I felt restless to do something. But what? I knew that they brewed alcohol a few lanes away. I was told that if one reported the goondas to the police they made one's life miserable. Well, I didn't even know whom to report to. In the entire building, taps dripped and drains overflowed. And I didn't have the faintest idea whom to inform. The neighbours also didn't know where to complain if a bad-natured woman living upstairs decided to empty her dustbin on someone's head. On such occasions the victim would look up and curse at the window above. Then he would go on his way wiping the dirt off his clothes.

I ran into Sakku Bai one day.

'You wretched woman, don't you feel any shame that the scoundrel gives you a drubbing everyday?'

'Not everyday, Bai,' she began to argue with me.

'Well, he beats you four or five times a month, doesn't he?'

'That he does, Bai. But I pay him back,' she laughed.

'Liar!'

'I swear on Pattu. I gave him a mild drubbing day before yesterday.'

'But don't you feel ashamed of yourself, being pummelled in this way by this white-skinned fellow?' Like a true patriot I began to lecture her. 'These plunderers have pillaged the country to its bare bones.' And so on and so forth.

'Don't say that, Bai. The Saab hasn't robbed anyone. These lumpens rob him day in and day out. Memsaheb left, and the bearers dispatched all the cutlery. The pants, coat, hat, first-class shoes – everything has vanished. Come to the bungalow and see for yourself. Nothing is left. You call Saab a robber. I say, if I weren't here, they would have torn the flesh off his body.'

'But why does your heart bleed for him?'

'Why not? He's my man, isn't he?' Sakku Bai smiled.

'How about Memsaheb?'

'She's a downright slut, yes –' Sakku Bai asserted with vehemence.

'We know her very well. She has many lovers in London. So she likes it there.' Here she mouthed a filthy abuse. 'And when she comes here she quarrels with Saab all day long. With the servants, too.'

I tried to explain to her that the Englishmen were about to leave the country. Saheb, too, would leave. But she was not convinced and said, 'Where will Saab go, leaving me here? He doesn't like England at all.'

After that I had to stay at Pune for a few years. The world had changed by then. The English had left the country for good. Partition had taken place. The white rulers had played the old trick, and the whole country bathed in blood.

When I returned to Bombay, the bungalow had undergone a transformation. Saheb was not there. A refugee family had taken possession of it. Sakku Bai was living in one of the rooms of the servants' quarters. Philomina had grown quite tall. She and Pattu went to an orphanage school in Mahim.

As soon as Sakku Bai heard of my arrival, she came to see me holding groundnut pods in her hand.

'How are you, Bai?' she asked me ritually as she massaged my knee.

'How are you? Where's your Saheb? Has he left for London?'

'No, Bai.' Sakku Bai's face went pale. 'I told him to go, but he didn't. His job ended as well. He was even ordered to leave India, but he didn't.'

'Where is he, then?'

'In the hospital.'

'Why? What's wrong?'

'Doctors say that too much drinking has affected his brain. They've sent him to the lunatic asylum.'

'But he was to return to England.'

'Everyone urged him to go. Me, too,' Sakku Bai was crying. 'But he didn't listen. He said to me "Sakku darling, I won't go, leaving you here."'

The sight of Sakku Bai crying for Jackson affected me deeply. I totally forgot that Saheb belonged to the community of oppressors who, joining the military service, had contributed to the subjugation of our country. He had sprayed children with bullets and showered fire from machine guns on unarmed people. He was a cog in the huge and hateful British imperial machine and had stained the road with the blood of our valorous fighters whose only fault was that they were demanding their rights. However, none of these occurred to my mind at that moment except that Sakku Bai's 'man' was in the asylum. I felt bad about getting so emotional because a patriot should never feel any sympathy or affection for any member of the colonizing race.

It was not I only; everyone had forgotten the past. All the young men of the mohalla were mad about Philomina. They didn't care whether the seed that begot her was black or white. When she returned from school their deep sighs and wistful gazes followed her. While falling in love no young man ever remembered the fact that she was the daughter of a white brute who had shed the blood of fourteen-year-old youths at the entrance of Hari Nivas, had fired on unarmed women right in front of the church because they were raising the slogan 'Quit India', had squeezed out the blood of youths on the sands of Chaupati and fired on a procession of hungry and downtrodden boys with machine guns! All of them had forgotten these. They only remembered that the girl had golden cheeks and blue eyes and that the swing of her hips was electrifying. And pearls dropped with the quiver of her succulent, big lips.

One day Sakku Bai came running carrying prasad. 'My Saab has returned,' she said in a voice filled with emotion. Her eyes shone like pearls. How much love there was in that word 'my'! The love that gave her life sustenance.

'Has he recovered?'

'Oh Bai, he was never mad. The Sahebs took him away and put him into the asylum without any good reason. He has run away from there,' she said conspiratorially.

I was alarmed, because not only was he a vanquished Englishman but a runaway from the lunatic asylum as well. But to whom could I report? No one wanted to be entangled in the wiles of the Bombay police. Let him be mad. I didn't have to be chummy with him.

But I was wrong. We grew more familiar. I was curious to know why he didn't want to join his wife in England. Would any person in his right mind want to give up paradise and stay in a shack? And I got my chance one day. After his arrival, he remained cooped up in his room for a few days, and then gradually began to come out and sit at the doorstep. He had grown thin as a wafer. His ruddy, beetroot complexion that reminded one of a monkey had now become a tanned brown and his hair had turned grey. Clad in a check lungi and dirty vest, he looked like the old Gurkhas scouring Indian streets. Now one could distinguish between his real eye and the artificial one. Though the glass was still bright, transparent and 'English', the real eye had lost its former lustre and sunk deep in its socket. Usually he went out without the glass eye. One day I saw him through the window standing under a jamun tree, picking up pebbles from the ground absent-mindedly. He looked at them and smiled like a child. Then he flung the pebbles with all his might. Seeing me he nodded and smiled.

'How are you, Saheb?' I asked, consumed with curiosity.

'Good, good.' He smiled and thanked me.

I went out to have a chat with him. Soon he opened up. I began to delve deeper. Several days' prodding revealed that he was the illegitimate son of an aristocratic lady. His grandfather had left him with a peasant and had paid for his upkeep. All this had been done with such finesse that even the peasant didn't know about the family of his ward. The peasant was a brute, and had several sons who tortured Jackson in various ways. He would be beaten up everyday. However, the meals were wholesome. When he was twelve or thirteen, he began to make plans to run away. He was successful in his mission after three years. Having knocked about at different places he eventually reached London. He tried his hand at various jobs but he had grown so deceitful and pig-headed that he couldn't stick to any one job for more than two days.

He was handsome, and that made him quite a success with girls. Dorothy, his wife, was from a snobbish, aristocratic family. She looked plain and was mean. Her father was a man with high connections. Jackson felt that his nomadic life had its disadvantages – he ran into trouble with the police and the court every other day. Marriage with Dorothy would put an end to all this.

Dorothy moved in high society and was beyond his reach. But at that time, both his eyes were real, and that did the trick. It was later when he fought with Dorothy and made pubs his home that the eye was injured during a drunken brawl. At that time, only his elder daughter had been born.

'Tell me how you trapped Dorothy?' I prodded him.

'Both my eyes were intact then.' He grinned.

Somehow, Dorothy fell into his hands. She was not even a virgin. Though her father objected to the match, she went ahead and married him. Perhaps she had lost all hope of marriage and was glad to have Jackson. The father understood the daughter's compulsion and finally acquiesced. Moreover, he was fed up with his wife's nagging on the subject. He got Jackson sent to India. It was a time when every worthless Englishman was being dispatched to India. He might have been an ordinary cobbler in England, but he would become a Pucca Saheb on his arrival in India.

Jackson was the limit. He turned out to be as worthless and wild as he had been in England. The worst fault he had was his lack of dignity. Instead of strutting and carrying himself about like a Pucca Saheb, he mingled with the damned natives. When he was posted in the department of forestry in the countryside, instead of clubs he would frequent the opium houses.

There were some bungalows around belonging to Englishmen who were mostly old and senile. The clubs, where Indians and dogs were not allowed to enter, were usually desolate. The wives of the officers stayed back in England. When a wife visited India, rather than bringing her to the jungle, the officer would take leave and carry her to Simla or Nainital. The wife would soon get fed up with the filth in India and return home while the husband would return to his post carrying sweet memories of his wife in his heart. Of course, the Sahebs would make do with the native women. Such liaisons benefited both the parties as they came cheap. The country, too, benefited from it – for one thing, the offspring of such unions used to be brown and, sometimes, quite fair. They were more fortunate than the natives because their influential fathers would establish orphanages and schools for them. Their educational expenses were borne by the government. In social status, the Anglo-Indian community came right after Englishmen. The boys found employment easily in the railways and the navy. Even ordinary-looking girls of the community would land better jobs than Indian girls and add glamour to schools, offices and hospitals. The fairer ones among them flourished in the red-light areas of big cities.

When Jackson came to India, he was richly endowed with all the evils associated with a one-eyed person. His tendency to get into brawls led to quick transfers from one place to another. He was shifted from the forestry to the police department. This disappointed him because he had fallen for a hillwoman. Having reached Jabalpur, he would have called her, but he fell so deeply in love with a rope dancer there that his wife spent her entire vacation in Nainital and he didn't visit her even once before she returned to England. His usual pretext was either too much work or lack of holidays. But Dorothy's father had many influential friends through whom he was granted leave – against his wish. He reached Nainital but didn't like it there. For one thing, the separation from Jackson had made Dorothy passionate, and she wanted a honeymoon all over again. But Jackson's mode of love disappointed her. His long stay in India had made him a stranger to her. Both the hillwoman and the rope dancer had spoilt him by doing his bidding like loyal Indian wives.

The wife who came to stay with him for only two months in a year had become a stranger. Moreover, Jackson had to abide by certain norms of etiquette with her.

One day when he was drunk, he demanded that his wife make

love like the hillwoman or the rope dancer. She flew into such a rage that Jackson had a hard time defending himself. She asked, 'Have you degenerated like the other low-born Englishmen who mess around with local native women?' Jackson swore again and again that it was not so. She had to be convinced of his faithfulness to her before she came to Jabalpur with him. Perhaps the heat and flies there drove her half mad. Perhaps she could have put up with that even, but one day when she found two eels crawling in her bathroom, she began to pack her luggage that very moment. Jackson tried to convince her that they were not snakes, nor did they bite. But she didn't listen to him and left for Delhi the next day.

From Delhi she pulled strings and got him transferred to Bombay. The Second World War had broken out. The separation from the rope dancer and Dorothy's permanent stay in Bombay made Jackson's life miserable. Sakku Bai was employed to help the ayah with the children. Fed up with the rains there, Dorothy left for England with the children and Jackson began to pay court to Sakku Bai. What a complicated story! Sakku Bai was, in fact, the mistress of Ganpat Rai, the head bearer who brought her from Pon Pol. He was a family man. To lighten his burden of responsibility, he got her employed as a charwoman to help the ayah. Sakku Bai was quite contented with her job, which entailed wiping the floors and washing the dishes in addition to keeping Ganpat in good humour.

Ganpat would sometimes lend her to a friend as a gesture of goodwill or as payment of a debt. But he did it with such subtle cunning that even Sakku Bai was unaware of it for quite sometime. Earlier she used to drink rarely. Now she began to drink country liquor with Ganpat every evening. Ganpat would bring the customer to his room. No one was afraid of Jackson. Abandoning household chores, the servants would spend time gambling and drinking country liquor. The moment Dorothy left, all the bad characters of Shivaji Park would assemble at the bungalow and make merry.

When the liquor went to his head, Ganpat would leave Sakku

Bai with the client on some pretext or the other. Sakku Bai thought that she was making a fool of Ganpat. And then, working for Saheb, she gradually began to play the role of his wife. That is how she got rid of Ganpat. That scoundrel used to take away all her wages. After that, Ganpat enrolled himself in the army as a bearer and left for the Middle East, and Sakku Bai consolidated herself in Memsaheb's position. When Memsaheb came to India Sakku Bai would shift to her shack. And when she called out for her in her fine, shrill voice, she would respond with a 'Yes, Memsaheb', with utmost promptness, leave all her chores and run to do her bidding. She thought herself quite an expert in the lingo. After all, what else was there in the English language except 'yes', 'no', 'damn fool' and 'swine'? The rulers could manage their work using these few words. They didn't need an elegant or literary language. All that the horse pulling the tonga needs to know are the sound of the whip and the clicking of his master's tongue. However, Sakku Bai didn't know that the frail horse yoked to the English cart had died, the cart had been sent home and that the reins of the country were now in others' hands. Her world was very small – it consisted of herself, her two children and her 'man'.

Whenever Memsaheb came to India, Sakku Bai would generously give up her place as Jackson's mistress and start working as the nanny's assistant. She never felt any jealousy towards Memsaheb. Memsaheb may have been considered beautiful by Western standards; however, if one judged her by Indian norms of beauty, she drew a blank. Her skin was rough like a raw turnip, as though it had been plucked before it was fully ripe. Or it was as though she had been left buried in some dark, cold grave for years and then taken out. Her untidy, thin hair made her look old. That is why people of Sakku Bai's class thought her an old woman, or an albino, who is considered an object of pity in India. When she washed her face, her eye-liner would vanish, and her face looked like a drawing disfigured by a cheap eraser.

Above all, Dorothy was frigid, and almost a stranger. Jackson's existence was an object of humiliation for her. She thought of herself as an unfortunate and oppressed woman, not responsible for her failed marriage. As for Jackson, even if he reached a high position, he could not take pride in it because he knew very well that he owed it to Dorothy's father. Any other person in his position, blessed with the munificence of Dorothy's father, would have made a spectacular rise in his career.

However, Sakku Bai was Jackson's own – she was warm to the touch. She was a bonfire where many could warm their hands. She had been Ganpat Rai's 'keep', and he lent her to his friends as though she were an old garment. Jackson Saheb was like a god to her, an embodiment of decency. There was a world of difference in the way he and Ganpat loved her. Ganpat used her to change the taste in his mouth, whereas Saheb, helpless and needy, treated her like nectar. His love was like that of a helpless baby.

When the British left bag and baggage, he didn't. Dorothy tried all means to call him back, even threatened him. But he resigned from his job and stayed back in India.

'Saheb, aren't you reminded of your children?'

'Yes, very much. Philo comes home late in the evening and Pattu goes out to play with other boys. I wish they would sit by me for a little while.' There was yearning in his voice.

'I don't mean Philomina and Pattu, but Esther and Liza,' I said brazenly.

'No, no . . .' He smiled as he shook his head. 'Pups get attached only to the bitch, not to the dog that is equally responsible for bringing them into the world,' he said as he winked at me with his real eye.

'Why doesn't he leave? Why rot here?' not only I but others in the neighbourhood wondered.

'He's a spy, left here on purpose to help the British re-establish their rule,' opined some. Even urchins would ask whenever they saw him:

'When will the Saab leave for Europe?'

'Why doesn't the Saab quit India?'

'Quit India, Saab!'

'The British have left.'

'The whites have left.'

'Why don't you leave?' the boys would shout as they trailed him in the street.

'Hum . . . m . . . m . . . I'll go . . . I'll go, baba.' He would shake his head, smile and return to his novel.

In those moments I felt deep pity for him. Where were the masters of the world who brought civilization to weaker nations, who clothed the naked in frocks and trousers and proclaimed the superiority of the white race? Jackson, their own flesh and blood, was shedding his garb, and no missionary was coming forth to cover his nakedness.

When the street urchins went their own way after teasing him, Jackson would sit outside his hovel and smoke bidis. His solitary eye looked into the far horizon that was a gateway to the world, where there was no discrimination between black and white, where there was no oppression, where sinful mothers could not leave their babies on others' doorsteps and go back to their world of respectability.

Sakku Bai earned good money working as a charwoman in the neighbouring houses. Moreover, she could make wicker baskets, tables, chairs, etc., which brought her a little extra money. Jackson, when not drunk, would also make baskets in his clumsy way. In the evening Sakku Bai would bring him a peg of country liquor, which he would gulp down immediately and then start a fight with her. One night, he kept drinking and somehow managed a whole bottle. At dawn, he lay down prostrate before the shack and slept. Philomina and Pattu jumped over him on their way to school. Sakku Bai also went out hurling abuses at him. He lay there till noon. When the children returned in the afternoon, they found him sitting, leaning against the wall. He had a high temperature, which turned into delirium the next day.

He kept muttering to himself the whole night. God knows who he was thinking of. Maybe his mother, whom he had never seen and who, in all probability, might have been giving lectures on morality at some august gathering; or his father, who had rendered his services like a bull to perpetuating the race, and who had given him no more importance than the filth released from his body – and who, perhaps, sitting in some other colonized country, was devising plans to consolidate imperial power. Or maybe he recalled Dorothy's reluctant favours, which lashed him throughout his life like the whip of a ruthless peasant; or the bullets fired from his machine gun that pierced the heart of innocent people, a fact that was now pricking his conscience. He kept on screaming and tossing in bed the whole night. His heart continued to beat. Every object in the house seemed to cry out:

You've no country . . . you've no race . . . no colour. Sakku Bai is your country, and your race, for she has given you unending love . . . Because she is among the wretched in her country . . . Exactly like you and like millions of other human beings who are born in different parts of the world . . . whose births are not celebrated and whose deaths are not mourned.

Day was dawning. Rows of workers were finding their way into mills as chimneys puffed out columns of smoke. The whores were exhausted after entertaining their clients through the night and bid them farewell.

'Hindustan chhor!'

'Quit India.'

Voices filled with contempt and hatred struck his brain like a hammer. He looked wistfully at his woman, who slept there resting her head on the threshold. Philomina was asleep on a piece of sack cloth in the kitchen. Pattu was lying nestled against her waist. A deep sigh went up from his heart, and a tear dropped from his real eye onto the dirty durrie.

The fading relic of the British Empire, Eric William Jackson, quit India.

The Survivor

The noon was hot like a kiln, without a trace of wind anywhere. The trees were absolutely bare and stood mute like beggars stretching their hands for alms. A mangy dog was sitting in the shade of the wall licking its wounds.

On the day of qiyamat, the sun will come down. The earth will rip off its chest gushing forth molten fire. Then all sinners will fall face down. But why did Maulvi Rifaqat Ali fall on his face as he slipped in the staircase of the mosque? He was a pious soul, adhering strictly to the injunction of religion. He never committed any sins. Be it a downpour or a hailstorm, he never missed his prayers in the mosque.

Within a moment, a crowd of people flocked there like so many insects coming out of their holes. Maulvi Saheb was writhing like a slaughtered chicken. Streams of sweat flowed from his body. People were making conjectures about his ailment. Some said it was colic pain while according to others it was a case of cardiac arrest. Well, it may have been a case of an ordinary fall, because he led quite a comfortable life and was not used to any hardship.

Just then Bachchan Babu reached there like an angel of God. He stopped his car, got off and picked his way through the crowd. Bachchan Babu was contesting the municipal election and was making rounds of the mohallas. In the mohalla where Maulvi Saheb lived people scarcely paid any heed when he arrived. They would pretend to be busy in their jobs; they would close their shops and gather in the mosque. It was a Muslim mohalla. How ironical it was that as enlightenment spread in the land, people were getting more and more communal!

Bachchan Babu could feel that the moment was pregnant with possibilities. He lifted Maulvi Saheb up and took him home. He phoned from the post office to call in a doctor. Maulvi Saheb's wife, the Begum, was standing behind the curtains wiping away tears in her spotless pallu. The children stared at each other.

Maulvi Rifaqat was lean and thin. He kept accounts at Lalaji's warehouse on a monthly salary of fifty-two rupees. He also taught children how to read the Quran. It was nothing short of a miracle how he maintained a brood of six children and a wife on such meagre income.

The doctor confirmed that it was indeed a cardiac arrest. The condition of the patient was critical; the slightest movement could cause death. However, Bachchan Babu came to his rescue. He got a bed brought from the hospital that could be heaved up and down by means of a handle. An oxygen cylinder was also brought in, which scared the Begum out of her wits. 'Why bring in this bomb here!' she exclaimed.

People from the entire mohalla converged there as though there was some circus going on. The nurse who came wearing a white sari with a green border impressed everyone. A photographer appeared from nowhere and began to click pictures. These pictures came out in the newspapers on the following day showing Bachchan Babu playing the role of a good Samaritan. There was one picture that showed the doctor administering oxygen to Maulvi Saheb while Bachchan Babu held the tube.

It hardly needs saying that Bachchan Babu won the election hands down. Everyone in the mohalla cast their vote in his favour.

Maulvi Saheb regained health, but Bachchan Babu's munificence did not subside. Newspapers published Maulvi Saheb's interview along with write-ups such as 'Great Scholar of Arabic and Farsi Starving', though, in fact, Maulvi Saheb had failed his matriculation exam. To meet the expenses of his medical treatment, Bachchan Babu opened a fund to which he contributed five thousand rupees out of his own pocket. He also managed a grant of ten thousand rupees from the Prime Minister's fund for Maulvi Saheb. On top of it, a letter came from the private secretary of Pandit Jawaharlal Nehru to Maulvi Saheb expressing sympathy.

Wealthy people contributed wholeheartedly to the fund. A purse consisting of forty thousand rupees was presented by the Governor of the state to Maulvi Rifaqat at an impressive function.

Bachchan Babu worked with great zeal to arrange functions for mobilizing funds. If he invited Dilip Kumar to chair one function, at another he invited Shakila Banu Bhopali to sing qawwali. Every function was a success. One of Bachchan Babu's flats was lying vacant. Maulvi Saheb shifted there. In a couple of years he underwent a great transformation. He got himself admitted to an English-medium school. His wife discarded her tight salwars and began wearing saris. She did not observe purdah anymore because now she had to preside over small meetings, etc., and had to travel a lot in connection with social work.

Maulvi Saheb's addresses were published regularly in papers and broadcast over the radio. The main point of his argument was 'We are one and will remain so.' There is no question of any discrimination. Everyone in the country is treated on equal terms. The leaders of the minorities have also a distinct voice.

Bachchan Babu had opened a proper Rifaqat Fund Office. A journal also came out under the patronage of Maulvi Saheb whose only slogan was 'Save Urdu'. This journal was waging a spirited struggle for the survival of Urdu. Bachchan Babu was the very soul of the Save Urdu Society. Urdu writers were given awards from the Rifaqat Fund. People usually find pleasure in levelling allegations. They alleged that all the awards went to Bachchan Babu's sycophants. Big film stars would attend these award functions. Nymphs from the film industry would distribute brochures and collect contributions from the people present there.

Maulvi Rifaqat steadily gained in health and put on quite a bit of weight. His tummy showed a bulge, which went well with his position. However, his wife became overweight and had to visit clinics for exercises.

Maulvi Saheb's visits to the mosque had got discontinued because of his ailment, though he went for Friday prayers off and on. However, he was very particular about attending the

Id-ul-Fitr and Bakr Id prayers. On his rare visits to his mohalla, people would take out processions in his honour. The residents of the mohalla took pride in the fact that Maulvi Saheb had once lived there. It was surprising that even after reaching such a position, he met poor people with such affability.

Meanwhile, Mrs Gandhi had come to power and was consolidating her position. As the representative of the minorities and in connection with the 'Save Urdu' movement, Maulvi Saheb had already had several fruitful meetings with her. His photographs with her were hung prominently at different places in his flat. His journal published regular columns that waxed eloquent on her political vision, her inherited brillance and her foresight. God had sent goddess Durga in the form of a woman for the welfare of Bharat. He composed a long poem on her achievements that was translated into various languages and dispatched to remote corners of the country. When he went to Delhi to present this poem personally to Mrs Gandhi, the historic event was recorded by television and Akashvani and presented to the public.

The Begum was drunk from the pleasure of her husband's meeting with the Prime Minister. She got the photograph of the meeting mounted on a golden frame and hung it in the drawing room, where every visitor got to see it. Then she would narrate to him at great length this pleasant meeting with such exaggerated details that the listener would be baffled. Some ill-tempered people had got bored listening to this great event again and again and would think twice before meeting the Begum. But when she said in a special tone with a faraway look in her eyes, 'Our Prime Minister is not an ordinary woman, she is a miracle,' all would nod their head in agreement. Maulvi Saheb was now in a different class. The Begum herself had become so well connected that people would line up for a recommendation from her. It was said that she could manage to get people awards and titles like Padmashri, etc.

That was how things stood when Maulvi Saheb had his second cardiac arrest. Some mean fellows believed that it was actually a rumour that Bachchan Babu had spread on purpose with the compliance of Maulvi Saheb. A second cardiac arrest had become necessary to provide an occasion for collecting funds anew. How crooked people could be! They burn with jealousy seeing someone prosper. Doesn't the prosperity of an industrialist lead to the prosperity of the country? Don't the skyscrapers raised in Bombay proclaim the grandeur of the city? Are these structures to be blamed if millions in the neighbourhood live on footpaths or in shacks? Well, it's just a coincidence that the greater part of the national income goes to a handful of people. It is up to God to bless whomever He wants with wealth and honour. If a particular class is dearer to God, why feel jealous of it?

Bachchan Babu had raised Maulvi Rifaqat from mean circumstances to great heights. Isn't it an indication of prosperity in the Muslim community? If the Harijans and Adivasis are looked after in the same way, the greatest problem facing the country may be solved in a minute! But it requires patriots like Bachchan Babu. Today it is Maulvi Saheb whose destiny has changed; tomorrow it would be the turn of the entire community.

After this cardiac arrest, Maulvi Saheb stayed in the best nursing home of the city. As people read about his ailment in newspapers, they assembled at the nursing home. Officers in high positions, even ministers, came to visit him. Some people said that the Governor also came accompanied by the First Lady. Jealous fellows asserted that it was only the Governor; the Lady could not make it. There were some madcaps who insisted that neither the Governor nor the First Lady came. These were rumours, spread on purpose to attract publicity.

Meetings were held with great fanfare and funds collected. Film shows were arranged and the tickets sold for as much as two hundred rupees. Advertisements were collected for the souvenir. Film stars made quite a bit of noise. However, it came out that the venture did not fetch the desired profits because the big stars, as usual, played truant and the small ones had sandals thrown at them by the audience. A nondescript film dancer presented a tumultuous dance number. Had he been in his old mohalla, Maulvi Saheb would have chanted, 'La hawla wala quwwat' to ward off evil. But now he thanked everyone tearfully – which unfortunately nobody heard in the enveloping din. The Prime Minister contributed twenty thousand rupees from her own fund along with a note wishing him quick recovery. The Begum made it a point to show the note to every visitor on some pretext or the other.

Then finally, it happened. Communalism is ingrained in our blood. People did not look upon the friendship of Bachchan Babu and Maulvi Rifaqat too kindly. They began to malign one to the other. They incited the Begum because mostly she lent them a patient ear. Women are, by nature, credulous. They told her that everything was not right with the Rifaqat Fund. Bachchan Babu was running several trades under assumed names. He was establishing factories, buying flats. He was robbing Maulvi Saheb of the funds that were collected in his name. He had bought several cinema halls in which Maulvi Saheb had no share. Maulvi Saheb was a simpleton, totally unaware of all this. Fed up with the Begum's constant nagging, Maulvi Saheb asked Bachchan Babu to show him the accounts. For some days Bachchan Babu evaded him. When Maulvi Saheb persisted with his demand, Bachchan Babu got into a rage. A bitter fight ensued. Bachchan Babu fumed. Maulvi Saheb was in dire straits. All his anger centred on the Begum: 'It all happened because of you! Bachchan Babu is very angry with me. What's to be done now?'

'So what? Let him be angry. Will there be no dawn if the cock does not crow?' said she spiritedly. 'Iftikhar Bhai says that our caravan is on the move, and no one can stop it.'

The wedding of Maulvi Rifaqat's elder daughter had been fixed. The bridegroom was to be paid seventy thousand rupees for his personal effects. The Begum began to have nightmares. She went to Bachchan Babu and fell at his feet. She pronounced that if Bachchan Babi did not come to attend the marriage, she would return the baraat and give poison to her daughter. Well, she could very well do so because Noor Jahan was only her adopted daughter! Bachchan Babu started crying.

The pomp and show that accompanied the wedding left everyone dazed. What a hoopla it was! Foreign liquor flowed like water for four days. Despite the famine prevailing in the country, hundreds of people helped themselves liberally to lunch and dinner. And it was nothing short of a royal fare on the actual day of the wedding. After all, one's friends should profit from one's position! Dayaramji, the sales tax officer, took upon himself the responsibility of catering. Goodies arrived from the few big hotels of the city. Such delicious fare and in such plenty! It would not have been possible to gather all the varieties at one place even before the Second World War! Electric bulbs lit up the whole house.

Some rioters decided to spoil the fun. The number of guests exceeded by ten times the legally permissible limit. The miscreants counted the number of cars and the guests and complained to the police. Maulvi Saheb suffered great humiliation. He contradicted the facts published in newspapers under oath, but there was quite a bit of fuss over it. Then, as happens in such cases, the issue died a natural death. Had not Bachchan Babu and his influential friends stood by him at that critical hour, Maulvi Saheb would have been in serious trouble. God is merciful and kind. He ignores men's inadequacies. The newspapers made a noise for some days and then gave up. Otherwise, the Prime Minister was famed to be like a naked sword, ruthless and unforgiving. Well, Bachchan Babu had also tamed many poisonous snakes. He could get his friends clean out of difficult situations. Actually, those were the days when the Emergency was declared and newspapers were being gagged. Only those papers that were ready to sing paeans to the Emergency prospered. No one knew how Bachchan Babu suppressed all complaints against Maulvi Saheb by giving them the appearance of propaganda against the minorities.

That night Maulvi Saheb wrote a stirring poem on the Emergency. He called the new law an auspicious window through which all the evil plaguing the land was driven out and all the bounties came in. It is through the promulgation of this law that the enemies of the country, that is, the smugglers, hoarders and profiteers, were severely dealt with. The rights of the backward communities and minorities were given due recognition. Poverty was vanishing rapidly and the common people were prospering.

That very evening he beat his servant Chotu within an inch of his life. He was alleged to have stolen the Begum's earrings. The police took Chotu away and tried to extract the things from him. When their daughter Sughra came back from her friend's party at night, they saw that the rings were shining in her ears. This made them break into a cold sweat. 'What can be done now, Begum? The case has gone to the police. It will be a scandal,' Maulvi Saheb said to his wife.

The daughter's marriage was solemnized with fanfare, but the Begum remained rather aloof. It was as though she was possessed by a spirit and showed extreme boorishness, refusing to come out. The assembly remained quite dull and lifeless without the hostess. Had Nirmala Khanna, Bachchan Babu's girlfriend, not played the hostess, it would have been disgraceful. Mrs Bachchan kept company with Mrs Rifaqat. Nirmala Khanna compensated adequately for this as well.

Things cooled off after the marriage. However, Maulvi Saheb was convinced by Bachchan Babu's argument that his personality could not shine as long as he did not have a young and beautiful hostess. High society was not the Begum's cup of tea. Her competence had remained confined to the four walls of the house. She lost her sense of proportion in society and had started suspecting Maulvi Saheb. Sometimes she would commit faux pas that stunned people from the upper classes. Had she put on a jorha inlaid with purple sequins as Nirmala had, she would have looked quite stunning.

Lots of educated and beautiful girls pine away their lives waiting to be married. They look for a groom with a fat salary. The jobs at school and offices are quite boring, but the job of a private secretary is looked upon as both interesting and respectable. Many wise fellows keep one or two flats tucked away somewhere without the knowledge of their wives where they entertain their friends without any inhibitions. If such a flat is endowed with an attractive hostess, it opens the doors to a thousand possibilities. A home is not a suitable place for arranging all those things required for good business transactions. During drinking bashes when friends get flushed with drink and make indecent overtures, the presence of wives and children acts as a dampener to the lively atmosphere.

Maulvi Saheb acted on Bachchan Babu's suggestion and bought a flat in the name of Saroj Bhatia, Nirmala's bosom friend, and got it furnished according to her taste. The Begum usually acted as a wet blanket during drinking assemblies. 'This skunk! How he swallows wine! He's swaying like a dying elephant!' she would say. Maulvi Saheb would try to pacify her, 'Why don't you understand? The quota for the newsprint is in his hands.' And the Begum would immediately understand because a greater part of the paper received through the quota was sold in the black market and the money went towards the maintenance of the journal, which was mostly distributed for free.

Saroj Bhatia turned out to be a wonderful hostess. Maulvi Saheb had a large circle of friends and acquaintances. He became a member of several high-power committees. His girlfriend was also given appropriate status. People forgot the Begum. Saroj Bhatia who was formerly a part-time teacher in a tiny school was now presiding over meetings like the wives of ministers. She would give away prizes and deliver speeches in schools and colleges.

The Begum fretted and fumed, but Maulvi Saheb told her sternly that Saroj Bhatia's presence was essential for maintaining his position. The Begum wept and cried. The daughters had been married off. The sons usually remained busy making rounds of Europe. She stayed all alone in the desolate flat while Saroj Bhatia's apartment buzzed with activities. The Begum's own daughters began to shy away from her. Whenever they came to see her, she would start off recounting her complaints against Saroj. On the contrary, there was always something interesting going on in Saroj's apartment. Big people would assemble there offering great promise for the future prospects of their husbands. That is why they would hover around their papa's girlfriend.

Maulvi Saheb had one foot planted in Delhi. He was a strong supporter of the Youth Congress and was involved wholeheartedly in the implementation of the twenty-point programme. The Youth Congress had resolved to change the whole complexion of the country and write its destiny anew. Its leader Sanjay Gandhi had inherited these patriotic feelings from his mother. Sanjayji was rather free with Maulvi Saheb. He would slap him on the back, asking endearingly, 'Hello, idiot, how are things with you, Maulvi?'

'Your blessings,' Maulvi Saheb would intone.

His poems on vasectomy were published regularly. They contained glowing descriptions of Youth Congress activities. Sanjay Gandhi, its leader, was slowly made out to be God's gift to India. Saroj Bhatia had made Rukhsana Sultana her sister. Together they would make plans for the welfare of the country.

The Mehfil was going on full blast. It was Saroj Bhatia's birthday. The invitees were hovering around, drink in hand. On the doctor's advice, Maulvi Saheb had begun soaking his tongue in wine, emptying a peg or two.

'What's you opinion?' Bachchan Babu asked.

'About what?'

'Madam does not take any step without being sure of success.'

'But what's the need for elections at this time?'

'She wants to demonstrate through these elections how strong her position is.'

'And if the Congress is defeated?'

'Tomorrow you'll say the sun may rise in the west!'

'But what's the sense of releasing the enemies from prison?'

'Arré, these enemies have no sting in them. They are all paper tigers. They made an alignment before but were defeated.'

At this point everyone requested Saroj to sing a song, and the issue remained unresolved.

Maulvi Saheb was sitting in his room and writing the editorial for the next issue of the journal. He demonstrated, quoting verses from the Quran and the Hadith, that Islam approves of vasectomy. The write-up was going to be a powerful one. Right at that moment entered Bachchan Babu – distraught, hair dishevelled, clothes dust laden.

'Have you any idea which way the wind is blowing?'

'What happened?'

'That which we did not dream in our wildest dreams. I'm coming straight from Rai Bareilly.'

'Are you serious?'

'Mianji, the Congress has tumbled.'

'Are you crazy? Bareilly is Madam's fortress.'

'Arré bhai, people do not even want to hear Deviji's name. Just look what they've done to me! They've broken the windscreen of the car. I've somehow managed to escape with my life.'

'Come on, you're getting panicky for nothing. This must be the handiwork of a few scoundrels.'

'These scoundrels have taken over the whole country. Throw away this editorial. It won't do now.'

'But the first instalment has already been sent to the press, and it has been printed. You get jittery over small things.'

'Look, Maulvi Saheb, I won't be responsible for the consequences.' He got up and left.

It came out in the evening news that Bachchan Babu had joined the Janata Party. Maulvi Saheb felt that the ground was receding from under his feet. He rushed to Bachchan Babu's place.

'It doesn't make much difference to you, Maulvi Saheb. You're the representative of a minority. You can get a place in any regime; it is only a question of minor adjustment. But my position is in serious jeopardy. I was so close to Deviji. How was I to know that all my running around would be in vain?'

Maulvi Saheb tore up the editorial. The issue of the journal being published was taken out of the machine and burnt that night. All irrelevant portraits were dismantled from their places: it was no longer safe to keep them in the house. The Begum took out her photograph with the Madam from the golden frame and replaced it with a coloured picture of Medina Sharif.

The next day Maulvi Saheb delivered a speech before a large gathering on the brutalities of the Emergency and declared that the Janata Party was the protector of democracy.

And the Janata Party accepted him with open arms.

God is bountiful.

He takes everyone's boat ashore.

Sacred Duty

The tiny bit of paper fluttered away from Siddiqi Saheb's hand and fell on his lap like a half-dead moth. He brushed it off as though its poisonous fangs would get stuck to his very being.

His wife was supervising the hanging of chandeliers and coloured lanterns outside. Sitting on a heap of rugs she was reading congratulatory telegrams and letters from faraway lands and from Delhi and other places inside the country on the occasion of their daughter's marriage. Samina was very dear to her parents and had passed B.Sc. that year with the highest honours.

The groom worked in Dubai on a monthly salary of twelve thousand, had free board and lodgings and was allowed a free vacation every year. Developments in the Arab world had opened up fortunes for many a nubile girl. The sudden spurt of wealth had brought prosperity to many a family. The boy was from a decent household and without much family encumbrances. The match had been settled over the phone. He was not very handsome and was a bit short as well. But the girl was not going to put her husband up for auction. One shouldn't bother about a man's physical features; it is his qualities that matter. Twelve thousand mattered a lot and ensured total comfort.

The daughter was delicate as a flower. She wanted to go in for higher studies, but an opportunity like this did not come every day. So she was silenced with a sharp reprimand. What benefit was to be had by doing an M.Sc. or becoming a doctor?

Samina didn't demur. On the contrary, she became absolutely quiet. These girls throw such tantrums, reflected the mother, as she put aside the letter she was reading. Well, she would go to see her daughter in Dubai in the month of Khali and, God willing, would perform hajj on her way back.

Siddiqi Saheb, in a dazed state at the moment, was staring in disbelief at the wretched bit of paper that had pulled his world from great heights into a bottomless abyss.

Papa, Mummy – I regret that I can't agree to this match: I'm going to Allahabad with Tushar Trivedi to his parents' home. We've been married in court. I'll consider myself fortunate if you can forgive me. Your daughter, Samina Trivedi.

May God help us! Siddiqi Saheb was a progressive, a supporter of education for girls and their freedom of choice in marriage. He also attended Id prayers, though he had not yet been called upon to participate in a crusade over Islamic principles or make any sacrifices for religion. Free from prejudices he lived a life of respectability among liberal-minded people. But that didn't mean that his blood wouldn't boil if his daughter went astray.

When Begum, his wife, heard this, she almost passed out.

There was just one thing to do – go to Allahabad and shoot them both. But Begum panicked at the mention of the word 'gun'. Ah! Her darling, her only daughter! God's curse on the worthless fellow! How innocent he looked when he came on Sundays and had tiffs with Samina as they both raised a racket! When did this blasted love intrude? How ungrateful the children had become to get married on the sly in this way giving no one the slightest inkling! How he would hug her calling her 'Mummy' – indeed the rogue had ended up making her his mummy. A generation of such deceitful youths! No, we've nothing against the Hindus. No one ever bothered about who was Hindu or Christian at Paplu's Sunday parties. Women had fancy nicknames. Pammy Deshmukh, for instance – was she Razzaq Deshmukh's wife or Chander Deshmukh's? Begum always thought Lily to be a Christian till she discovered one day that she was Laila Razdan. The Razdans made it all the more confusing. Tirmila Razdan – who called herself Nikki, swore in English at the slightest provocation and sprinkled her conversation liberally with invectives like 'shut up' and 'hell' (she was hell-bound, for sure) – was from a highly respected Shia family. As for Razdan Saheb – Mohammad Ismail Razdan – he had performed hajj thrice already. Nikki, too, was a Haji. What beautiful saris and cosmetics she had brought back from Mecca this time! She brought us a gift of the holy water zamzam and rosaries along with an inch-long snippet of the sheet that covered the Kaaba. She had used the nail scissors expertly to rip off that swatch, and the folds fell so neatly that no one suspected it.

They sat late into the night, calling people on the phone and sending telegrams to all invitees to tell them that Samina was down with pneumonia. That she was in intensive care. The wedding had been postponed for the time being. If she survived, they would be informed about the future programme.

How to kill the daughter and the son-in-law? There wasn't even a sharp knife in the house! They had to forget about the gun. A licence was hard to get. How were they to know? Otherwise they could've procured one beforehand. They had good connections. Now by the time the licence would come through, the couple might even have a child born to them. The very thought of the child made their blood curdle.

Well, God had blessed them with two hands, which were enough to wring the daughter's neck. They must lie in ambush behind some shrubbery near the house of her in-laws. No one knew if there was any in the vicinity where the villains lived. This was like demanding the river to be full before one jumped into it to drown. If their luck had not run out, their daughter wouldn't have run off bringing them disrepute.

But it would be sheer injustice to let that scoundrel Tushar, who had seduced their daughter, escape without severe punishment. The screwdriver, properly sharpened, would do. The sharpening man used to sit in front of the gate every day. He was threatened with police action and ordered to sit elsewhere. What a horrible grating noise the grinding stone made! As though one's teeth were cutting through a handful of sand.

Such a delicate matter could not be shared even with friends.

But Jawwad was like a member of the family. He had a thriving practice in Allahabad. They called him on the phone and sought his advice. He promised to come at teatime the following day.

Meanwhile a bomb exploded.

A newspaper was sent to them from Allahabad that had splashed the wedding photographs of Samina and Tushar. A civil marriage was not considered enough by Seth Saheb, Tushar's father. He had arranged a ceremony according to Arya Samaj rituals, complete with a havan and a pandit. Snapshots were taken showing the rituals, the girl changing her faith, taking a dip in the Ganges at Allahabad where she had been flown. The girl was so shameless that even after all this she was smiling and looking demurely at Tushar.

Siddiqi Saheb got himself into such a rage that he very nearly had a heart attack. Had Jawwad Saheb not arrived at the right moment something disastrous might have happened. Tushar's father had taken such an unfair advantage of the situation. He was a rabid Mahasabhai. By getting those photographs printed with such gusto he had added to Siddiqi Saheb's abject humiliation.

Now, the entire family deserved to be blown up with a bomb. But where could one get a bomb? Siddiqi Saheb who used to get upset even by the fireworks at Diwali and Shab-e-baraat had been totally shattered by this explosion. This was a nation of the Hindus, no doubt about that! What lucrative jobs were offered him in Pakistan! He had rejected all those because of his progressive leanings – sheer stupidity! 'I can't leave my own country. I'll be buried in the land I was born' – he had asserted using the Hindi word 'janam' for birth. What a shame! 'Janam' was not to be uttered by someone from a respectable Muslim family with pronounced religious feelings.

Jawwad Saheb had a hard time pacifying him. Both of them had a prolonged tête-à-tête behind closed doors. Then the scheme was revealed to Begum, who was simply thrilled. What a crafty man this Jawwad Saheb was! Although a Shia, he had been Siddiqi Saheb's friend for years. A Siddiqi–Jafri alliance may seem improbable, but there never appeared any chink in their friendship in spite of the traditional Shia–Sunni conflict. Often a man's faith comes in the way of his friendship, but it is mostly love and friendship that triumph. Life is full of contradictions that can make it tragic. But principles easily fall a victim to love and friendship.

Siddiqi Saheb asked the driver to wait and rang the doorbell.

After a few moments, his dear daughter was clinging to him, smiling through her tears. A daughter is deeply anguished when she acts against the will of her parents and never finds peace until she is forgiven. It was at her parents' home that Samina had discovered Tushar's love, which gradually overwhelmed her. Had her parents been not enlightened, would they have allowed Tushar to pay court to her under their own roof?

And Tushar was standing there grinning shamefacedly. He hadn't liked the newspaper stunt his father had pulled off. But he was the only brother of four sisters, and one day he had to perform the funeral rites of his father. Sethji would remind him of this duty time and again. His sisters, all older to him, were well settled with families of their own. Nirmal, the youngest, had fallen for a dark-complexioned Christian professor. Sethji had manoeuvred to get him sent to England on a government scholarship. The fellow left the arena of love without protest. Sethji was known to have made the career of many politicians. Although he had never accepted any position himself, many of his protégés were members of many state assemblies and various committees. He was a successful 'king-maker'. He didn't align himself with any particular political group and would be seen to support the party in power. He played his part in the rise and fall of those parties. His was a multifaceted personality.

Jawwad Saheb's advice acted like a magic and transformed Siddiqi Saheb. He was a new person, his heart beating within his chest in a new rhythm. In high-flown and chaste Hindi, studded like diamonds with Sanskrit words, Siddiqi Saheb conveyed to Sethji how grateful he was to him for relieving him of a great burden, that of an unwed daughter, and was thus obliged to him for generations. All faiths are sacred, he said, and the greatest one consists of the love and affection that an enlightened father-in-law bestows on his daughter-in-law. To be able to give one's faith to one's daughter-in-law and one's son was a noble act. And Ganga was everyone's mother, be he a Hindu, a Muslim or a Christian. Her holy waters made no distinctions between the Brahmin and the untouchable but quenched everyone's thirst.

Addressing Sethji as 'Sayyid Saheb' he said, 'I'm a human being. I've inherited the religion I profess and gathered knowledge from books. Your Bhagwan and my Allah are two names for the same power.' He quoted profusely from the Bible and the Gita besides the Quran. Sethji was highly impressed. His wife got her neighbour, Miss Rosa, to make a sumptuous murgh musallam for the guest. Everyone was very excited. Sethji's samdhi, a great scholar and of scrupulous principles, came to bless his daughter and son-in-law. How liberally he doled out those fifty-rupee bills to the servants! Siddiqi Saheb was invited to lunches and dinners, where he refused to eat chicken. 'Meat is not conducive to knowledge and austerity,' he proclaimed.

'You have fulfilled your wishes,' he said to Sethji, 'now you must allow me to do the duty I owe to my friends and relatives. The girl's mother has been crying her heart out, though the photographs provided her some relief.' (Actually Begum wanted the photographs to be torn to shreds and thrown into the fire.)

Sethji's wife didn't want to hand over the diamond necklace to the daughter-in-law at the time of her departure. Sethji admonished her, 'Don't be mean. Our samdhi is a wise and generous person. See how gracefully he has overlooked all our unfair acts. And here you are, crying over a few pieces of glass!'

Siddiqi Saheb brought his daughter and son-in-law to Delhi with great fanfare. He had phoned up friends and relatives, who were present at the station with bouquets and garlands. For good luck, Jawwad Saheb had accompanied the party from Allahabad.

Begum was boiling with rage. 'Kill him. His body will make good compost for the garden,' she said about the son-in-law.

'Are you crazy? Just wait and see what drama unfolds. Tushar is Samina's husband now. Proposal and acceptance – whatever the language and whoever the persons present – has already made them man and wife. And both are dear to us.'

The marquee was set up in the afternoon, and guests in the city were invited with utmost haste over the telephone or by visiting them in person.

Tushar was unnerved for a few moments when he was asked to convert to Islam. He looked fearfully at Jawwad Saheb and Siddiqi Saheb and was probably planning to jump out of the window.

'Abbaji, what's this nonsense? First it was Papa who forced me to become a Hindu, got me to take a dip in the Ganga and compelled me to chant mantras that sounded like gibberish. And now you want us to go through this farce. We wouldn't submit to your petty politicking. When we return to Allahabad, we'll be required to take dips again, and photographs would be taken and . . .'

Begum started crying. Siddiqi Saheb was confounded.

'There's just one way out,' he said, clasping his wife's hand. 'Let's go and drown ourselves in the Jamuna.'

'How can you drown, Papa?' asked their daughter. 'You know how to swim. You'll drown Mummy and come out of the river safe and sound. Good for your girlfriend Miss Farzana.'

'Shut up, Sami,' Tushar admonished her. 'Papa, I mean Siddiqi Saheb, I'm ready to become a Muslim.'

'Shut up, you idiot. I'm not prepared to be reconverted. Don't you remember how lovingly Mataji had put the mangalsutra around my neck? These are diamonds, you know. How beautiful they are!'

'You can wear the mangalsutra as a Muslim, too!' Tushar admonished her once again.

'Kill the two, and that's the end of it. God's curse on them!' Begum said. 'What an ungrateful daughter! He's ready to become a Muslim, but she's spoiling the case.'

'Will you shut up, you chatterbox?' Tushar snubbed Samina. 'When I had refused to obey Pitaji, you opposed me tooth and nail and threatened to jump out of the window. Did you know that there was a mouse burrow under the window where a fat mouse lives? If it had been surprised out of its hole, you would've got a heart attack!'

'Look, the Maulvi Saheb has been waiting a long time. He hasn't even taken a cup of tea, says he'll have breakfast after performing the sacred duty of conversion. He's a glutton, for sure,' said someone.

'I'm ready. Two slaps across her face, and she'll agree. Darling, did you lose anything by becoming a Hindu? Why are you being so obstinate?'

'Oh . . . and what about the aarti I performed and the nice mangalsutra you gave me? But what stinking socks you wear! Your feet smelled awfully when I bent down to touch them.'

'What's this nonsense!' Siddiqi Saheb roared. 'Everything is a big joke to you. Tushar, are you ready to embrace Islam and thus become musharraf?'

'Musharraf? You mean Musharraf Hamidullah who is a crook and a mean pilferer? He always cheated in the exams to get through. Do you remember, Samina, how when Sir caught him cheating, he pulled out a knife?'

'You're the pampered son of a Seth. He's the son of a poor orderly. What injustice! Have you ever cared to know how he manages to survive, you bloody capitalist bloodsucker?'

'Look, Mummy, she's calling me names. I'll hit her.'

'They've perished, those hitters. Hunh!'

'How long will this farce continue?' Begum asked. 'Good God, I forgot the pudding in the oven.' She leapt towards the kitchen.

'Oh dear, these kids are driving me mad. Brother Jawwad . . .' Siddiqi Saheb sounded desperate.

'What is it?' asked Jawwad, who had been listening to the exchanges quietly all this while and smiling to himself.

'I'm acting according to your instructions. Now tell me what to do.'

'Convert me to Islam and hurry, please. We've booked seats for the matinee and must reach the cinema hall by three.'

'And here the maulvi is starving and cursing us. Skip the matinee. We've arranged for an "at-home" in the evening.'

'But that's at eight.'

Siddiqi Saheb's plans were going awry.

'Look here, children . . .' Jawwad Saheb cleared his throat.

'Yes, uncle,' Tushar responded promptly.

'Did you have a civil marriage?'

'Yes. The certificate has been put in a safe by Mataji at Allahabad.'

'Did you read the forms carefully before signing them?'

'Yes, I did. But Samina was too nervous to read them. I asked her to sign quickly and be done with them.'

'How could I sign quickly with your terrible pen? You can buy dozens of shoes, can't you buy a decent pen?'

'Just see her manners! . . . We've been married twice – first the civil marriage and then a Hindu one. I had refused it straightaway, but she found it romantic to be led around the sacred fire. She opposed all my moves just so she could please my parents.'

'Yes, it was romantic like the marriage of fishermen. The pandit was chanting mantras, "shutram, shutram", and Papaji was pouring spoonfuls of pure ghee into the fire. It was as though someone was frying carrot halwa. Wonderful!'

'Baby, have you ever smelt pure ghee burning in a funeral pyre?'

'You bloody sadist! Just shut your trap.' Samina folded the newspaper and pounded Tushar's head.

'Oh God, it's crazy!' Siddiqi Saheb was losing his bearings.

'What a calamity! How long will this farce go on?' Begum asked as she entered the room.

'Let me handle this.' Jawwad Saheb came forward and said in a gentle voice, 'Listen to me, children, and don't interrupt while I'm talking. It's bad manners. I'm asking you a very important question. Before the civil marriage, did you read the clause in the form which states that neither of you professes any religion?'

'I don't think so, but that doesn't matter. I always acted according to my parents' instructions. As a matter of fact, I've never pondered much over questions of faith. Religion is for the elderly. In the convent we were Christ's lambs. In Mathura, Krishnaji reigned supreme. Once Musharraf took me to a dargah where, imitating him, I cupped my hands in prayer and moved my lips.'

'Does that mean that you've never thought seriously about Ishwar or Allah?'

'Hmm . . . Have you ever thought about Dilip Kumar?'

'Well, Mataji was his fan at one time. As for me, I prefer Amit, Mithun and . . .'

'That's enough! Now this means that no other ceremony has any validity unless your civil marriage is dissolved first.'

'So the circumambulations were no good?' Tushar asked excitedly.

'Nonsense! Tushi, it won't help you harping about them. You can divorce me if you want, but I'll never return the mangalsutra.'

'Ugh, what a mean girl you are! We're discussing serious matters and you're obsessed with the mangalsutra. Tell me the truth – if Mataji hadn't shown you the mangalsutra and the rest of the jewellery, would you have agreed to go around the fire?'

'You're so mean, Tushi! You think I'm so greedy, you scoundrel? Papa, marry me off to any dumb fool. I took this idiot as my protector, touched his feet covered in stinking socks . . . this . . . this . . . Oh my God!' Samina clenched her fists and leapt towards Tushar. It would have led to a serious scuffle had not Begum threatened them with an attack of hysteria.

'Jawwad, I don't agree with you at all on this new point.'

'But perhaps the law . . .'

'To hell with the law! I've to give an appropriate answer to Sethji's superciliousness. We must have the nikah even if I've to go to jail or be hanged for it. He made me appear a fool before the whole world, and I'm not going to let him get away with it.'

'Will someone tell me what's the problem now when both are ready to become Muslims?' Begum asked impatiently.

'My wife's right. After all she's the daughter of a maulvi.'

'And she beats everyone at rummy, too,' Samina piped in.

'Shut up, wicked girl! Don't interfere in everything.'

Qazi Saheb arrived. Samina stopped grinning and covered her head. The photographer offered Tushar his karakuli cap recently brought from Pakistan. Samina's eyes lit up when she saw Tushar so handsomely turned out.

Both received the honour of embracing Islam. Both had difficulty reciting verses from the Quran. Tushar was in a cold sweat. Maulvi Saheb was very gentle, the atmosphere was just right. Jawwad Saheb was ready to act as both counsellor and witness. One more witness was required.

'Let Ammi be the witness,' Samina suggested.

'Then one more woman will be required.'

'Why?'

'One man's testimony is equal to that of two women. Why not use Shakura, the boy-servant?'

'Ammi is better than ten Shakuras put together,' asserted Samina stubbornly.

'Just be quiet, girl. Don't keep butting in. Ah, here's your father.'

'Can I be a witness?' asked Siddiqi Saheb suddenly.

'Undoubtedly.'

Qazi Saheb was feeling annoyed. Residents of mansions and bungalows were so unpredictable. This man, a university professor, didn't know a thing about his religion!

The nikah was over. Dry dates were distributed. The photographer was clicking away at every stage of the ceremony. If a close-up shot of the couple affixing the signature on the wedding documents could have been taken, it would have been enough to devastate Sethji. But there was no time for all this.

The photos were splashed prominently in the newspaper the next morning along with the information that the couple had left for Bombay by air. From there they would depart for England. God willing, they would perform hajj before they returned home.

The couple was put up at the Ashoka Hotel for the night. All their things were taken there. The bride's family returned home from the hotel at about two, and everyone hit the bed immediately. Siddiqi Saheb realized, for the first time, that the marriage of a daughter was not an easy job. Parents await this day with trepidation. However, a sense of victory made him feel light-hearted the next morning. Jawwad Saheb had given a nice twist to the whole affair. The papers would be in Sethji's hands by now. He must be in the habit of rising early for his ritual bath and prayers.

Siddiqi Saheb was pleased with himself.

'I say, Sethji's samdhi, can we have some breakfast?' Jawwad Saheb bellowed from the doorway. 'Why, it seems you've grown taller by six inches – you're looking great!'

'Not just six inches, at least a yard. By God, I've beaten the rogue. He must be writhing! How about breakfast at the Ashoka?'

'Wonderful idea.'

'What do you say, Begum?'

'I'll be ready in a moment.'

The three of them reached the hotel.

'Sir, they've checked out,' the clerk at the reception informed them.

'What? Where have they gone? When?'

'The moment you left, they called a taxi. I told them repeatedly that they could stay here till tomorrow night, but as soon as they finished talking on the phone . . .'

'Talking on the phone?' To whom?'

'To someone at Allahabad. I got the call through. Seth . . .'

'Seth!' They were stunned. 'So they've pulled a fast one on us.'

'Did they say they were going to Allahabad?'

'No, sir, they didn't say any such thing.'

'He'll raise a storm again, the rogue. Did Tushar make the call?'

'Yes, sir, I mean both did, sir. Baby was with him in the

telephone booth, and they talked for about twenty-five minutes. Oh, they've left a letter to be sent to you, sir.'

The envelope was quite heavy, or maybe Siddiqi Saheb's hands were trembling too much to grip it. The letter was in English, written in two hands. Samina and Tushar had taken turns in writing every alternate sentence:

Dear Papa, Mummy, Uncle Jawwad:

The only decent option before us is to leave. No, not for Allahabad, for there, too, a stubborn father and a sobbing mother await us. Like good human beings, we've known each other for four years and fallen in love. We opted for civil marriage after a good deal of thought. I'm not very brave, but Sami is a great coward. No, that's not really true. I had suggested to her in the beginning that we elope and get away from here to some far-off place. With this in mind, I had phoned up my father at Allahabad. He invited us lovingly to Allahabad, said that my mother was crying her heart out and that I must console her. When we reached there he arranged this marriage around the holy fire. We thought, what's the harm? But then he played other tricks. We put up with all that. Then, Papa, you appeared on the scene. You're such a good actor! How you won over Papaji with your sweet talk! I was so touched that my eyes became moist. My father's so broad-minded, I thought. Papaji played a dirty trick on us and managed to take us to Benaras with the help of his cronies. On top of it Sami makes things difficult for me. First it was Papa who waved the magic wand at us, and then you showed your generosity by forgiving us. But when you brought us to Delhi you revealed yourself as someone petty and mean. You made us do the monkey dance before you. We took all this as a big joke, this farce too. Don't worry, we haven't exposed you to Papa. He will explode when he gets to read the newspaper tomorrow. We've just said goodbye to them from here. We bid goodbye to all of you. No, don't bother about where we're going. Papa, Tushar is indulging in sweet talk, but he's calling you names. He also calls himself 'medieval' i.e., a crazy buffalo. We beg forgiveness if we've hurt you. No, we haven't hurt you. Rather, you should ask us for forgiveness because you've made us look ridiculous. Good parents you are, to have made us dance like monkeys to any tune you like.

I've told Papaji and now I'm telling you that we don't have any religion. All religions are gifts from that Supreme Being who is called Bhagwan or God. You know him only as Khuda, but we know of his thousand other names –

He who is powerful and compassionate (The Quran)
Who is within and without
Who is above and below
Who exists in darkness and in light
In presence as in absences
In negation as in affirmation (Bhagwad Gita).

The letter ended with their signatures.

Begum began to cry spasmodically. Siddiqi Saheb proceeded to make wry remarks on women's tears.

Jawwad Saheb was scraping his pipe intently as though he were trying to escape into it. This is because he was the maker of this prescription à la Galen. No one knew which ingredient had proved uncongenial so that the prescription had lost its potency and rendered the world of two pairs of parents desolate.

Tiny's Granny

God knows what her real name was. No one had ever called her by it. When she was a little snotty-nosed girl roaming about the alleys, people used to call her 'Bafatan's kid'. Then she was 'Bashira's daughter-in-law', and then, 'Bismillah's mother'; and when Bismillah died in childbirth leaving Tiny an orphan, she become 'Tiny's Granny' to her dying day.

There was no occupation which Tiny's Granny had not tried at some stage of her life. From the time she was old enough to hold her own cup, she had started working at odd jobs in people's houses in return for her two meals a day and cast-off clothes. Exactly what the words 'odd jobs' mean, only those know who have been kept at them at an age when they ought to have been laughing and playing with other children. Anything from the uninteresting duty of shaking the baby's rattle to massaging the master's head comes under the category of 'odd jobs'. As she grew older, she learnt to do a bit of cooking, and she spent some years of her life as a cook. But when her sight began to fail and she began to cook lizards in the lentils and knead flies into the bread, she had to retire. All she was fit for after that was gossiping and tale-bearing. But that also was a fairly paying trade. In every mohalla there is always some quarrel going on, and one who has the wit to carry information to the enemy camp can be sure of a hospitable reception. But it's a game that doesn't last. People began to call her a tell-tale, and when she saw that there was no future there, she took up her last and most profitable profession: she became a polished and accomplished beggar.

At mealtimes, Granny would dilate her nostrils to smell what was cooking, single out the smell she liked best and be off on its track until she reached the house it was coming from.

'Lady, are you cooking aravi with the meat?' she would ask with a disinterested air.

'No, Granny. The aravi you get these days doesn't get soft. I'm cooking potatoes with it.'

'Potatoes! What a lovely smell! Bismillah's father, God rest him, used to love meat and potatoes. Every day it was the same thing: "Let's have meat and potatoes", and now (she would heave a sigh), I don't see meat and potatoes for months together.' Then, suddenly getting anxious, 'Lady, have you put any coriander leaves in the meat?'

'No, Granny. All our coriander was ruined. The confounded water carrier's dog got into the garden and rolled over it.'

'That's a pity. A bit of coriander leaves in meat and potatoes makes all the difference. Hakeemji's got plenty in his garden.'

'That's no good to me, Granny. Yesterday his boy cut my Shabban Mian's kite string, and I told him that if he showed his face again, he'd better look out for himself.'

'Good heavens, I shan't say it's for you.' And Granny would arrange her burkha and be off with slippers clacking, to Hakeemji's. She'd get into the garden on the plea of wanting to sit in the sun, and then edge towards the coriander bed. Then she'd pluck a leaf and crush it between her finger and thumb and savour the pleasant smell and as soon as the Hakeemji's daughter-in-law turned her back, Granny would make a grab. And obviously, when she had provided the coriander leaf, she would hardly be refused a bite to eat.

Granny was famed throughout the mohalla for her sleight of hand. You couldn't leave food and drink lying unwatched when Granny was about. She would pick up the children's milk and drink it straight from the pan: two swallows and it would be gone. She'd put a little sugar in the palm of her hand and toss it straight into her mouth. Or press a lump of gur to her palate, and sit in the sun sucking it at her ease. She made good use of her waistband too. She would whip up an areca nut and tuck it in. Or stuff in a couple of chapatis, half in and half out, but with her thick kurta concealing them from view, and hobble away, groaning and grunting in her usual style. Everyone knew all about these things, but no one had the courage to say anything, first because her old hands were as quick as lightning, and moreover, when in a tight corner, she had no objection to swallowing whole whatever was in her mouth; and second, because if anyone expressed the slightest suspicion of her, she made such a fuss that they soon thought better of it. She would swear her innocence by all that was sacred, and threaten to take an oath on the Holy Quran. And who would disgrace himself in the next world by directly inviting her to swear a false oath on the Quran?

Granny was not only a tale-bearer, thief and cheat. She was also a first-rate liar. And her biggest lie was her burkha, which she always wore.

At one time it had had a veil, but when one by one the old men of the mohalla died, or their eyesight failed, Granny said goodbye to her veil. But you never saw her without the cap of her burkha with its fashionably serrated pattern, as though it were stuck to her skull, and though she might have left the burkha open down the front (even when she was wearing a transparent kurta with no vest underneath), it would billow out behind her like a king's robe. This burkha was not simply for keeping her head modestly covered. She put it to every possible and impossible use. It served her as bedclothes: bundled up, it became a pillow. On the rare occasions when she bathed, she used it as a towel. At the five times of prayer, it was her prayer mat. When the local dogs bared their teeth at her, it became a serviceable shield for her protection. As the dog leapt at her calves it would find the voluminous folds of Granny's burkha hissing in its face. Granny was exceedingly fond of her burkha, and in her spare moments would sit and lament with the keenest regret over its advancing old age. To forestall further wear and tear, she would patch it with any scrap of cloth that came her way, and she trembled at the very thought of the day when it would be no more. Where would she get eight yards of white cloth to make another one? She would be lucky if she could get as much together for her shroud.

Granny had no permanent headquarters. Like a soldier, she was always on the march – today in someone's veranda, tomorrow in someone else's backyard, the next day in some abandoned room. Wherever she spied a suitable site she would pitch camp and, when they turned her out, would move on. With half her burkha laid out under her and the other half wrapped around her, she would lie down and be at ease.

But even more than she worried about her burkha, she worried about her only granddaughter, Tiny. Like a broody old hen, she would always have her safe under her sheltering wing and never let her out of her sight. But a time came when Granny could no longer get about so easily, and when the people of the mohalla had got wise to her ways, as soon as they heard the shuffle of her slippers approaching, they sounded the alert and took up positions of defence; and then all Granny's broad hints and suggestions would fall on deaf ears. So there was nothing that Granny could do except put Tiny to her ancestral trade, doing odd jobs in people's houses. She thought about it for a long time, and then got her a job at the Deputy Saheb's for her food, clothing and one and a half rupees a month. She was never far away, though, and stuck to Tiny like a shadow. The moment Tiny was out of sight she would set up a hullabaloo.

But a pair of old hands cannot wipe out what is inscribed in a person's fate. It was midday. The deputy's wife had gone off to her brother's to discuss the possibility of marrying her son to his daughter. Granny was sitting at the edge of the garden, taking a nap under the shade of a tree. The lord and master was taking his siesta in a room enclosed by water-cooled screens. And Tiny, who was supposed to be pulling the rope of the ceiling fan, was dozing with the rope in her hand. The fan stopped moving, the lord and master woke up, his sexual appetite was whetted, and Tiny's fate was sealed.

They say that to ward off the failing powers of old age, hakeems and vaids, besides all the medicine and ointments that they employ, also prescribe chicken broth; well, the nine-year-old Tiny was no more than a chicken herself.

When Tiny's Granny awoke from her nap, Tiny had disappeared. She searched the whole mohalla, but there was no sign of her anywhere. But when she returned tired out to her room at night, there was Tiny in a corner leaning against the wall, staring about her with listless eyes like a wounded bird. Granny was almost too terrified to speak, but to conceal the weakness she felt, she began swearing at Tiny. 'You little whore, so this is where you've got to! And I've been all over the place looking for you until my poor old legs are all swollen. Just wait till I tell the master. I'll get you thrashed within an inch of your life!'

But Tiny couldn't conceal what had happened to her for long, and when Granny found out, she beat her head and shrieked. When the woman next door was told, she clutched her head in horror. If the deputy's son had done it, then perhaps something might have been said. But the deputy himself . . . one of the leading men in the mohalla, grandfather to three grandchildren, a religious man who regularly said his five daily prayers and had only recently provided mats and water vessels to the local mosque – how could anyone raise a voice against him?

So Granny, who was used to being at the mercy of others, swallowed her sorrow, applied hot compresses to Tiny's back, gave her sweets to comfort her and bore her trouble as best she might. Tiny spent a day or two in bed, and then was up and about again. And in a few days, she had forgotten all about it.

Not so the gentlewomen of the mohalla. They would send for her on the quiet and ask her all about it.

'No, Granny will smack me.' Tiny would try to get out of it.

'Here, take these bangles . . . Granny won't know anything about it,' the eager ladies would coax her.

'What happened? How did it happen?' They would ask for all the details, and Tiny, who was too young and innocent to understand entirely what it all meant, would tell them as well as she could and they would cover their faces and laugh delightedly.

Tiny might forget, but nature cannot. If you pluck a flower in the bud and make it bloom before it is ready, its petals fall and only the stump is left. Who knows how many innocent petals Tiny's face had shed? It acquired a forward, brazen look, a look older than its years. Tiny did not grow from a child into a girl, but at one leap became a woman, and not a fully fashioned woman moulded by nature's skilled and practised hands, but one like a figure on whom some giant with feet two yards long had trodden – squat, fat, puffy, like a clay toy which the potter had knelt on before it had hardened.

When a rag is all dirty and greasy, no one minds too much if someone wipes his nose on it. The boys would pinch her playfully in the open street and give her sweets to eat. Tiny's eyes began to dance with an evil light . . . And now Granny no longer stuffed her with sweets; she beat her black and blue instead. But you can't shake the dust off a greasy cloth. Tiny was like a rubber ball: hit it, and it comes bouncing back at you.

Within a few years Tiny's promiscuity had made her the pest of the whole mohalla. It was rumoured that the Deputy Saheb and his son had quarrelled over her . . . then that Rajva, the palanquin bearer, had given the mullah a thorough thrashing . . . then that she had taken up regularly with the nephew of Siddiq the wrestler. Every day Tiny came near to losing her nose, and there were fights and brawls in the alleys.

The place became too hot to hold her. There was nowhere she could safely set foot anymore. Thanks to Tiny's youthful charms and Siddiq's nephew's youthful strength, life in the mohalla became intolerable. They say that in places like Delhi and Bombay there is huge demand for their kind. Perhaps the two of them migrated there. The day Tiny ran away, Granny had not the slightest suspicion of what was afoot. For several days the little wretch had been unusually quiet. She hadn't sworn at Granny, but had spent a lot of time sitting quietly on her own, staring into space.

'Come and get your dinner, Tiny,' Granny would say.

'I'm not hungry, Granny.'

'Tiny, it's getting late. Go to bed.'

'I don't feel sleepy, Granny.'

That night she began to massage Granny's feet for her. 'Granny . . . Granny; just hear me recite the "Subhanakallahumma", and see if I have got it right.' Granny heard it. Tiny had it pat.

'All right, dear. Off you go now. It's time you were asleep.' And Granny turned over and tried to sleep.

A little later she could hear Tiny moving about in the yard.

'What the devil is she up to now?' she muttered. 'What b— has she brought home now? Little whore. She's got to use even the backyard now!' But when she peered down into the yard, Granny was filled with awe. Tiny was saying her isha prayer. And in the morning, she was gone.

People who return to this place from journeyings far afield sometimes bring news of her. One says that a great lord has made her his mistress and that she is living in fine style like a lady, with a carriage and an abundance of gold. Another says she has been seen in Faras Road or in Sona Gachi.

But Granny's story is that Tiny had had a sudden attack of cholera and was dead before anyone knew it. After her period of mourning for Tiny, Granny's mind started to wander. People passing her in the street would tease her and make jokes at her expense.

'Granny, why don't you get married?' my sister would say.

Granny would get annoyed. 'To whom? Your husband?'

'Why not marry the mullah? I tell you, he's crazy about you. By God he is!'

Then the swearing would begin, and Granny's swearing was so novel and colourful that people could only stare aghast.

'That pimp! Just see what happens if I get hold of him! If I don't pull his beard out, you can call me what you like.' But whenever she met the mullah at the corner of the street, then, believe it or not, she would go all shy.

Apart from the urchins of the mohalla, Granny's lifelong enemies were the monkeys – 'the confounded, blasted monkeys'.

They had been settled in the mohalla for generations and knew all about everyone who lived there. They knew that men were dangerous and children mischievous, but that women were only afraid of them. But then Granny too had spent all her life among them. She'd got hold of some child's catapult to frighten them with, and when she wound her burkha round her head like a great turban and pounced upon them with her catapult at the ready, the monkeys really did panic for a moment before returning to their usual attitude of indifference towards her.

Day in and day out, Granny and the monkeys used to fight over her bits and pieces of stale food. Whenever there was a wedding in the mohalla, or a funeral feast, or the celebrations that mark the fortieth day after childbirth, Granny would be there, gathering up the scraps left over as though she were under contract to do so. Where free food was being distributed she would contrive to come up for her share four times over. In this way she would pile up a regular stack of food, and then she would gaze at it regretfully, wishing that God had arranged her stomach like the camel's so that she could tuck away four days' supply. Why should He be so utterly haphazard? Why had He provided her with a machine for eating so defective that if she had more than two meals' supply at any one time, it simply couldn't cope with it? So what she used to do was to spread out the food to dry on bits of sacking and then put them in a pitcher. When she felt hungry she would take some out and crumble it up, add a dash of water and a pinch of chillies and salt, and there was a tasty mash all ready to eat. But during the summer and during the rains this recipe had often given her severe diarrhoea. So when her bits of food got stale and began to smell she would with the greatest reluctance sell them to people for whatever price she could get to feed to their dogs and goats. The trouble was that generally the stomachs of the dogs and the goats proved less brazen than Granny's, and people would not take her dainties as a gift, let alone buy them.

And yet these bits and pieces were dearer to Granny than life itself; she put up with countless kicks and curses to get them and dry them in the sun even though this meant waging holy war against the whole monkey race. She would no sooner spread them out than the news would, as though by wireless, reach the monkey tribes, and band upon band of them would come and take up their positions on the wall or frisk about on the tiles raising a din. They would pull out the straws from the thatch and chatter and scold passers-by. Granny would take the field against them. Swathing her burkha round her head and taking her catapult in her hand, she would take her stand. The battle would rage all day, Granny scaring the monkeys off again and again. And when evening came she would gather up what was left after their depredations and, cursing them from the bottom of her heart, creep exhausted into her little room to sleep.

The monkeys must have developed a personal grudge against Granny. How else can you explain the fact that they turned their backs on everything else the world had to offer and concentrated all their attacks on Granny's scraps of food? And how else can you explain the fact that a big rascally, red-bottomed monkey ran off with her pillow, which she loved more than her life? Once Tiny had gone, this pillow was the only thing left in the world that was near and dear to her. She fussed and worried over it as much as she did over her burkha. She was forever repairing its seams with stout stitches. Time and again she would sit herself down in some secluded corner and start playing with it as if it were a doll. She had none but the pillow now to tell all her troubles to and so, lighten her burden. And the greater the love she felt for her pillow, the more stout stitches she would put into it to strengthen its seams.

And now see what trick Fate played on her. She was sitting leaning against the parapet with her burkha wrapped around her, picking the lice out of her waistband, when suddenly a monkey flopped down, whipped up her pillow and was off. You would have thought that someone had plucked Granny's heart out of her breast. She wept and screamed and carried on so much that the whole mohalla came flocking.

You know what monkeys are like. They wait until no one is looking and then run off with a glass or a katora, go and sit on the parapet, and taking it in both hands start rubbing it against the wall. The person it belongs to stands there looking up and making coaxing noises and holding out bread or an onion, but the monkey takes his time and, when he has had his bellyful of fun, throws the thing down and goes his own way. Granny poured out the whole contents of a pitcher, but the b— monkey had set his heart on the pillow, and that was that. She did all she could to coax him, but his heart would not melt and he proceeded with the greatest enjoyment to peel the manifold coverings off the pillow as though he were peeling the successive skins off an onion – those same coverings over which Granny had pored with her weak and watering eyes, trying to hold them together with stitching. As every fresh cover came off, Granny's hysterical wailing grew louder. And now the last covering was off, and the monkey began bit by bit to throw down the contents . . . not cotton wadding but . . . Shabban's quilted jacket . . . Bannu the water carrier's waist cloth . . . Hasina's bodice . . . the baggy trousers belonging to little Munni's doll . . . Rahmat's little dupatta and Khairati's knickers . . . Khairati's little boy's pistol . . . Munshiji's muffler . . . the sleeve (with cuff) of Ibrahim's shirt . . . a piece of Siddiq's loincloth . . . Amina's collyrium bottle and Bafatan's kajal box . . . Sakina's box of tinsel clippings . . . the big bead of Mullan's rosary and Baqir Mian's prayer board . . . Bismillah's dried navel string, the knob of turmeric in its sachet from Tiny's first birthday, some lucky grass, and a silver ring . . . and Bashir Khan's gilt medal conferred on him by the government for having returned safe and sound from the war.

But it was not Granny's own trinkets that interested the onlookers. What they had their eyes on was her precious stock of stolen goods which Granny had got together by years of raiding.

'Thief! . . . Swindler! . . . Old hag! Turn the old devil out! . . . Hand her over to the police! Search her bedding, you might find a lot more stuff in it!' In short, they came straight out with anything they felt like saying.

Granny's shrieking suddenly stopped. Her tears dried up, her head drooped, and she stood there stunned and speechless . . . She passed that night sitting on her haunches, her hands grasping her knees, rocking backwards and forwards, her body shaken by dry sobbing, lamenting and calling the names of now her mother and father, now her husband, now her daughter Bismillah, and her granddaughter Tiny. Every now and then, just for a moment, she would doze, then wake with a cry, as though ants were stinging an old sore. At times she would laugh and cry hysterically, at times talk to herself, then suddenly, for no reason, break into a smile. Then out of the darkness some old recollection would hurl its spear at her, and like a sick dog howling in a half-human voice, she would rouse the whole mohalla with her cries.

Two days passed in this way, and the people of the mohalla gradually began to feel sorry for what they had done. After all, no one had the slightest need of any of these things. They had disappeared years ago, and though there had been weeping and wailing over them at the time, they had long since been forgotten. It was just that they themselves were no millionaires, and sometimes on such occasions a mere straw weighs down upon you like a great beam. But the loss of these things had not killed them. Shabban's quilted jacket had long since lost any ability to grapple with the cold, and he couldn't stop himself growing up while he waited for it to be found. Hasina had long felt she was past the age for wearing a bodice. Of what use to Munni were her doll's baggy trousers? She had long passed the stage of playing with dolls and graduated to toy cooking posts. And none of the people of the mohalla were out for Granny's blood.

In old days there lived a giant. This giant's life was in a big black bee. Across the seven seas in a cave there was a big chest, and in it another chest, and inside that was a little box, in which there was a big black bee. A brave prince came . . . and first he tore off the bee's legs and, by the power of the spell, one of the giant's legs broke. Then the prince broke another leg, and the giant's other leg broke. And then he crushed the bee, and the giant died.

Granny's life was in the pillow, and the monkey had torn the enchanted pillow with his teeth and so thrust a red-hot iron bar into Granny's heart.

There was no sorrow in the world, no humiliation, no disgrace, which Fate had not brought to Granny. When her husband died and her bangles were broken, Granny had thought she had not many more days to live; when Bismillah was wrapped in her shroud, she felt certain that this was the last straw on the camel's back. And when Tiny brought disgrace upon her and ran away, Granny had thought that this was the death blow.

From the day of her birth onwards, every conceivable illness had assailed her. Smallpox had left its marks upon her face. Every year at some festival she would contract severe diarrhoea.

Her fingers were worn to the bone by years of cleaning up other people's filth, and she had scoured pots and pans until her hands were all pitted and marked. Some time every year she would fall down the stairs in the dark, take to bed for a day or two and then start dragging herself about again. In her last birth Granny surely must have been a dog tick; that's why she was so hard to kill. It seemed as though death always gave her a wide berth. She'd wander about with her clothes hanging in tatters, but she would never accept the clothes of anyone who had died, nor even let them come into contact with her. The dead person might have hidden death in the seams to jump out and grab the delicately nurtured Granny. Who could have imagined that in the end it would be the monkeys who would settle her account? Early in the morning, when the water carrier came with his water skin, he saw that Granny was sitting on her haunches on the steps. Her mouth was open and flies were crawling in the corners of her half-closed eyes.

People had often seen Granny asleep just like this, and had feared she was dead. But Granny had always started up, cleared her throat and spat out the phlegm and poured out a shower of abuse on the person who had disturbed her. But that day Granny remained sitting on her haunches on the stairs. Fixed in death, she showered continuous abuse upon the world. Her whole life through she had never known a moment's ease and wherever she had laid herself down there had been thorns. Granny was shrouded just as she was, squatting on her haunches. Her body had set fast, and no amount of pulling and tugging could straighten it.

On Judgement Day, the trumpet sounded, and Granny woke with a start and got up coughing and clearing her throat, as though her ears had caught the sound of free food being doled out . . . Cursing and swearing at the angels, she dragged herself somehow or other doubled up as she was over the Bridge of Sirat and burst into the presence of God, the All Powerful and All Kind . . . And God, beholding the degradation of humanity, bowed His head in shame and wept tears, and those divine tears of blood fell upon Granny's rough grave, and bright red poppies sprang up there and began to dance in the breeze.

Translated by Ralph Russell

Vocation

I was sure that she was a courtesan. The dyed hair, tight outfits and the rush of men at all hours. Dance, music, loud and shrill guffaws that made me reel in my room. We women can outwit great wrestlers, but when we encounter a courtesan all our feminine wiles seem to vanish. That is why at the time of singing lullabies to her child, a mother emphasizes that a courtesan is a dragon, a serpent and heaven knows what else!

This childhood abhorrence of courtesans seems to be running in my bloodstream even today. A thousand women may walk past me without making me self-conscious, but the mere scent of a courtesan makes me excitable as an antelope. I still remember this smell of which I had the first experience when I was a mere child. There used to be a gathering of courtesans at the shrine of Syed Mian of Bahraich on Thursdays. On those auspicious days God-fearing people would throng the place. One day an old courtesan had picked me up in her arms under the influence of some strange emotions. Oh! That slippery dress and the peculiar scent of her breast! I immediately climbed down from her arms.

That day everyone had teased me, saying with disdain that I was touched by a whore, and I kept crying for a long time from a sense of humiliation. Then one day an aunt of mine visited us. As she caressed me, I felt the same shimmering dress and aromatic breast! I ran away from her. Yes, I guessed right. The gorgeous woman did not stay with us for a month when Abbajan, a father of ten children, fell for her badly. My poor Ammi just took it lying down. How could an ordinary paan kiosk compete with a thriving restaurant? Well, black magic was resorted to; she developed a pain in the neck and departed. What I mean to say is that we women can smell courtesans from a distance and want to erect protective walls against their onslaught.

She was coming down the stairs as I was going up when I smelt her. Good God, where had I landed? What would people say? And the bunch of ill-tempered fellows in my office? It is they more than the neighbours who had a flair for such gossip.

It was the day of Id. But what is Id or Muharram to one living as humbly as I? I had not even changed my dress and was skimming through the newspaper in bed. One could hear the clatter of crockery in the neighbour's apartment from the wee hours. The poor souls had to take care about offerings and prayers. I still lay in bed and was taking breakfast when she knocked and then barged into the room before I could get up.

Who could foretell the events that were going to unfold? This was the first occasion when a courtesan had imposed herself on me. So I was visibly shaken. 'Oh dear, I hope you haven't taken your breakfast yet. I've brought you delicious sewaiyaan' – she hissed from her tight outfit. Silly thing! She didn't have time to reflect that the days for such tight outfits for her were over. In them she looked like uneven lumps of yeasted dough tied up in shoelaces.

'I don't take sweets in the morning,' I said tartly as a proud housewife.

'Oh no! Not on the day of Id. You must taste a bit, for my sake.' She sat down on the bed with an air of easy familiarity.

Good God! Did she take me for a courtesan like her and had come to wash my sins with the sacred offerings? How could I tell her that I was chaste and pure? And her urgings! Well, she must have urged thousands of her admirers in this way. I got annoyed, but, as she kept on insisting brazenly, I tasted two morsels.

'The cook said that you're a Muslim. Since then I have been looking forward to meeting you . . . but you're not to be seen during daytime.' Someone called for her, and she left.

I took two more spoonfuls. But then I felt like thrusting a finger in my gullet to throw up. Whatever had come upon me that I partook of a prostitute's earnings? The money earned through selling her chastity. The money of an obscene whore!

But then all sorts of rebellious thoughts came to my mind. The prostitute's wealth was, in reality, the wealth of my ancestors. I had an uncle who spent as much as thirty thousand rupees in a matter of three weeks in whoring. What do I care who that prostitute was? She could well be the sister or niece of this red-haired woman! With this thought I started taking the sewaiyaan with great relish as though I was retrieving lost wealth! At least I was making a rich person somewhat poor. I took another morsel soaked in rose water and garnished with dry fruits. A big pistachio got stuck between my teeth. Tiny bubbles of fat started dancing in my mouth as though I had chewed up a burly moneylender. The thought of his plentiful fat made me feel nauseated. I experienced the satisfaction that rebels felt in burning British clothes. Our revengeful eyes find solace in conjuring up figures of fancy to fill empty dresses.

I took up the matriculation examination scripts from the bed-side table and started to evaluate them. Id or not, I had yet to examine three hundred scripts. But when my mind begins to wander, it is difficult to control it. Irritated, I failed a few unfortunate examinees, threw away the scripts and stretched myself on the bed. The weather here is also rather peculiar – mushy and soggy. One feels drowsy and indolent, the body seems heavy as though someone has spread glue over it and let it dry. A strange sort of intoxication overwhelms one. And then the hearty guffaws from the neighbour's apartment.

Poor woman! I felt pity for her. It is quite possible that she was compelled to part with her precious virginity. Perhaps some brute had violated her chastity, thus forcing her to become a public commodity. I felt a sudden affection for her. As children whenever we fought over some eatables, Amma would lose her temper and throw the entire basket at us, saying, 'Here you are, the eternally hungry brats! Now eat to your death!'

But as always, evil thoughts invariably followed the noble ones in my mind. As soon as the noble thoughts retreated, evil thoughts raised their head. This red-haired one must have become a courtesan for the fun of it. Sheer laziness. She could not do anything else, so she took to this vocation, which suited her admirably. Oh yes, could the neighbour ever do such household jobs as sewing or grinding wheat? There are hundreds of irritants in other vocations. Husband, wife, children – then the tiffs with mother-in-law and sisters-in-law. Disgusting! Could the neighbour have managed to look so youthful if she had had a few mothers-in-law and sisters-in-law? No way.

One day it so happened that as soon as I entered my apartment, I heard screams and yells from the neighbour's. I could not be sure of some peaceful moments here at the end of a gruelling day. After school I felt so worn out that I needed to lie down still for a few hours to shed the exhaustion. It seemed that the girls in the class squeezed the brain as one sucks sugar cane dry before spitting it out. Revive this sucked-out sugar cane with utmost effort and the next morning face the same gnawing teeth once more! Follow this routine for 260 days in a year and then start the process all over again!

The door opened, and she sauntered in clicking her heels. 'I'm fed up with Nigar. God knows why she makes so much fuss about school and study . . .' Oho! Even the daughters of courtesans had become so sensitive to studies that their mothers had to make a to-do about it!

'Why send her to school at all? . . . Withdraw her.'

'Withdraw her? What a piece of advice! Ai bi, whoever cares for an illiterate girl nowadays? Fellows only want memsahebs who can spout English.'

What a revelation! Education was necessary even in their calling! Probably they had to quote Shakespeare and Wordsworth as well!

'What's the problem?'

'Well, I urged her to wear khara pyjamas today. But she doesn't listen to me . . . wants to wear only those wretched frocks. She might listen to you. Actually some people are coming from Delhi.' She confided to me in a hushed tone, and I felt like scratching her beetroot-tinted face. It was as though my Bachelor of Teachers' Training degree had equipped me to advise the daughters of prostitutes on how to use their wiles. How would I teach them to wear pyjamas for Delhiites, saris for Calcuttans and salwars for Lahoris? Splendid! On top of it I did not much care for Nigar Malati. Just think of her name – was it a symbol of Hindu–Muslim unity or Hindu–Muslim discord? Real leaders had admitted defeat over the issue that she solved by a single stroke! But it has become a habit with me that I consider everyone a victim of circumstances. Perhaps the red-haired Sethani was also helpless, unable to decide whose seed was this Nigar and took care of the rights of both. Anyway.

'Why don't you come over to our place sometimes,' she said brazenly and, before I could think of a rude reply, added, 'Nigar has learnt a new dance form.'

If I ever feel kindly towards a courtesan, it is when she actually performs a dance. Then she becomes exactly like a hard-working labourer yoked to capitalism or a housewife grinding the mill. Dancing is no joke, every tiny bit of the flesh is thoroughly shaken as though one has ground ten seers of grains. Actually I don't detest the seamy side of a courtesan's life because it is somewhat different. Not at all. Rather – out of sheer necessity – well, it is difficult to explain.

The next day I gathered some courage and went to her apartment. I wanted to see how their homes looked from inside. Gosh! It looked like the house of a small king or minister – complete with life-size portraits and statues of nude women. Why do these courtesans hang pictures of naked women on the walls? What's the use? Perhaps the sethani intended to hide her hideous wrinkles in the shadow of these well-endowed figures. This must be one of their celebrated wiles!

Nigar turned so coy at seeing me, as though she was not used to seeing strangers, and came before me after a good deal of fuss. On the sethani's reprimand she put a record on the gramophone and began to dance. These whores! I was told that their bodies rot away, but the sethani looked solid like an iron pillar and her young one was beyond all compare. What a supple and delicate figure! As though a cobra was stretching itself sensuously. One wrist upon another, when she gestured a knot and hit the earth with her tiny heels, the whole world seemed to swing with her. My heart missed a beat. No one knew how many men would be stung by this serpent! How many heads would tumble! A woman usually gets jealous of other women, but God save us from prostitutes. This world is like a market where everyone claims his share. A woman takes her share – a man – and moves away. But not so a prostitute. It can be understood through this analogy – ordinary people buy their groceries according to needs from the shop and move away, but big fellows stuff their basement with sacks and sacks of food-grains. If you have studied economics you would know the result – paucity of food. Thus our struggle against courtesans that has been going on is, in fact, the struggle of workers against capitalists. One suffers and another reaps the benefit. People say that a blast of whirlwind will come one day and the workers will wipe out the capitalists and snatch away their wealth. Perhaps women will lead a similar attack on the courtesans one day and rob them of their 'capital'. Well, perhaps!

The clients began to arrive at sundown. I was looking for a chance to take flight and dived to a corner in sheer embarrassment lest they take me for a prostitute. That is what happened. She fixed me up with a dimwit editor. I could not utter a word, and she struck the deal.

Soon the hall became chock-full of gorgeous women and fun-loving men, and it reverberated with hearty guffaws. A few started boozing and gambling in one corner. Nigar was showing herself off amidst a group of admirers. She was the centre of attraction for everyone. A middle-aged fellow was trying to pull her to his lap while she hit at him, laughing.

But it was the sethani who brightened up the whole atmosphere. She had worn a dark-coloured gaudy dress that had looked rather dull in the daylight but was sparkling now. Powdered and rouged, she was looking like a new bride, making demure gestures at the young men who surrounded her. A real stunner, she looked much younger than her age. Sitting there, I kept wondering whether youth depended on age or coquetry.

Meanwhile, the editor was at his game. Sophisticated and clever talk that left me stammering. His attention was concentrated on the nude paintings that were hung near me – rather it seemed that they were stuck on my body. He dwelt at length on their excellence, touching different parts of the figures. I felt alarmed and pretended to look into my purse for some important object. Undeterred, he came back again and again to the issue of the height of female breasts and, creating romance in his watery eyes, explained things to me as he made suggestive gestures with his withered hands. Despite being quite brazen, I had to fix my eyes on the figures in the carpet. Every gesture of his made me feel that he was kneading my body like flour with his leg and, when it was thin as wafer, disfiguring it. He must have been enjoying himself thoroughly, squeezing me out in this fashion, which was evident from his perpetual smile. I felt like doing the same with a part of his body so that the eyes wearing the ugly smile dropped down in shame. But a sense of decency stopped me.

I rushed into my room at the first opportunity. Near the gallery I saw an officer clawing Nigar zestfully while she was crooning and scratching him.

I lay down in bed, but could neither sleep nor do any other work. The inspector was coming to visit the school the following day. I had to play a hundred tricks to impress her – the lesson must be effective, the conversations engaging, the dress dignified and the manners mild but firm. An attentive class, proper use of the blackboard, the importance of dialogic method – these were the ingredients of my noble profession. Without any thought I started doing physical exercises in bed, but then the thought of someone seeing me in this condition restrained me. This thought also made me feel terribly lonely. How lonely I was, except for the guffaws from the sethani's apartment, which descended on me like frightening rocks and hit my brain! The jingling of bells and the sound of clapping crept into my body and began to vibrate through my whole being – and then evil thoughts began to raise their heads.

Heaven knows what would happen if anyone had the slightest inkling of these thoughts! For instance, it seemed to me that the sethani tempted her clients with her get-up for the sake of livelihood. I also do the same – making myself presentable I go to the court of my clients. The only difference was that my intellect was a squeezed-out sugar cane while the sethani was a pitcherful of nectar. I sold my brain and she her body! The value of my brain was equal to that of a second-hand tyre, that is, seventy rupees. And the sethani? She earned much more in one sensuous gesture than my father, a highly placed officer of the British government, did in his whole life. Both of us were sitting in the marketplace displaying our wares. Different wares, but the objective was the same. What was the worth of my squeezed-up brain before her stately physique? A mere paan–biri kiosk in front of a cricket club! I was sure to be beaten. The thought made me burn with jealousy. People feel pity for courtesans and endeavour to improve their lot – no, they should not completely disappear – but those living poorly should live better! Their shabby clothes be replaced by sparkling ones! Their dwellings on drains and sewers be transferred to Marine Drive! The clients should come, but not so many that they can't take good care of! On the other hand, no one seems to care if our salary goes down year after year. Let the number of students, all troublemakers, increase twofold; the headmistress sucks you dry, the clerks in the office claw you and the committee members swallow you up – no one gives a damn! Lady teachers are moulding children's minds just as courtesans are providing succour to 'orphans'. Both are doing their duty – then why this discrimination?

Having spent the night in such mental gymnastics, there was little strength left to charm and flatter the inspector the next day. The result was that any hope of the job becoming permanent that year was lost. A heart-warming prospect came to an end. This was the lot for one who had decided to dedicate her life to the nation! Oh . . . but the nation had had enough of these half-dead cows – these sick goats – their very sight was repulsive to the nation!

The sethani came again the next day and deluged me with advice with such easy familiarity as though I were very close to her and led my life blindfolded.

'What's this – study, study at all hours! Your poor brain must have gone numb.'

I mumbled something to excuse myself.

'Just see what you've made of yourself!' she said in a pitying tone and my rebellious self came to the fore. What right did she have to tease me like this? Oh my God, where have I landed myself? From all appearances, the building seemed to be the abode of decent people. The name plates indicated as much – Miss Cotino, Miss Walker, Mrs Abdullah, Miss Rasheeda, Mrs . . .

'Mr Hameed desires to see you again.' He was the same editor! So she had decided to enlist me in her profession and send the thinnest and dullest of her clients to me!

'I must take you to see a movie today,' she coaxed me.

'But I've to . . .' It must be made clear that my vocation, besides being respectable, was quite exciting.

'Come on, you're always neck-deep in work. Hameed Saheb has brought the passes especially for you, and here you are making excuses! Arré, this is the age to enjoy life.'

Good God! So this was the end of my noble profession and the beginning of 'fun and frolic'. What a shock it would be to my poor mother if she were to know that her innocent daughter was being led astray and bargained for! Today came the passes, tomorrow it would be a Benarasi sari, then diamond tops and, eventually, the fellow himself with his painterly ideas! His rough and withered hands making suggestive gestures . . . Oh God!

I refused curtly, and she left disappointed. Her parting shot was, 'Well what was wrong in it? It is rightly said that girls should not be highly educated.'

I started arranging the answer scripts. Oh God, these stupid fellows who failed gave me trouble deliberately. If there were a score lower than zero I would have awarded it to them! I was so cut up that I felt like failing even those who did not actually fail so that each one of them, like the sethani, may go to hell. Well, this punishment was rather unwarranted. I would rather make them courageous and hard-working teachers like me so that – so that – they also . . . I could not think further.

The sethani and Nigar went out grinning and giggling with Hameed Saheb and several other zestful admirers. I was still awake when they returned. The moment I began to doze off, dragons attacked me baring their teeth. How could one work in such a situation? I knew what was going to happen to me if I stayed for a few more days in close proximity with that whore. I was getting more confused every day. I was even afraid of looking deep into my heart lest my conscience pricked me. I kept sitting on the bed holding my head.

Tired and exhausted, the sethani was fast asleep. The apartment was drowned in silence. Some unsavoury thoughts invaded my mind. I indulged them a bit and a whole host of them crashed in. Guffaws were reverberating in my brain, but there was no smile on my face. Respectability, chastity – if you kept these eggs warm under your wings, would a peacock hatch out of them? And the irony is, no one gives you any credit for hatching those eggs. The nation does not give a damn – that a devi has kept herself chaste! I felt like breaking that illusion in a single stroke so that everyone knew about the filth within.

I kept wondering at the state of my mind. This was the result of staying close to that whorehouse. I was reminded of my friend Veena. How beautiful and lively she was! Nine years of continuous teaching in a school had taken its toll. Then one day, she married a filthy old fogey in a panic. She used to say that she had fallen in love with him because of his patriotism. He had spent sixteen years in prison and had been quite handsome once. But I know that Veena was using patriotism as a shield as the sethani used the nude pictures as a convenient façade. The fact is, when hungry, even a piece of wood tastes like papad.

I resolved to shift out. Otherwise the pearl would sink in filth and the treasure for which a woman from the Orient gives away her life would be thrown in dirt. Chastity is something that one woman trades for livelihood while another gives her life to protect. Eventually this is the trump card she uses at all critical moments!

Totally drained by the tangle of thoughts, I tried to go to sleep.

I met the sethani the following morning as I was going down. She was arguing with a fruit vendor. She turned away her face as she saw me. My head rose high with pride. She had finally realized that I was respectable – and she an object of the marketplace.

After a couple of days, my cousin came to visit me with his wife. Since I had moved into the apartment I was worried. He would be furious if he came to know that I was living in such a neighbourhood. The moment he came in, guffaws began to tumble down like huge rocks from the sethani's apartment. I got up and shut the door in disgust.

'Vulgar woman! Some mischief or the other is going on all the time!'

'Where?'

'Up there. A saucy courtesan lives upstairs. There's a big rush all the time.'

'Courtesan? Here? But this was Nigar laughing, wasn't it?' he exclaimed.

'Yes. So you're familiar with them?' I gave a knowing wink to his wife.

'Oh, yes. Didn't you meet them? I operated on Nigar when she had tonsillitis. They come from a reputed family.'

'You mean – this sethani?'

'Of course. She is Sheikh Abdullah's wife – from the lineage of Sir Abdul Karim. His wife is from Delhi – a descendent of the Chishtias. And she is Razia's khala.'

'Mumani,' Razia corrected him.

I had a hard time concealing my terrible discomfiture. I was stunned as though I had kicked the holy scripture. And the penance was beyond me.

'Then – well, it must be some other apartment.'

All Alone

'How about Rasheed?'

'La hawla wala quwwat!'

'Naeem?'

'He's a dwarf.'

'But his father has tons of wealth . . .'

'Darling, I wear shoes with five-inch high heels.'

'Okay. But how about Dilshad Mirza?'

'Hmm . . .' Shahzad's rosy lips became moist. Her pupils constricted and then dilated. A ringlet from her wild hair fell, nestling her cheek. Tumultuous desires made her forget herself for a moment. Dilshad Mirza, six feet two inches tall, overwhelmed her, like the Qutb Minar in its overpowering height. Then the minaret spread its wings and enveloped her. She, all too eager to surrender herself, melted in its embrace. The smell of ubtan and freshly ground henna made her head swirl as though she had drunk several pegs of cognac. A mad cobra began to dance as wedding music rang in her ears.

That lasted only for a moment. She kicked away this maddening tumult of emotions that drowned her and rose to the surface of the sea, as it were. She pulled the stray ringlet from her cheek and tucked it into her bun. Then she brushed her moist lips with the back of her palm, rose above the tumultuous sea and put her feet firmly on the sand.

'A pauper!'

'Come to your senses!' Farida was piqued. She was one of those girls who thought any man was good enough for a woman and never dreamt of stealing a glance at Dilshad Mirza even in her imagination. She derived the pleasures of the love-game by helping students find a partner of the opposite sex. While others played at love, she bore with its agony. Of course, while acting as messenger, she sometimes enjoyed the bonus of reading missives filled with extravagant emotions.

'He'll become a lecturer as soon as he completes his dissertation.'

'First a lecturer, then a professor and then, if luck favours, the principal of the college.'

'Sure. Dilshad's very promising . . .'

'But, darling, tell me one thing – this college, students, library, common room, annual fête, prize distribution, seminars, conferences – don't you sometimes want to dump the textbook on the professor's head, run away to some distant place and fly kites?'

'By God, you're a bit mad.'

'Not a bit dear, quite a bit.'

'Fine. Leave Dilshad Mian alone. It doesn't help to get married to a very handsome man.'

'That leaves Tamizuddin, but you say his is an old-fashioned, indecent name!'

'On top of it, he writes verses. Further, he's not content to just write but insists on reciting his poetry!'

'He has a good voice.'

'That's the pity. Had his voice been bad he'd not have been able to mix bhimpalasi with todi. He'd be caught right away.'

'Oh dear, now you're taking on the mantle of an ustad of classical music. Granted that you've sometimes trained yourself under Ustad Ashiq Hussain . . .' Seeing Shahzad smile, Farida flared up and said, 'So you want a cricket champion like Rasheed, a millionaire like Naeem, a glamour boy like Dilshad Mirza . . .'

'A witty fellow like Manjhli Aapa's husband,' Shahzad added.

'Henpecked like Tasneem's husband, a patriot like Tilak, daring like Bhagat Singh and as . . . as Tagore.'

The defiant ringlets danced on her cheeks again, sometimes on the right and sometimes on the left. Once again, Shahzad's lips became honey-moist. 'You look like an ass, but there's some grey matter in some corner of your brain.'

'And like Gama, the wrestler . . .'

'Shut up. The issue is closed. You can't say anything more.'

Suddenly a rickety old car pulled up close by and disgorged as many as eleven passengers. Then Dilshad Mirza, the driver, emerged tottering and swooned on the bonnet. However, he leapt up immediately because not only the bonnet but the whole car was groaning.

Those were the heady and carefree days! Life was a Milky Way without end, free from the shackles of days and nights. One didn't have a surfeit of films those days. Students were not crazy about film stars. Today's blockbusters chock-full of fights and songs were looked down upon. Only the servants would care to hang up posters of actresses like Sulochana Billimoria in the kitchen. Students patronized films produced only in the New Theatre, Prabhat and Bombay Talkies. Rather than gossiping about film stars, students would hold political debates and mushairas in the common room. The British were the oppressors, and the leaders of the freedom struggle were heroes. After the Second World War, along with Independence, the partition of the country was a controversial issue. A particular section of people believed that Partition was not necessary. In any case, the twin issues of Independence and Partition were rather paradoxical. Among the dozen-odd students, there were Shamsa and Sushila, Kumud Bhatnagar and Tamizuddin, Alice Thomas and Dilshad Mirza. They were known for their chaste Urdu laced with formal English words and phrases. This class consisted of the offspring of feudal and service gentry; they went to the best English-medium schools and colleges. Their future was bright and full of promise. The poison-spewing youths who came from the lower classes looked famished. Their future was uncertain, and they suffered from an inferiority complex vis-à-vis the charmed circle in which they could not enter. If anyone managed to do it through some good references or through his unusual merit, he would slough off his skin and wear a new one for the rest of his life and conceal his roots from all.

Dilshad Mirza came from a declining Mughal family of Agra. He was the fifth among the nine-odd siblings. His father was a munshi in the household of Nawab Mahmud Ali Sherwani. His family lived huddled with several other families in a ramshackle house surrounded by dirty, narrow streets in Mohalla Panjshahi. His four elder brothers preferred kite flying and kabaddi to study; his three younger sisters, having learnt to read the Quran and some Urdu, were waiting to get married. Dilshad Mirza was fortunate in having the company of Nawab Saheb's sons. His extraordinary brilliance impressed Nawab Saheb, who sent him to Aligarh. A fellowship helped him obtain a first class in his exams all through. He lived in style, and everyone thought that he was some relative of Nawab Saheb.

God help parents looking for suitable boys for their girls! Agra was not far from Aligarh. Therefore, it soon became known that Dilshad Mirza was the son of a poor official in the employ of Nawab Saheb. Dilshad moved to Lucknow to do his M.A. and Ph.D., and buried deep his past. His parents did not know where he had disappeared. This was because when he had passed his F.A. two of his aunts fought bitterly over him to make him their son-in-law. However, Dilshad Mirza had utter contempt for the anaemic, hysteria-prone cousins on both his mother's and father's sides. After the exposure at Aligarh, he had taken refuge in distant Lucknow. He was a good orator and earned a fair amount by writing newspaper columns. He had many rich friends, and he was always welcome in their houses. Despite inflation, it was not difficult for a smart fellow like Dilshad Mirza to live in style. But he was rather pig-headed insofar as he never accorded any importance to love or romance. His mind was totally preoccupied with the thought of his future career.

And such is the irony of fate that, despite being always on guard, Dilshad Mirza could not remain immune to Shahzad Hasan's charm. Many young men of the college were her admirers. Some young professors, too. Of course, there was no age bar among Shahzad's admirers. Dilshad Mirza called all these people donkeys but ended up being smitten by her. Coming from a prosperous bourgeois family, Shahzad was a vain and clever woman.

She was highly conscious of her beauty and brilliance and used to give away her heart with abandon. She was witty and silenced her admirers easily with the sting of her repartee. But when they – Dilshad and Shahzad – met each other at some solitary spot, all their eloquence left them. Shahzad's eyes would become downcast, a restless lock would descend on her cheek, caressing it, and her lips would become moist. The nonsensical, matter-of-fact and outspoken Dilshad Mirza would scratch his nape stupidly and start rubbing his eyes as though splinters had fallen in them. In one hand, they held their books, but they did not know what to do with the other. Their hearts and bodies called out to each other, but their verbal exchanges would remain inane and rough. Then when they heard someone's resounding laughter or someone's approaching footsteps, they would snap out of it hastily as though they had some urgent task to do. Shahzad would go to the library, open a weighty tome and start looking for something very important in her effort to suppress the wild beating of her heart. She did not know this ignorant, timid girl who lay hidden in her and who always yearned to have a glimpse of Dilshad. As soon as she saw him every pore of her body opened up and Shahzad's self-image suffered a setback. As though she was not really Shahzad but the ghost of some silly girl brought up in an inhibiting environment that possessed her in those moments.

With great zest, she would think of some stinging phrase of self-reproach and plan out a strategy to control her feelings. What stupidity this was! Would she be swallowed by it? When the carefree youths met in the chandukhana, they indulged in jokes at each other's expense. As the baitbazi went on full steam, Dilshad Mirza would also participate in the exchange and repartee. Maybe out of revenge, she sounded more enthusiastic than the others. And she would find fault with whatever he said.

And fanciful Farida would curse both of them in her mind. 'What a lovely couple they would make! He's a six-footer Mughal; she's a charming, portly sayyidani. If one's complexion is glowing wheatish, the other's is molten gold with a tinge of vermilion. If their union doesn't take place, the whole of creation will remain unsatisfied.'

As soon as Shahzad passed her B.A., she was inundated with marriage proposals. But she didn't find any to her taste. She joined the Arts College. Painting had always interested her. She had received prizes in several painting competitions while in school. Besides, she needed something to occupy herself until marriage. The very idea of teaching in a school repelled her.

However, this preoccupation turned out to be the real objective of her life. The stifled love in her heart, hatred, disappointments, the unknown, unfathomable desires hidden in the soul began to take shape on the canvas in colours. For two months, she made rounds of art galleries, mosques, temples, shrines, the caves of Ajanta and Ellora to acquaint herself with the life captured in colours and stones. She struck deep bonds with the churches of Goa, the echoing, resounding bells of temples in the south and the tumultuous sea waves in Bombay. As the waves touched her bare feet, she often broke into tears. Why was it so? She didn't have answers to such questions. Why was she always reminded of Dilshad Mirza? What was he to her? What deep bond bound them? Or, was he an enemy that his remembrance brought nothing but pain?

The partition of the country was old history now. The world had disintegrated. After the death of her mother, she could not leave this land. However, in connection with an exhibition, she went to France and then travelled through Europe. The art galleries brought her some relief. Some disquiet too. Time slipped by imperceptibly. As she looked in the mirror she gave a start and bent her head. It's impossible! Perhaps the thread of the pillow cover had got entangled in her hair. She hastily ran the comb through her hair. The threads were still there. How could this be? Was the calendar hung upside down? 1975! No, it must be 1957. Fifty-seven – that is, ten years had passed after the vivisection of the land. Oh no! She was wrong. The calendar was hung all right. It's thirty years! She was afraid to count the years. Maybe she had not seen herself in the mirror for a long time. There must be some mistake.

Her steps automatically led her towards the hairdressing salon. When she came out after about an hour, the grey streaks were no longer there. Her body was still supple and graceful, the features well proportioned. The premature wrinkles disappeared if one did not wear glasses.

Her fame had spread in the art world, and she was counted among the top-notch painters. Her masterpieces celebrated the beauty of the country and its glorious heritage. She could capture in colours the musical sound of the temple bells as well as the azan in the mosque. The present and the future derive inspiration from the past. The past never dies. If a nation considers its past dead, it remains ever confused.

The past lives in us. Thus, as the grey streaks disappeared from her hair, the past returned. 'Bibi, a two-penny-worth lecturer! Oh my God' – Manjhli Khala had sneered when she had heard the rumours about Dilshad Mirza. Then there were Naeem, Ahmad Jamal ICS, Anwarul Haq T'aluqadar who was a bit older but very smart, Javed Zaidi – all of them were genuine sayyids and belonged to the gentry. But she did not care a hoot for any of them.

'Naeem?' 'Phew . . .' Ahmad Jamal was jet black, the veritable wrong side of the tawa.

Anwarul Haq was opposed by the whole family. There was a difference of fifteen to twenty years in their age. That left Javed Zaidi, whose family was so conservative that women still lived in purdah there, what to speak of their moving in high society!

And Dilshad Mirza? He got a lectureship in the university at Aligarh. However, the likelihood of climbing up the professional ladder was rather remote. So, in 1953 he migrated to Pakistan. He did not manage to get a foothold in Pakistan and moved to England. Those who leave – do they ever return?

Now her tresses do not dance on her cheeks anymore. Nor do the thoughts of Dilshad Mirza make her eyelids droop. But her heart still feels the pain – thank God, it's still alive. Even if it had died, what could she have done? She had dissolved the pangs of her heart in variegated hues – the pangs she felt when she saw children rummaging in dustbins for apple skins and licking the leaf wrappings of chaat at Chaupatti. Behind the railings on Faras Road, she saw an eleven-year-old girl, lips heavy with lipstick and wearing a see-through dress in order to attract customers. One could glimpse her tiny breasts through her dress. She had also watched the mother who beat her child mercilessly for not bringing enough 'pickings' after begging the whole day on the road.

'Why're you beating him?' she had asked.

'He's a little bastard, memsaheb. Spends the whole day playing one game or the other and blows up whatever he gets from begging, in eating chaat masala' – the woman was heavily pregnant and panting for breath.

'Why do you send them to beg?'

'What else can I do, memsaheb?'

'Where's their father?'

'Ran away with a slut.'

Shahzad did not pull back the tress that fell on her cheek. It was stinging her. When Lord Shiva had drunk the poison of the earth, his throat had turned pale. The poison that she had to swallow went right to her heart, which she, in turn, poured out onto the canvas.

'So, this is love.' Her mind wandered as she dipped the brush in blue. It is said that when a woman gets pregnant, each part of her body glistens like gold. However, sometimes pregnancy can turn out to be a cancer as well. Well, how could one who was a stranger to the touch of the male body know the pleasure and pain of pregnancy? Shahzad was a barren island. There was no possibility of any buds blossoming on it. She would shrink within herself when she saw people look pityingly at her.

Time wore on. Then the telephone rang one day.

'I want to talk to Shahzad Hasan.'

'Who's on the line, please?'

'Dilshad Mirza.' She froze.

'Hullo? Hullo,' the voice was growing impatient.

'This is Shahzad speaking.' She was surprised that her voice did not quiver.

'Ah, at last! Adaab arz.'

'Adab arz. How did you trace me?'

'Well, England may be beyond the seven seas, but it's on this planet. Besides, a famed personality like you . . . Even an illiterate person like me knows . . .'

'So, still practising targets?'

'Several members of our group are here in search of a livelihood.'

'Great!'

'Well, tell me, do I have to talk to your secretary for an appointment?'

'Arré, you're under some strange delusion. I am not such a big shot as to engage secretaries.'

'What hour can one meet you?'

'Any auspicious hour that suits you.'

'If one says now, this moment!'

'Sure.'

'Well . . . I mean, my wife will be with me.' The innumerable wings of the Qutb Minar began to drop off one by one. But she said hastily, 'Sure, children too?'

'There are no children.'

'You mean they didn't come with you.'

'We don't have children.'

'Oh, I'm sorry.'

'It's all right. We'll be on our way.'

For a few moments, Shahzad sat like a stone holding the silent receiver.

In the room, things were in a mess – colour tubes, brushes, cushions, discarded nightclothes and teacups. She began cleaning up the mess and swept the garbage to the other room. Then she took out the purple kanjivaram sari, but it looked rather dull. So, she brought out the peacock-blue tanchoi. She was determined that Dilshad Mirza should not be given the slightest reason to feel pity for her. He would come swaggering with his wife to show off his success in life and would pity me for my lonely existence. Damn! I . . .

As the doorbell rang, she took a final look in the mirror. A light stroke of lipstick and mascara had brought freshness to her face. She opened the door and stood dead in her tracks.

Standing before her was a lanky, shrivelled and completely bald Englishman grinning out of his dentures. Holding his hand was a portly old woman who barely reached his waist even though she was wearing high heels.

'Dilshad Mirza. Sylvia – my wife,' said Dilshad in English.

'Shahzad. Come on in.'

'She's still beautiful!' Sylvia gushed to her husband. She looked older than him by a few years.

No one spoke for a while.

Oh God, will the tongues remain tied even now? Only the heart will beat wildly, thought Shahzad. But her heart neither beat wildly, nor did it leap up.

'I'm down with ulcers. In fact, we owe our marriage to our common ailment. We met at the doctor's who was treating both of us. Then we continued seeing each other. Sylvia's ailment was older than mine. She helped me a lot with her advice.'

'Dilli is very careless. Drinking has ruined him.'

'Sylvia has given me a new lease of life.'

'Your marriage . . .'

'This is the fourth year of our marriage. In fact, we'll complete four in October.'

'Dilli was in love with you.' Sylvia smiled mischievously and started making tea.

'Please, Sylvia.' Dilshad Mirza's yellow face was turning pale.

'Nonsense! Miss Hasan, were you also in love with him?'

'Sylvia!'

'Here, if a woman expresses her love for someone, it's looked upon as audacity.' Shahzad endeavoured to turn the whole thing into a joke.

'You must have been in love with him. It's unlikely that Dilli's love was one-sided. It was so intense. No, impossible.'

'Why talk about it? What's the use?' Dilshad Mirza leant back on the sofa and closed his eyes.

'How silly! Why didn't you marry, then? Just because the conservative elders in your families opposed it?'

'No.'

'Then?'

'You won't understand.'

'Why?'

'It's rather complex. We Indian women are both free and fettered.'

'How's that?'

'Our enlightened elders leave us free to choose our life partners but then they very cleverly put doubts in our mind about the person we've chosen.'

'That's just not fair! It's inhuman!' Sylvia lost her temper.

'But you cannot call them guilty of any misconduct.'

'Is it because they're very clever?'

'No, they think that they do it for our good.'

'Sylvia, what a pity that all three of us had to suffer for our parents. But none of us knows about children. So, this debate is pointless. Talk of something else.'

'Well, what brings you to India after all these years?' Shahzad changed the topic.

'The memory of this land has brought me back.'

'But you had migrated to Pakistan.'

'Pakistan's also my land. I go there every alternate year or so.'

'And India?'

'India is the land of my ancestors. The land where I was born, where my ancestors are buried. I grew up playing and dancing on its soil. How can I forget the waters of the Yamuna where I learnt swimming? Those labyrinthine lanes of Agra, Muharram taziyas, the riot of colours at Holi and the illumination of Diwali? I'm a British citizen. But that does not mean that the shopping sprees at

Anarkali, the lively assemblies of Karachi, the literary and educational seminars, Hawk's Bay, Sands Pit, picnic parties, Faiz Ahmad Faiz, Mehdi Hasan are not part of my heritage. In fact, when I come to think of it, the whole world seems to be my home.'

A strange silence descended once again. A feeling of desolation, too.

'And now,' Dilshad Mirza resumed, 'after spending almost half of my life in England it has become my third home. My tummy upsets remain under control there. I've got so used to that life that I do not feel at home anywhere else. Could those who migrated from Iran and the Arab world forget their fatherland even after centuries? Don't we love them, as did our ancestors? I love all these three countries. To love one of them is not to betray another. How many people emigrated from India and Pakistan to other lands and were driven out from there to somewhere else! I met people who call themselves Indians and their hearts bleed for Africa from where they were driven out. They've settled down in England and feel at home there.

'Take the Chinese – even after staying in India for centuries they call themselves Chinese. Though India fought a war with China they were not proved traitors. Even if they want, they cannot go back to the land of their ancestors. The Iranians, settled here in Bombay, have not forgotten the land of their ancestors, but their security is ensured if India is secure.'

'Oh, you're boring me to death. Your explanation is unsatisfactory' – Sylvia was irritated.

'Which explanation?' asked Shahzad.

'That parents do not bring any pressure to bear on you and even then, you stifle your love. Why didn't you elope?'

'What a cruel wife you are, to suggest that your husband elope with another woman!'

'I was not your wife then. Had you eloped, I would not have even known about it.'

'Do all the girls in your country who elope against the wishes of their parents and marry lead a successful married life?'

'Oh no, it's ridiculous to suggest it. There's no guarantee at all.'

'Now you're talking nonsense,' Dilshad smiled. 'If the parents arrange the marriage, and it turns out to be a failure, then they are to blame. And if the sons and daughters marry of their own choice they say, "If you had listened to us you would have led a happy life." '

Sylvia got up to make tea. Dilshad Mirza and Shahzad kept sitting like two guilty souls.

'For God's sake, say something. Don't feel shy. I'm not listening,' Sylvia yelled from the kitchen.

Dilshad looked Shahzad in the eye and said bitterly, 'I've made my life a farce because of my love for you. For God's sake, just tell me that I was not a fool. That the feeling was not one-sided, that you were also touched by it.'

'Is confession necessary?' Shahzad's eyelashes became heavy. The tresses danced down and caressed her cheeks. After ages the lips quivered and became moist. The tresses seemed to her to be Dilshad Mirza's lips. She did not tuck them into the bun.

'Every moment of my life has been filled with thought of you, with music and emotion. This would not have been possible if I hadn't known you.'

'And if you had been depressed, I'd have divorced you by now,' cut in Sylvia as she brought the tea tray. 'Sorry, I was listening. I know this much Urdu.'

'Well, Sylvia, why did you marry so late?'

'Do you Indians think that only you know the ways of love?'

'What do you mean?'

'I mean that my fiancé died in an accident in a factory.'

'And you wasted the best years of your life living alone.'

'This is a classic case of the pot calling the kettle black. Dear girl, you have not been less silly than I.'

All three broke into laughter.

'How stupid we are!'

'Well, we're still alive.'

'In fact, our hearts are still alive,' Shahzad chirruped.

'Well, Shahzad, I'm deeply in love with Sylvia. I hope you don't mind?'

'Tauba!' Shahzad was outwitted. 'If I say I also like Sylvia, will you have any objection to that?'

Even after the couple had left, Shahzad remained in a trance. Do children take birth only in the womb? Do the heart and the brain have nothing to do with it? Today my heart and brain are 'pregnant' with new emotions. They're my children, loved by my admirers as well. Don't I have children, then? She looked at the half-finished painting wistfully.

Am I lonely? Someone has been living his life beyond the seven seas enshrining me in his heart. Whenever I had wanted, I took refuge in his arms. My art and my imprisonment are of my own choice. My desires are under my control. Besides, I also feel a bond with the homes where my paintings are hung. I have brought to life sky-kissing minarets, temples, urchins playing on the road, birds flying in the air, lush green harvest, laughter and sighs, the whistle of the train and captured them on my canvas.

Am I alone? Stupid girl, answer me.

Suddenly the room became filled with the aroma of ubtan and freshly ground henna. And the shehnai began to warble wedding songs.

The sound of a baby's laughter rang out in the distance. The sky was bathed in twilight.

Shahzad picked up the brush and dipped it in orange.

The Invalid

His fever would rise. The teeth would make a constant clatter. It seemed as though the bones rattled, and the whole body burnt to a cinder. A veritable water wheel ran through his gullet – chukh . . . chrr . . . shrr – and then he got drowned in repeated fits of a racking cough.

His tongue had turned into the sole of an old shoe – dead and insensitive as a result of gulping queer, tasteless medicines interminably. He could remember, when he was a boy, how bitter the quinine tasted, how sour was the tamarind and how sweet the sugar pills! What a sensitive tongue he had had! But it had become so shamelessly dull that it didn't feel anything now.

The children romped in the courtyard, and he felt as though they were trampling over his body. They ran out, banging the door, chasing one another, and his almost lifeless body shivered all over. There were other sounds as well – lorries lumbering along, cars honking and bicycle bells ringing out. It seemed as though all these vehicles were running over his chest.

'Ram Naam sat hai' – he heard the chant, and his heart sank. 'Hurry up . . . quick!' someone called out, and he hid his face under the hemp-smeared quilt, fearing that mobs were coming to kill him.

And dogs? Well, they were kings. Given a chance they would have liked to lie down in his lap and go on barking. And the cats felt it necessary to come to his room for their nightly courtship. As he tried to shoo them away, the female of the pair merely smiled while she kept gazing at her mate dreamily, uttering an endearing 'mew' now and then. Initially they were somewhat scared of him, but gradually they realized that it was silly to run away.

Then there was the wind! It came through every chink and

crevice and smote his body. It rustled as it entered through his ears, then passed through the gullet and finally froze in his chest. In the summer, the wind brought sizzling particles of sand, plastered them on his body, and he savoured the feeling of lying in a furnace.

However, it was his burly neighbour who rankled him the most. He had a beetroot-tinted face adorned with a thick moustache. He would come and plonk down, filling the entire morha. 'How do you do?' he would ask in his dull, uniform tone that never varied.

And then his neighbour would ask of his wife, 'Bhabi, get me a paan please.' The wrinkled, wilted face of his wife – mother of six children – would light up for a few moments. He would make further demands: 'Do prepare some dahi vadas sometimes,' or 'I'll not budge without tasting your matar pulao today.' The eyes of his wife, hollowed out because of keeping constant vigil, would start dancing. She would take the neighbour to the other veranda to give him some jam or pickle, and from there would come the sound of her laughter and the loud clicking of the neighbour's tongue as he savoured the goodies.

In those moments, he felt a sudden urge to go to the toilet, or he felt thirsty, or felt a sudden need to get some or the other part of his body massaged. When he had called her several times, she would come in a huff – her eyes rolling and her body tense – as though it was not she who had let off those guffaws that had driven him mad a while ago but someone else. He would keep staring at her face as though he expected to find something there.

He would get tired of drinking water and getting his arms massaged. But the jaws of the neighbour continued to move unabated, like a millstone, as though they were determined to do away with his existence altogether.

So what if he was an invalid? His heart had not died yet.

But how could the wife be blamed? She was young; warm blood was coursing through her veins. Whenever he made an effort to get intimate with her, she would dismiss his overtures. 'I don't like your silly romance,' she would say in a gesture of dismissal, and his straw-thin hand would remain dangling in mid-air. There was a time when she was so enamoured of this 'silly romance' that she could not stay back at her parents' place even for a few hours. Sometimes they would stay alone in the room for the entire day with the doors shut. His hands were so agile and mischievous. But now the neighbour had spelt doom for him. If he did not come, he would send his shirt to get the buttons fixed. And the wife would do so keeping it close to her lap though she could have easily avoided it. Thus even if the neighbour was not there, his shirts, pyjamas or socks would be there to make his life hell. There were only a few drops of blood left in his body that kept boiling. How he wished to tear off layers of flesh from the body of his podgy neighbour with his dried-up fingers and smear it with salt and pepper! His tongue shed some of its bluntness at these appetizing thoughts.

Sitting on the bed he would notice his wife absorbed in her chores. Must be thinking of the neighbour, of that he was sure! If he could only imprison the thoughts of that loose woman! If it were in his power, he would not have allowed her to think!

But she seemed to tantalize him – 'Come on, hold the thread of my thoughts if you can.' He was piqued and his doubts would intensify. It seemed to him that all his children resembled the neighbour – the same rolling eyes, plump physique, curled feet and swollen ankles! He would call them to his side and peer at them closely. Sometimes his doubts were allayed; sometimes they increased and made him crazy. His mind would be in a whirl, so much so that he would see the neighbour's child in her womb! Restless, he would get up, beckon his wife to his side and scrutinize her. How stupid the washerwoman was! Why did she put so much starch in saris? One looked twice one's size, for no reason.

'Tell that silly washerwoman not to use so much starch,' he would say hotly, and the wife would snap, 'Why, now you want to dictate in matters of starch and saris as well!' Certainly he did not want to dictate about starch and saris. But why not? . . . And then his temperature would shoot up once again, his withered shins throb, his lungs writhe like wounded pigeons, and his temples flutter. He wanted to catch his wife by the throat and wring it to his heart's content, breaking the windpipe. And then he would slash her nose. Well, slashing the nose was no longer considered fashionable, but he spent most of the time doing this in his imagination. He liked to imagine that he had slashed her nose and was making fine squares on her face with the tip of the knife. He would give a start and look at his wife. Without doubt there were fine lines on her face. People said that they were the result of constant worry, but he only smiled because he knew better. They were the lines he had drawn in his imagination.

The temperature would increase by leaps and bounds at night. Some parts of the body turned ice cold while other parts blazed like embers. The eyes blazed while the nose turned into an ice cube, the palms burnt as the fingers melted away. The nape froze. It seemed as though someone was churning milk in his throat. The doctor looked for a bit of flesh to push needles into. The scattered lumps in the buttocks smote him like a noose.

If the eyes closed for a while he felt as though someone had poured bundles of cotton on him and he was diving through them, sobbing. Giant-like creatures danced on his chest. Someone seemed to lash his calf. Hundreds of withered, bony hands stretched out at him. Soft, inhuman fingers crawled on his temples. All his dead relatives beckoned him with outstretched hands. The old grandmother coaxed him, wagging her head. But he courteously refused to oblige them and returned safe. It is believed that if any dead relative calls one in a dream and if one accompanies him, then one dies in a few days. He knew all these tricks of the dead and was no dimwit to fall prey to the trap. After all, why should he die? He would live with a vengeance. Why did people expect him to die? He wouldn't, come what may!

He lay down in his bed and swaggered when people came to see him. At the slightest provocation, he would growl like an excitable and valorous youth. He got furious as he saw people's worn faces tinged with sympathy. He wanted to smash their chins. Finding him so energetic, the visitors, shaking their heads, would say, 'He's recovering.'

He did not know what people really thought about him. There was a time when all the unmarried girls in the extended family were protected from him as though he would gobble them up. The girls also got nervous fits at his very sight – faces flustered, they would leave the chores they were doing and run for cover. They stumbled if they tried to run away. If they wanted to cover their face, the dupatta slipped off, leaving them at his mercy. And he was indeed ruthless!

So many girls came to his view who felt coy at his sight that it was difficult for him to make a choice. Sometimes he would fall for Manjhu, at other times for Jaani. Sometimes he would forget them altogether and become a devotee of Munni. Then there were moments when he felt so confused that he pounced on all of them.

But now they have stopped feeling shy anymore in his presence. The young daughter-in-law of the cleaning woman looked straight into his eyes and discussed such topics with him as though he were a cat or a mouse and not a man! And Manjhu to whom he was all but engaged and who used to have fits of hysteria whenever she heard of his arrival now breastfed her baby before him nonchalantly. And Jaani would openly discuss her private ailments with his doctor right before him! They had forgiven him for his youthful indiscretions and now considered him absolutely harmless. Once when he wanted to shock them out of their complacency and muttered something into the ears of the young maid, she was in jitters. 'Ai, Bhaiya's fever is going up,' she yelled. Since the time he had fallen sick, people started to address him as 'Bhaiya'. The old fogeys swaggered before him and expected that he would kick the bucket any moment and depart for the other world. Hunh! Let people die of expectations. He wouldn't die. He would live! Let all his children resemble the neighbour. Let everyone resemble the neighbour – his father, mother, brother and sister. Let them have the same roving eyes, crooked feet and swollen ankles! Still he would live! He would live for revenge! They were fools if they thought that he would die to provide them relief.

He could measure a person at a glance. He would peer into the faces of those who came to see him. If they looked sad he lost his temper. They were all hypocrites! He would adopt a cutting tone while talking to them. Those who smiled to cheer him up were also impostors. Did they consider him a dimwit? They came just to mouth platitudes like 'Get well soon', 'God willing, you'll be all right', etc. He would start discussing their private affairs. The smiles on their faces vanished in a moment, leaving them awe-struck. If a person's face remained devoid of any expression, he considered him an utter fool and advised him on the benefits of incurring losses, facing humiliations, inviting plunder and litigation and smiled contentedly when the visitors showed visible signs of anxiety and disquiet. 'Come again, will you? Without waiting for an occasion?' he would ask them mentally.

Doctors came one after another and prescribed him tasteless medicines. As they gave him injections, and his wife massaged his chest, they would try to get closer to her on the pretext of helping her. Then they tried to touch her fingers and advised her to take protein-rich food and increase her blood count. They also prescribed tasty medicines for her. There was hardly any doctor who did not write prescription after prescription for his wife with utmost promptness. He cursed all of them and tore up the prescriptions. Had it been in his power, he would have held her firmly and fed her a handful of the viruses that had afflicted him.

His wife had once promised to be a companion through life and death. But now she was scared of the viruses, washed her hands with carbolic acid and gargled with soda water. What a wide gulf there was between them now!

And then his temperature would rise, the lungs swell up, the throat constrict, the bones rattle and he would drown in the sea of physical and mental torment.

Mother-in-law

The sun was blazing in the sky. It seemed to shower all its heat and light on the crone's hut. She changed the position of the cot to escape the sun, but in vain. Then, as she tried to doze off, loud bangs and peals of laughter came from the roof.

'May God ruin her!' The mother-in-law cursed her bahu – the daughter-in-law – who was playing kabaddi and having fun with the urchins of the mohalla. Why would anyone wish to live if one had such a bahu, wondered the mother-in-law. Come noon and she is up on the roof. Hordes of boys and girls arrive. One can't get a wink of sleep.

'Bahu . . . u . . . u . . . u . . .' screamed the crone through the thick layer of phlegm accumulated in her windpipe.

'Hey . . . bahu . . . u . . . u!'

'Just coming,' replied the bahu after many yells but kept on prancing. It seemed as though ghosts were dancing in her brain.

'Arré, come fast or else . . .' The bahu came down the stairs banging her feet while her anklets tinkled. She was followed by a troupe of urchins – naked, half naked, freckled – their noses running. They hid their shy faces behind the column and kept on grinning.

'Oh God, let this litter of bastards die, or send death to me. I don't know why these brats come here to torture me. Offspring of worthless chaps who procreate like hell and send them here to make my life miserable!' And so on. But the children kept on grinning, aiming their fists at one another.

'I say, have your houses caught fire that . . .'

'Why Bashariya, you died . . .' The bahu nudged the girl standing close to her.

Assuming that the jibe was directed at her, the crone screeched,

'I hurl brooms at your face. Death to all your near and dear ones! . . . Your . . .'

'Bah, we're not talking about you,' the bahu said endearingly. But the crone kept on fuming. She reprimanded the children so severely that they had to run away. The bahu sat down on the cot.

'Does anyone's daughter-in-law prance about with lads like you do? Come day, it's the lads, come night . . .' The mother-in-law seemed to be fed up with life.

'Ghun . . . ghun . . . ghun,' the bahu mumbled as she pulled the straws from the hand fan and thrust them into the parrot's cage. 'Ti . . . ti . . .' croaked the parrot.

'Why the hell are you torturing the parrot now?' the mother-in-law growled.

'Why doesn't he talk?'

'So what? It's his wish . . . Does your father feed him?' the mother-in-law turned around and yelled.

'I'll make him talk.' The bahu thrust a straw into the parrot's claw.

'Ai, ai . . . I say, have you gone crazy? Will you move, or shall I give you one or two . . .'

As the bahu continued to provoke her, she picked up one of her crooked shoes and flung it at her with such force that it hit the dog lying under the gharaunchi, making it sneak away, whining. The bahu broke into heart-warming laughter. The crone picked up the other shoe, and the bahu hid herself behind the column.

'Let that fellow Asghar come . . .'

'Fellow!' Instead of feeling shy at the mention of her husband, the bahu could barely suppress her laughter.

'Curse on your life! Why, if you could give birth to a child, your life would have been worth something. You spelt ruin for the house the day you entered it!'

The bahu smiled and gave a push to the parrot's cage.

'Why the hell are you after the parrot's life?'

'Why doesn't he talk . . . ? I'll make him.'

The crone boiled with rage. 'If you go on like this, by God I'll get a second wife for my son.'

The sun had now reached the gharaunchi and beyond. The mother-in-law kept on muttering to herself – 'What did the fellows give their daughter as dowry? . . . Ai, what wonderful gifts! Imitation bangles and chrome-plated tops. And . . .'

'Well, what can I do about that?' The bahu was put off by this show of boorishness and stretched herself on the cot.

'And those aluminium . . .' intoned the crone as she yawned. Then she rested her head on the basket and stretched her legs. However, before she finally dozed off, she continued with her interminable litany about the samdhan's gulbadan pyjamas that were frayed at the bottom, the tasteless zarda served during the wedding feast and the wooden bed with moth-eaten legs that was given as dowry. But the shameless bahu, her body lying half on the cot, half on the ground, was fast asleep. Soon the crone's mutterings also gave way to snoring.

Asghar came home, placed his umbrella against the column, took off his blue waistcoat and wiped off the profusely flowing sweat with his shirt as he entered the house. Like a mischievous boy he cast a furtive glance first at his mother and then at his wife. He laid the sack filled with mangoes and melons on the floor and scratched his head for a few moments. Then he bent over and shook the arm of his wife.

'Unh . . .' His wife frowned and snatched away her arm. Then she turned over on her side and was asleep again.

Asghar lifted the sack, fiddled with the bangles in his pocket and went into the inner room. Like a cunning cat on the prowl, the bahu craned her neck to have a look at the crone and rushed into the room holding her dupatta.

The loo had stopped. Furrows of sweat flowed unceasingly . . . The flies had had enough of the mango peelings and the garbage heap. They were now crawling on the crone's body. Some of them favoured the paan juice stuck on her lips while some entered the deep-set sockets of her eyes . . . From the inner room came the sound of groaning accompanied by moans. One could also hear the sound of mangoes and melons being peeled.

The flies made it impossible for the crone to sleep, and she got up. These flies were after one's life. They would sit on the baby's face after its birth, scenting the gripe water and then remain stuck to the body throughout life – whether one was awake or asleep – as though they were a part of one's body like one's eyes, nose or lips. One particular fly had been her mortal enemy for years. It had stung her when she was in Lucknow . . . Then she moved to Unnao. It stung her again during the rainy season. From Unnao she had moved to Sandila. It pursued her there as well. Had it been attached to any particular part of her body, she would have chopped off that part and given it to the fly. But it crawled all over her body. Sometimes she would closely watch that fly – the same spotted wings, curly legs and bulbous head. She used to take aim and hit it fiercely . . . but the fly would just hop away nonchalantly. Dear God, how she wished that some day she would be able to kill it. Or at least be able to maim it or twist its legs and enjoy the pleasure of seeing it writhe in pain. But that was not to be. Maybe God himself had admitted defeat to this fly as He had done to the Devil and it was left free to plague humanity. Well, she was sure that this fly would be consigned to hell. She would appeal to the Almighty against it, and angels would feed it on blood and pus and make it lie on thorns. But . . . will the flies also go to heaven and pollute the atmosphere there? The crone made a swipe of her fan and struck her own face, hands and dried-up legs.

'Bahu . . . bahu . . . Where on earth are you?' The crone called out. The bahu rushed out of the inner room. No dupatta on her and the front of her kurta wide open. She held a mango seed in her hand as though she had been wrestling with someone. Then she rushed back into the room, put the dupatta over her shoulder and came out wiping her hand on the pallu.

'Arré bahu . . . I was saying . . . I was thirsty.'

Asghar also came out shaking the grime off his salwar and rubbing his neck with his shirt.

'Here you are, Amma. Look, what juicy mangoes!' he said as he put the sack in her lap. Then he sat cross-legged on the cot.

As the crone smelt the mangoes and melons, she forgot the injustice done to her by the flies. From her lips they had now descended on the mangoes.

'Ai bahu, bring a knife.'

The bahu licked the mango juice on her lips as she held the tumbler. Asghar stretched his legs and dug his toe into her ankle. The water splashed and the crone yelled, 'Have you turned blind that you're emptying the tumbler on my feet?' And she struck her so fiercely that the thick-bottomed tumbler fell on the bahu's feet. The bahu clenched her teeth, glared at Asghar and left in a huff.

'Amma, here's water,' said Asghar like an obedient son. 'The bahu has become wild!'

'Judge for yourself,' complained the crone.

'Kick out the bitch. Ammi, let's bring another woman. This one . . .' said Asghar as he looked at his wife affectionately.

'Hold your tongue, you scoundrel!' the crone screeched as she slit a mango.

'Why Ammi? Just see how she's getting fat like a buffalo,' Asghar said and dug his finger into the bahu's waist when his mother was not watching. The bahu threatened to throw the knife at Asghar; but it landed on the sack in front of the crone.

'Did you see, Amma? . . . Shall I give her a good bashing? Asghar leapt up, planted a hefty blow on his wife's back and then sat cross-legged on the cot. He had the aspect of an obedient son.

'Beware! . . . Listen, I'll break your hands if you raise them to hit her again,' the crone spoke in support of her enemy. 'You had a decent marriage. Did she elope with you that you're treating her like this? . . . Hey girl, get some water, quick,' she commanded the bahu in a peremptory tone.

The bahu sat against the column, sulking. She pressed the tumbler on the bruised toe and blood oozed out while the crone licked the mango seeds testily. Then, as the bahu held out the tin of sugar to her mother-in-law, the crone had a glimpse of her blood-stained toe.

'Good God, it's blood! What's happened?' But the bahu kept on sulking behind the column and let the blood flow.

'Ai, come here . . . let me see it . . .' said the crone solicitously.

The bahu did not budge from her position.

'Just see how you're bleeding! Asghar, get up and pour some cold water on her leg.' Mothers-in-law are chameleons.

'I can't,' said Asghar wrinkling his nose.

'Bastard!' The crone got up dragging her feet. 'Come, girl, lie down on the bed. I say, this tumbler weighs no less than a kilo. I asked the scoundrel umpteen times to get an aluminium one. But he's a bastard! Come, try to get up.' The bahu did not budge an inch. She continued to sulk as she wiped her nose with the dupatta.

'Pour the water from the pitcher,' commanded the crone, and Asghar had to get up reluctantly. The crone began to wash away the blood with her withered, trembling hands. But she lost all self-control when she found that instead of pouring water on his wife's wound Asghar was peeping into her bosom. She could also sense that the bahu was eagerly waiting to bite his ear as he came closer.

'May worms eat up your body!' The crone's paws landed on Asghar's shoulder. He was piqued and poured all the water on the bahu. Then he went away to eat mangoes. The mother began to invoke instant death on the son.

'Just wait, you scoundrel. Let your uncle come, I'll get you skinned . . .' She threatened Asghar as she tied the bandage with a dirty rag.

'Come on, lie down for sometime.' The crone said that the wound was quite serious and asked Asghar to carry her to the cot.

'I can't lift her. She's huge as a buffalo.'

'You have to . . . Now, will you listen to me or . . .' As he kept sitting the crone herself tried to take the bahu in her arms.

'Amma, I'll get up on my own,' said the bahu, scared as she was of the tickle the crone gave her.

'No, daughter . . . I . . .' She glared at Asghar as though threatening him with dire consequences.

Asghar got up in a huff, lifted the bahu in his arms in a jiffy and sprinted towards the cot. Taking advantage of the situation, the bahu dug her teeth into his shoulder where a few moments ago, the crone had struck with her paws. Checkmated, Asghar threw her down on the cot and smacked her rosy lips.

The bahu kept on smiling triumphantly while Asghar grumbled as he rubbed his shoulder that had gone pale. The mother-in-law was doing her wazu and was muttering to herself, looking up at the sky. Who could say what she was muttering? Maybe she was cursing her shameless daughter-in-law.

Roots

The faces were pale. No food was cooked in the house. It was the sixth day of the forced holiday from school for children who were making life miserable for the adults in the house – the same childish tiffs, wrangles, noise and somersaults as though the fifteenth of August had not come at all. The wretched urchins did not realize that the English had left and, while leaving, had inflicted such a deadly wound that it would fester for years to come. India was operated upon by such clumsy hands and blunt knives that thousands of arteries were left open. Rivers of blood flowed, and no one had the strength left to stitch the wounds.

Had it been a normal day, the little devils would have been sent outdoors. But for the last couple of days the atmosphere had become so foul that the Muslims of the city were virtually living under siege. The houses were padlocked, and the police patrolled outside. So the children were free to let loose their terror inside the house. Of course, the Civil Lines was quiet as usual. In any case, filth spreads where there is a surfeit of children, poverty and ignorance – preying grounds for religious fanaticism, the seeds of which had already been sown. On top of it, the swelling number of refugees from Punjab created panic among the minority Muslim community. The garbage dump was being raked, and the filth had come on to the road.

There were open skirmishes at two places. However, in the state of Marwar, Hindus and Muslims had much in common and could not be distinguished from one another by their names, features or attire. Those Muslims who came from outside Marwar could be identified easily: they had already crossed the border to Pakistan when they got wind of what was to happen on the fifteenth of August. As far as the old inhabitants of the state were concerned, they had neither the sense nor the status for anyone to talk to them about the complicated India–Pakistan problem. Those who had any sense, understood the situation and had prepared for their security. Among the rest were those who were tempted to go to Pakistan by the rumours that four seers of wheat cost only one rupee there and a cubit-long naan only four annas. They were returning as they realized that to buy four seers of wheat, they needed one rupee and though a cubit-long naan cost a quarter, it still had to be paid for. And those rupees and coins were neither sold nor did they grow in fields. To acquire them was as difficult as was the struggle for existence.

So a serious problem arose when it was openly decided to throw out members of the minority community. The Thakurs told the officer in clear terms: 'Look, the people are so intermingled that, for combing Muslims out, you need staff, which involves wasteful expense. However, if you want to buy a plot of land for the refugees, that can be arranged. Only animals live in the forest, and they can be driven away any moment.'

Only a few select families remained – they were mostly in the employ of the Maharaja, and there was no question of their leaving. There were also those who were packing their bags and preparing to leave. Ours was one such family. Till Barré Bhai returned from Ajmer, there was no urgency. But as soon as he returned, he tried to create panic, yet no one paid heed. As a matter of fact, no one would have taken him seriously if Chabban Mian – may Allah grant him prosperity – had not played a trick. Having tried in vain to persuade his family to emigrate to Pakistan, Barré Bhai had almost given up when Chabban Mian decided to inscribe 'Pakistan Zindabad' on the school wall. Roopchandji's children were up in arms and wrote 'Akhand Hindustan'. This led to a fight, to intimidation and death threats. As the matter got out of hand, the police were called in, and the few Muslim children on the spot were put into a lorry and sent home.

Now behold! When these children reached home their mothers, who were always too ready to curse them invoking cholera and plague on their head, ran out of their houses solicitously and held them to their bosom. In normal circumstances, if Chabba had come home after a fight with Roopchandji's children, Dulhan Bhabi would have served him a few resounding slaps and sent him to Roopchandji for administering a castor oil and quinine mixture. Roopchandji was not only our family doctor but was Abba's longstanding friend as well. His sons were my brothers' friends and his daughters-in-law were friends of my sisters-in-law. This close friendship extended to the children. The two families were so close to each other over three generations that no one had the slightest suspicion that the country's partition would rupture their relationship.

There were, of course, members of the Muslim League, the Congress and the Hindu Mahasabha in both families, who held fierce debates on religious and political matters. But it was more like a football or a cricket match. If Abba was a Congresswala, Doctor Saheb and Barré Bhai were supporters of the League. Gyan Chand was a Mahasabhai while Manjhle Bhai was a communist and Gulab Chand a socialist. Women and children supported the party patronized by their husband or father. When an argument ensued, it was usually the Congress supporters who tipped the scales. Abuses were hurled at the socialists and the communists, but they would both end up siding with the Congress. That would leave the League and the Mahasabha to act in unison. They were each other's enemy but invariably got together to attack the Congress.

However, over the last couple of years, there was a groundswell of support for both the League and the Mahasabha. The Congress was in disarray. The entire new crop of the family, with the exception of one or two impartial Congressmen, spruced themselves up like the National Guards under the command of Barré Bhai. On the other side, a small group of Sevak Sangh was raised under Gyan Chand's leadership. But this did not strain mutual affection and friendship.

'My Lallu will marry none but Munni,' the Mahasabhai Gyan

Chand would tell Munni's father, the Leaguer. 'We'll bring gold anklets for her.'

'Yaar, I hope they won't simply be gold-plated.' Barré Bhai would have a dig at Gyan Chand's trade.

If the National Guards wrote 'Pakistan Zindabad' on the walls, the party of Sevak Sangh would wipe it out and write 'Akhand Hindustan'. This was the time when the formation of Pakistan was still a matter of jokes and jibes.

Abba and Roopchandji would listen to all this and smile. They would make plans for a United Asia.

Untouched by politics, Amma and Chachi would talk of spices like coriander and turmeric and their daughters' dowries. The daughters-in-law were busy aping each other's fashions. Besides salt, pepper, etc., medicines also came from Doctor Saheb's place. If one sneezed, one ran there. If anyone fell sick, Amma would make rotis thick with pulses, and dahi vadas. An invitation would be sent to Doctor Saheb, who would arrive holding the hands of his grandsons.

His wife would say, 'Don't eat there, do you hear?'

'And how would I collect my fees, then? Listen, send Lala and Chunni as well.'

'Hai Ram, you've no shame,' Chachi would mutter.

It was great fun when Amma fell sick. 'No, I'll not allow this joker to treat me,' she would say. But who would go to call in a doctor from the city when there was one at home. Doctor Saheb would come as soon as he heard of Amma's illness.

He'd tease, 'If you gobble up all pulao-zarda, how can you avoid falling ill?' Amma would retort from behind the purdah, 'Everyone's not like you.'

'Well, why make excuses? If you want to see me, just send word, and I'll be here. You need not fake illness!' he'd say with a mischievous smile. Amma would jerk her hand back in mock anger and mutter curses. Abba would smile indulgently.

If Doctor Saheb came to see a patient, everyone else would line up for a check-up. If one had stomach problems, another a pimple; others had either an inflammation of the ear or a swollen nose.

'What a nuisance, Deputy Saheb! I'll give poison to one or two. Do you take me for a vet that you pounce on me like a pack of animals?' Doctor Saheb would go on muttering while examining them.

Whenever he came to know that a new baby was expected, he would explode: 'Hunh! The doctor's for free. Procreate as many times as you want, and make my life miserable!'

But as soon as the labour pain started, he would pace restlessly between our veranda and his. He caused panic with his screams and shouts, rendering it difficult for the neighbours to come. The would-be father would be slapped vigorously and castigated for his foolhardiness.

But as soon as the newborn's cry reached his ears, he would leap from the veranda to the door and then into the room, followed by Abba in a state of nervousness. The women would resent and curse them and then go behind the purdah. He would examine the pulse of the mother and pat her back. 'Good show, my lioness.' Then he would cut the umbilical cord and bathe the baby. Abba would nervously act as a clumsy nurse to him. Then Amma would start screaming, 'God's curse! These men have no business to be here.' Under the circumstances, both would slink away like two chastised children.

When Abba was paralysed, Roopchandji had retired and his medical practice was restricted to his own house and ours. Abba was being treated by some other doctors, but Roopchandji would keep constant vigil along with Amma and the nurses . . . After Abba's passing away, he felt a new sense of responsibility besides the affection he had towards the members of our family. He would go to the children's school to get the fees waived, prevent Gyan Chand from charging on the girls' dowry. In the house, nothing was done without consulting him. So much so that when it was suggested that two rooms be added to the western wing of the house, the plan was scrapped at Doctor Saheb's instance.

'Why don't you build two rooms upstairs, instead,' he suggested, and it was acted upon. Fajjan was not ready to opt for science in F.A.; Doctor Saheb thrashed him with his shoes, and the issue was resolved. When Farida fought with her husband and returned home, her husband sought Doctor Saheb's help. As Sheela entered his family as the wife of his younger son, the problem of having to hunt for a midwife was solved. She would run from the hospital as soon as word was sent. Forget about charging a fee, she'd present the baby with a cap and a kurta on the sixth day.

But today, when Chabba returned after the fight, he was fêted as a crusader, a mard-i-ghazi having won a battle. Everyone asked him about his daring acts. Only Amma was mute, as she had been from the fifteenth of August when the tricolour was hoisted on the roof of Doctor Saheb's house and the Muslim League flag on ours. Between these two flags there was a chasm miles wide. Amma would look at its bottomless depth with her melancholy eyes and shudder. Then, like a deluge, refugees began to arrive. As the relatives of the eldest daughter-in-law arrived from Bhawalpur having lost all their possessions and somehow escaping with their lives, the chasm widened. And then, when the in-laws of Nirmala arrived from Bhawalpur in a half-dead state, the chasm became filled with venom-spewing snakes.

When Choti Bhabi sent word that her son had a stomach ailment, Sheela Bhabi drove the servant away. No one made any comment. Neither did anyone speak about one's ailment in the house. Barri Bhabi forgot her fits of hysteria and began to pack up her belongings in haste.

'Don't touch my trunk.' Amma at last broke her silence. Everyone was stunned.

'Aren't you coming with us?' Barré Bhai asked sharply.

'No. Do you think I'll go to die among those Sindhis? God's curse on them! They wander about in flowing burkhas and pyjamas.'

'Why doesn't she go to the younger son in Dhaka?'

'Aye, why should she go to Dhaka? Those headhunting Bengalis knead rice in their hands and then slurp it down,' taunted Mumani Bi, Sanjhle Bhai's mother-in-law.

'Then go and stay with Farida at Rawalpindi,' Khala suggested.

'Tauba! May Allah save us from the Punjabis. They speak

like the denizens of hell.' My taciturn Amma was rather voluble that day.

'Aye, Bua, you're acting like a woman who would rather sit in the wilderness than seek shelter in anyone's house. Aye, Bi, stop throwing tantrums as though the emperor has invited you, sending his elephants and black horses to pick you up . . .' In spite of the grim atmosphere, peals of laughter rang out. Amma's face fell further.

'Stop behaving like children,' Sardar Ali, the leader of the National Guards reprimanded.

'You're talking nonsense. Do you want us to stay back and get killed?'

'You all go. As for me, where shall I go at this age?'

'At the end, do you want your ruin at the hands of these kafirs?'

Khala Bi kept count of her luggage. Along with gold and silver, she also stuffed bone powder, dry fenugreek and Multani mitti in bundles. She was taking them along with such care as though the sterling reserves in Pakistani banks would fall without them. Getting angry, Barré Bhai threw away these bundles three times, but she screamed so loudly it was as if Pakistan would become poor without this 'wealth'. Eventually one had to take out the cotton from the mattresses soaked with children's urine and pack them in bundles. Utensils were stuffed into gunny bags, beds dismantled and their legs tied together with rope. Right before our eyes the well-equipped house slowly turned into misshapen bundles and boxes.

Now the luggage seemed to have grown legs and danced through the house.

Amma's trunk, however, rested immobile.

'If you have decided to die here, no one can stop you,' Bhai Saheb said finally. And my simple, innocent-looking Amma stared at the sky with her wandering eyes as though asking herself, 'Who could kill me? When?'

'Amma has become senile. She's not all there,' Manjhle Bhai whispered.

'What does she know how the kafirs have tortured innocents! At least life and property will be safe if we have a land of our own.'

If my taciturn Amma had had a sharp tongue, she would have retorted: 'What's this strange bird called "our land"? Tell me where's that land? This is the place where one was born, one grew up in body and mind. If this cannot be one's own land, then how can the place where one simply goes and settles down for a couple of days be one's own? And who knows whether one won't be driven out from there as well and be told "Go and inhabit a new land"? I am like a lamp in its last gasp. A mild gust of wind and all this fuss about choosing a land will be over. After all, this game of one's land vanishing, and inhabiting a new land, is not very interesting. There was a time when the Mughals left their country to inhabit a new country. And today you want to establish a new one. As though the land is no better than a pair of shoes – if it gets a little tight, throw it away and get a new one.' But she was silent, and her face looked more weary than before, as though she, after her quest for a land over centuries, was exhausted. And she seemed to have lost herself in that quest.

Time passed on, but Amma stayed steadfast in her position like a banyan tree that stands upright through storms and blizzards. But when the caravan consisting of her sons and daughters, sons-in-law, daughters-in-law and grandchildren passed through the big gate and got on to the lorries under police supervision, her heart fluttered. Her restless eyes gazed helplessly towards the other side of the chasm. The house on the other side seemed as far removed as a fleeting cloud in the distant sky. The veranda of Roopchandji's house was desolate. Once or twice when the children came out, they were dragged in quickly. But Amma's tearful eyes caught glimpses of those eyes behind the door and chiks, eyes that were brimming over with tears.

When the lorries left kicking up a lot of dust, some dead soul on the left side seemed to take a breather. The door opened and Roopchandji emerged with heavy steps and gazed at the vacant house like a thief. For some time he tried to trace the images of those who had left in the dust haze. Failing, his gaze wandered for a while in the desolation and got fixed to the ground.

Having surrendered all the assets of her life to the mercy of God, Amma stood in the desolate courtyard. Her heart sank, and she got scared like a small child, as though ghosts would pounce on her from all sides. She felt giddy and supported herself against a pillar. As she turned to the room in front, her heart came to her mouth. It was here that the ghunghat was lifted from the moon-like face of the young and timorous bride who had surrendered her life to her husband. In the room on the other side, her eldest daughter had been born, whose memory pierced through her heart like lightning. There, in the corner, her umbilical cord was buried . . . In fact, all her children had their umbilical cords buried there. Ten images of flesh and blood – ten human beings were born in that hallowed room from the sacred womb which they left behind that day. They had left her hung in thorns like an old snake-slough and made good their escape. In search of peace and contentment, looking for the place where wheat was sold for four seers a rupee. The voices of her children filled the room. She ran towards it with outstretched arms, but her lap was empty. The lap that newly wedded brides touched for luck, so that their wombs would not remain barren. The room lay desolate, and she returned, terror-stricken.

However, she could not stop the flight of her imagination. Tottering, she ran to another room, the one where her life-partner had breathed his last after fifty years of married life. Wrapped in the shroud, his body had been laid near the door. The whole family had stood around it. He was fortunate to have passed away, lamented by his dear ones. But he left me behind, I who lie here today like an enshrouded corpse, uncared for. Her legs gave way, and she slumped at the spot where the head of her dead husband had rested and where she had been lighting lamps with trembling hands for the last ten years. But there was no oil in the lamp that day, and the wick had burnt out.

Roopchandji was pacing up and down his veranda. He was

cursing everyone – his wife, children, the government and the silent street that stretched before him – also the bricks and stones, the knives and daggers. Indeed, the whole universe seemed to be afraid and cringe before his torrent of curses. His special target was the vacant house that stood across the road and seemed to taunt him as though he had broken it, brick by brick, with his own hands. He was wrenching out the things that were deeply entrenched in his very existence, like roots, but felt as though his flesh would come off his body with them. Eventually, he gave up the effort with a groan, and his curses stopped abruptly. He stopped pacing, got into the car and sped away.

As night descended and the street corner became desolate, Roopchandji's wife entered our house stealthily through the back door holding two trays of food. The two old women sat across from each other silently. They were mute, but the eyes communicated everything. The food trays remained untouched. When two women indulge in backbiting, their tongues run like scissors; but when they are overwhelmed with emotion, their lips get sealed.

Alone in the house, Amma was oppressed by painful thoughts throughout the night. 'I hope they won't be done away with on the way. Nowadays, whole trainloads of people are being slaughtered' – so ran her thoughts. She had nursed the crop with her heart's blood through fifty years, and that day it had been exiled from its own land to find a new land. 'Who knows whether the new soil will be conducive to these saplings or make them wilt. These poor saplings! Choti Bahu – may Allah protect her – her baby is due any moment. Who knows in which wilderness she will deliver it. They left everything – their homestead, job, business. Have the vultures left anything for them in the new land? Or will they have to return soon? When they return, will they get the opportunity to develop their roots again? Who knows whether this old skeleton of mine will be a witness to the return of spring?'

She kept on muttering to herself for hours, clutching the walls and parapets of the house. Then she slumped on the floor. There was no question of sleep amidst the nightmare in which she saw the mutilated corpse of her youthful daughter, her young daughter-in-law being paraded naked and the grandchildren being cut to pieces. Perhaps she had dozed off for a moment or two when she heard a great commotion at the door. One may not care for one's life, but even a lamp whose oil has run out shudders before its final gasp. 'Is natural death less terrifying that it should come in the form of men who have turned into demons? People say that they catch even old women by their locks and drag them along the street so violently that their skins come off revealing the bones. And then, the horrors of the world are let loose in such a manner that the horrors of hell pale into insignificance!'

The pounding on the door became more violent. Malik-ul-Maut, the angel of death, seemed to be in a hurry. The lights came on. A voice came from afar, as though from the bottom of a well. Perhaps the eldest son was calling out. No, it seemed like the voice of the younger ones from some hidden corner of the other world.

So everyone has reached the new land? So fast? She could clearly see the younger son and the youngest standing along with their wives and children. Then, all of a sudden, the whole house came back to life. The souls came alive and stood around the grieving mother. The hands of the old and the young touched her tenderly. Soft smiles spread on her dry lips. Apprehensions swirled and vanished in the overwhelming tumult of happiness.

As she opened her eyes, she felt the touch of familiar fingers on her pulse. 'Sorry, Bhabi, if you want to see me, just send word, and I'll be here. You need not fake illness!' Roopchandji said from behind the curtain. 'Bhabi, today I must be paid my fees. Look, I have brought back your good-for-nothing children from Loni junction. Scoundrels! They were running away. They were not ready to trust even the police superintendent.'

Again a smile blossomed forth on the old lips. She sat up. There was silence for a while. Then two pearls of warm tears trickled down and fell on Roopchandji's wrinkled hands.

Hell-bound

As long as college dominated my life, reading and writing took up all my time, and I couldn't give any attention to literature; and as soon as I left college I got it into my head that anything written even two years earlier was rotten stuff, false and uninteresting. The 'new literature' was the literature of today or yesterday. And this 'new literature' made such an impact on me that God knows how many books there were that I dismissed when I'd done no more than look at their titles and written them off as worthless. And the books that seemed most worthless of all were those of Azim Beg Chughtai. 'A prophet is not without honour . . .' It was a case of that.

His books were scattered all over the house, but no one except my mother and a few of my old-fashioned sisters-in-law paid the least attention to them. I used to think, 'What's the point in reading them? They're not literature – nothing but clowning and buffoonery, rotten, old-fashioned love stories and the sort of stuff that it makes you cross to read.' In other words, I'd made up my mind about them without even reading them. I myself didn't really know why I'd not read my brother's stories. There may have been a bit of arrogance in my attitude, priding myself that I was a 'new' writer and he an old one.*

One day in a moment of idleness my eye lighted on his essay 'Ekka'. Asim and I began to read it. God knows what mood we were in, but we began to laugh, and we laughed so much that we could hardly go on reading. While we were reading it Azim came in. He saw that we were reading his book and was very pleased.

* The first part of this piece is extracted from a brief autobiographical essay, included here because it forms a good introduction to the rest.

But we were annoyed at this and made a face. He knew what he was about. 'Give it to me,' he said, 'I'll read to you.' He read two or three of his pieces and had us literally rolling about. All our pretence was gone. It was not only what he was reading, but the fact that it was he who was reading it. It was as though there was laughter everywhere, like sparks flying. When he'd made us look properly foolish, he said, 'You lot say that there's nothing in my writings,' and started teasing us. We were crestfallen, but we gradually recovered and got really cross with him. God knows what absurd things we said to him. We were very put out, and began to dislike his books even more than before.

While he was alive, I never praised his writings, though when he read what I wrote, he was more pleased with them than words can say, and very generous in his praise. But I'd got into the habit of taking offence at everything he said. I thought he was making fun of me – and, by God, when he *did* make fun of people, his sarcasm and bitter smile and cutting remarks would make them feel like getting down on the floor and kicking and crying like a child. I was always afraid that he'd make fun of me, and I'd swear at him. Sometimes he'd say, 'I'm afraid that you might start writing better than I do.' And that too, when I'd only written a few things. That's why I got angry and thought he was making fun of me.

After he died, for some reason I began to feel an attachment to everything that was his. Every word he had written began to have an impact on me, and now, for the first time in my life, I got down to reading his books. Got down to! That's absurd. I didn't need to 'get down to' it. I positively wanted to. 'Good God!' I would think. 'That's how he wrote!'

When I began to read his books, every word in them evoked the picture of how he had looked in his last years. Within moments I would see his eyes, struggling to smile through all the pain that racked him all the time. I saw his dense hair falling over his dark, wasted, melancholy face, over which it seemed as if dark rain clouds had gathered; his bluish-yellow high forehead; his shrunken, purple lips; his uneven prematurely broken teeth; his dried-up, emaciated hands, with their long delicate fingers like a girl's, bloated from the medicine he was taking. And then the swelling attacked his hands. I saw his thin matchstick legs, ending in ugly, swollen feet, which we felt afraid to look at and so always went to the head of his bed. I saw his cage-like chest, working like a bellows, and the clothes and vests on his body worn layer upon layer. And that breast held an ever-lively, ever-high-spirited heart. God, how that man could laugh! Like a demon or a jinn, ready to grapple with every power in the universe. Never defeated, always smiling. A wrathful and tyrannical God visited upon him every torture that his constant coughing and asthma could bring him, and he responded to all of them with a laugh. No pain that this world or the next could produce was spared him, but nothing could reduce him to tears. One would have thought it beyond the power of any human being to laugh in all this pain and distress, let alone to make others laugh too. My uncle used to say, 'He's a living corpse.' Well, by God, if corpses were so lively, so restless, so active, one could wish that everyone on earth was a corpse.

When I looked at him not with a sister's eyes but simply with the detached eyes of a fellow human being, it made me reel. What a stubborn heart he had! How full of life he was! There was almost no flesh on his face, but soon after it had begun to swell he began to fill out. A death-like radiance came to his face, and a sort of magical greenness like that of an embalmed mummy. But his eyes were the eyes of a mischievous boy, dancing in response to every little thing, or sometimes the merry eyes of a youngster. And these same eyes, when an attack of severe pain was upon him, would scream out and the clear bluish surface of his skin would turn a muddy yellow, and his helpless hands would tremble, and it seemed as though his breast would burst. And when the attack was over, again the same radiance, the same dancing brightness.

Only a few days ago I read his 'Khanam' for the first time. He is not its hero. Its hero is someone much stronger and healthier than he was, the embodiment of the hero he could imagine that he might have been, like the active vigorous youngster in whom a lame man would like to see himself; not him, but his hamzad, whom he watched getting up to all the tricks that he, lying there a helpless prey to illness, could not get up to. Others may think that 'Khanam' is nothing much. But all its characters except his hero are accurately portrayed, living characters – all exactly like the people who made up, and still do make up, a family. At any rate that's what *my* family was like, and every word is true to life. Azim watched all of us in action in the home and when he wrote he portrayed accurately all that he saw . . . Everyone is there – and always will be. It is as though, when he wrote, all of us acted parts for him, all of us were moving puppets in his hands, and he produced a faithful picture of it all.

He loved talking to people and would make friends with absolutely anyone. There was an old mirasan. He would sit for hours and talk nonsense with her. People were astonished. They'd think, 'Good God! What have *those* two got to talk about?' But everything in his story 'Khurpa Bahadur' is what this old mirasan told him. He would even stop the sweeper or the water carrier or anyone passing in the street to talk to him or her. Once he had to go to hospital for some days, and at nights, when everything was quiet, he'd secretly gather all the patients together to chat with them. They would tell each other innumerable stories, and these were the bases for the things he wrote. It used to give him great pleasure to encounter liars and cheats. He'd say, 'Tricking people and deceiving them is no joke. You need intelligence for things like that.' Everything he wrote, he took from life, including the lies in which life abounds. He wrote many improbable things, because his poetic imagination could accept all of them.

He used to love to watch singing and dancing – but the kind of dancing he liked was the kind that wandering holy men would perform. He'd often give them money and then watch them dance to the beat of the drum, watching so intently that you'd envy him his enjoyment. God knows what he could see in their naked, hungry dancing.

He had for ages been opposed to purdah, and in the end he used to say, 'All that is out of date. They can't preserve purdah now, no matter how they try. We've finished with that now. Now there are fresh things to worry about.'

He did not take much interest in politics. He used to say, 'I can't be a leader, so what's the point? People say, "Show us some results," but this wretched cough and asthma plague me all the time.' Many years ago he wrote some articles on politics and economics that were published in *Riyasat*. God knows what became of them.

His writings cut no ice with us present-day writers. The world has changed, and people's ideas have changed. We're outspoken and abusive. When we feel pain, we cry. Capitalism, socialism, unemployment – these things have seared us with their flames. We grind our teeth as we write and spit out the poison we brew from our secret griefs and crushed emotions. He too felt pain – he was poor, ill and destitute. He too was oppressed by capitalism, and yet with all that, he had the courage to make faces at life and to laugh at his distress. It was not only in his stories that he laughed; in every department of life he defeated distress with laughter.

One of the reasons that Azim is not popular with contemporary, that is, *completely* contemporary readers, is that he did not write as openly and directly as the new writers do. He could see women's beauty, but he hardly saw their bodies. In the old masnavis like *Zahr-e-Ishq*, the description of women's physical form is quite prominent. After a while, this kind of writing became old-fashioned. And now, this old fashion has revived, and the new literature is full of rising and falling breasts, shapely calves and soft thighs. He used to consider such 'naked' writing pornographic and fought shy of it, though his writing abounds in the portrayal of naked emotions, and he would write without hesitation of really filthy things. He would portray a woman's naked emotions, but the woman would always be fully clothed. He never spoke very freely with me, because he looked upon me as a child. And he never discussed sexual problems with anyone at all. The most he said, speaking to a friend, was 'The new writers are all very spirited, but they're hungry, and very much under the influence of sex. In everything they write you feel as though they're saying, "Mummy, I'm hungry."' He used to also say that in every age Indian literature has borne the clear imprint of sex. 'Our people are much affected by it. Our poetry, our painting and even our ancient styles of worship all express our sexual hunger. If they forget love and sex even for a moment, they lose their popularity.' And that is why his way of writing was soon abandoned and the old *Thousand and One Nights*-style of writing prevailed.

He was especially fond of Hijab Imtiyaz Ali's stories. (I must say, with apologies to the lady, that the secret of why he liked them has died with him.) He used to complain to me, saying, 'I wrote the kind of lies that made no sense to them,' that *my* lies were the cry of a hungry man, while *his* lies were the smiles of a hungry man. God knows what he meant by that.

We generally used to tell him his stories were 'all lies'. Whenever he started talking my father would say to him, 'Have you started your castles in the air again?' . . . Azim would tell him, 'My dear sir, it's lies that give colour to life. If you want to make what you say interesting, you must mix lies with truth.' And he would say, 'The descriptions of heaven and hell too are no more than castles in the air.' At this my uncle would say, 'Stop this living corpse saying such things. It's blasphemy.' And Azim would mock him and his in-laws and tell them that they were a superstitious lot.

I never saw him saying his prayers. He used to read the Quran lying down. He showed no respect for it and would fall asleep as he read. When he was rebuked for this, he put it in paper covers and would tell people he was reading a law book. He used to study the Traditions a lot and make it a point to memorize very strange ones so that he could argue with people over them. He would read them out and argue over them. People were at a loss and found it difficult to keep up. He used to memorize verses of the Quran too and never tire of referring to them; and if you cast doubt upon them, he would get out the Quran from his bedside and show them to you.

He was a great admirer of Yazid and talked a lot of nonsense about Imam Husain. He would argue for hours on this theme. He used to say, 'I dreamt that Hazrat Imam Husain was standing somewhere when Yazid the accursed came along, fell at his feet, and humbly joined hands in supplication to him. At this, Husain was deeply moved. He raised him up and embraced him. From that day I too began to revere Yazid. In Paradise they were reconciled. So why should we fight over them?'

He used to think that piri muridi was a hoax. But he would say, 'All hoaxes are attractive lies; and lies are in themselves attractive.' He used to say, 'If my health had permitted, I would have got people to worship at my father's grave. I would have arranged qawwalis for two years and got people to donate coverings for his tomb. It would have been a fine and enjoyable way to earn an income.'

He was addicted to religious controversy, but in the end he stopped arguing so much. He would say, 'You lot are strong and healthy, and I'm dying. And if by any chance it turns out that there *is* a heaven and a hell, what shall I do? Best keep quiet.' When people used to tell him he would go to hell he used to say, 'And what sort of Paradise has the good Lord given me here that threats of hell should deter me? I don't care. I'm used to hell. If the good Lord burns me in hell, He'll be wasting his sticks and coal because there's no suffering I haven't got used to.' Sometimes he said, 'If I go to hell, then at any rate these germs will be killed. If I go to heaven I'll infect all the maulvis with my TB.'

And that's why everybody call him a hell-bound rebel.

It seems as though he was *born* crying, and he was reared with all care and attention. People saw how weak he was and forgave him everything. He would hit his big stalwart brother, who would just bow his head and take it. Because he was so weak, my father would excuse him no matter what he did. Everyone tried all the time to please him, but when you're forever telling someone who is ill that he's ill, how can you please him? All our kindnesses to him only made him feel his weakness the more. He got more and more rebellious, more and more angry, but he was helpless. All of us began to adopt Gandhi's policy of non-violence, but what he wanted was to be counted with others as a member of the human race, to be scolded as others are scolded, to be numbered among the living. And he worked out that the way to achieve this was to be a troublemaker. Whenever he felt like it, he could get any two people to quarrel with each other. God had given him a good brain, an astonishing imagination and a sharp tongue, which he would ply with great enjoyment and to great effect. His brothers and sisters and our mother and father all began to loathe him. Our home became a fair old battlefield, and it was he who caused it all. What more could he want? All his self-regarding emotions were satisfied, and the weak, helpless, ever-ailing villain of the piece became a hero. He made all his weaknesses his weapons.

But he didn't really want people to abandon him. The more his family avoided him, the tighter he clung to them. In the end, may God forgive us, we all came to loathe the very sight of him and, for all his pleadings, to regard him as our enemy. His wife didn't look upon him as a husband, nor his children as a father. His sisters told him, 'You're no brother to me.' And his brothers would turn away in disgust at the sound of his voice. My mother would say, 'I gave birth to a snake, not a child.'

Before he died, he was in a pitiable state. Not as his sister but simply as a human being, I tell you that I wished he would die and get it over. But even then he never stopped hurting people. He was like the torments of hell. The hero of a thousand stories had become a villain, and his ambition was satisfied. Yet even then he wanted people to love him, wanted his wife to worship him, and his children to look affectionately upon him, and his sisters to feel ready to do everything for him and his mother to take him to her bosom.

And his mother *did* that, returning to the path from which she'd strayed. She was his mother, after all. But the others still hated him, until the time came when his lungs packed up, the swelling got worse, his eyesight failed, and he would grope his way like a blind man and still not find it. He had made himself a hero, but in the end he was defeated. He never got what he had wanted. What he got instead was hatred, revulsion and contempt . . . Such was the man, who with ulcers in his lungs, and legs that had been stiff for ages, and arm pierced with innumerable injections, and boils on his hips the size of apples, that he laughed as he lay there dying. Ants had begun to crawl over his body, and he looked at one of them and said, 'How impatient my lady ant is! She's here to claim her portion before time.' This was two days before he died. What a heart he must have had to joke like this when he was dying!

At four o'clock one morning, he who had been born forty-two years earlier as a weak little baby had played out his role in the drama of life. At six in the morning on 20th August, Shamim came and told me to get up, because Azim was dying.

'He'll never die,' I said crossly. 'Don't wake me up for nothing.' And I tried to sleep again in the cool of the morning.

Shamim got worried and shook me. 'Get up, you wretch. He's asking for you.'

'Tell him I'll see him on Judgement Day,' I said. 'I tell you, Shamim, he *can't* be dying.'

But when I went down, he could no longer speak. All the furniture, all the junk, all the books had been cleared from the room. Medicine bottles were rolling uselessly about. Two of the little children were staring anxiously at the door. My sister-in-law was making them drink their tea. There were no tears in her eyes.

I leant over him. 'Murine Bhai,' I said. For a moment, his eyes focused, and he compressed his lips. Then he lapsed into a coma once again. We all sat waiting outside his room, and for four hours watched the battle that his dried-up, lifeless hands were waging. It looked as though there was a chance of Azrail, the Angel of Death, losing.

'He's dead.' I don't know who it was who told us.

I thought to myself, 'He isn't. He can never die.'

And today I look at his books and say, 'Impossible! He can never die. He's still fighting. What difference does death make?'

For me it was his death that brought him to life, and God knows how many more there will be – how many there will continue to be – for whom he will be born after his death.

His message was, 'Fight pain, fight hatred, and go on fighting even after you're dead.' He'll never die. No one can kill his rebellious spirit. He was not a virtuous man. If his health had been good he would not have been an abstemious man either. He was a liar. His life was a lie – the biggest lie of all. His tears were a lie, and his laughter was a lie. People say, 'He caused nothing but pain to his mother and father, and to his wife, and to his children, and to the whole of creation. He was a malevolent spirit sent into the world to plague it, and now the only proper place for him is hell.'

Wherever he is, whether it's in heaven or in hell, I want to see him. I'm certain that he's laughing even now. Worms will be eating his body, and his bones will be crumbling to dust, and his neck will be bowed under the burden of the fatwas of the mullahs, and the saw will be tearing at his body. But he'll still be laughing. His mischievous eyes will still be dancing, his blue, dead lips will be moving in bitterness, but no one will be able to reduce him to tears. Wherever he is, I want to see him, to see if his sharp tongue is at work there too, see whether he's making love to the houris in heaven or laughing as he angers the angels in hell, whether he's quarrelling with the maulvis or whether in the leaping flames of hell his cough resounds and he's breathing with difficulty, and the angels are giving him his injections. What difference does it make to go from one hell into another? Where else would the 'hell-bound' be?

Translated by Ralph Russell

My Friend, My Enemy!

I was filled with trepidation as we climbed the wooden stairs of Adelfi Chambers. The kind of trepidation that one feels while entering the examination hall. I usually had apprehensions while meeting strangers. But here the 'stranger' was Manto, whom I was going to meet for the first time. My apprehensions soon turned into worry, and I said to Shahid, 'Let's go back. It seems Manto is not home.' But Shahid would have none of it.

'He is usually at home in the evening. This is his boozing time.' This was too much to handle. A sober Manto was trouble enough, but a drunk Manto was more than one could deal with. I gathered the courage to face him – well, he couldn't devour me! It might be that he had a barbed tongue that would leave its sting. I was not a bubble that would burst if he blew on it. We climbed the dusty stairs and reached the second floor. The door of the flat was ajar. There was a sofa set lying in the space that was the drawing room. A white bed lay on the other side. There was a thin, spiderlike man sitting on his haunches before a table near the window.

'Come on in, please.' Manto got up cheerfully. Manto used to sit curled up in his chair, which gave him the look of a midget. But when he stood up and straightened himself, he looked fairly tall. He was wearing a khaddar kurta-pyjama and a Jawahar waistcoat.

'You know, I had imagined you to be a dark, shrivelled-up creature.'

'And I had thought that you would be a hefty Punjabi, singing heer in a full-throated voice.' I was determined to give him tit for tat so that he didn't get an upper hand right from the start.

And in a few moments we began to argue vociferously. It was as though we had suffered a great loss from not having met each other for a long time and were now impatient to make good the loss. Our jaws moved rapidly through a host of subjects like machines. It soon became apparent that Manto, like me, was accustomed to cut others in mid-sentence. He would start his retort without listening to his interlocutor in full. The discussion soon turned into a debate, and the debate gave way to nit-picking. And on the strength of a few hours' acquaintance we called each other silly, ignorant, hair-splitter and so on, though all in very elegant language.

During the stormy discussions I sidled up to him and looked at him closely – big eyes with dark pupils leaping behind large eyeglasses that reminded me of a peacock feather. What could be the similarity between peacock feathers and human eyes? This always eluded me. But whenever I saw his eyes I was reminded of peacock feathers. Perhaps the combination of pride, irreverence and freshness in him reminded me of peacocks. Seeing those eyes, my heart missed a beat. I had already seen them before, from very close quarters . . . The same delicate hands and legs, a luxuriant crop of hair on the head, two shrivelled up, yellowish cheeks and some uneven teeth. While drinking, Manto choked, and he began to cough. My senses became alert. This cough was familiar. I had heard it right from childhood. I began to feel uneasy and said in reference to something, 'This is absolutely wrong!' And we began to fight.

'You're indulging in hair-splitting.'

'This is silly!'

'This is fraud, Sister Ismat.'

'Why are you calling me "sister"?' I was peeved.

'Just like that. Normally, I don't call women "sisters". My own sister is not an exception.'

'So you're calling me "sister" just to tease me?'

'Not at all. Why do you think so?'

'Because my own brothers always teased me and bashed me up. Or they saw to it that I was beaten.'

Manto burst out laughing. 'Then I'll certainly call you "sister", and nothing else.'

'In that case, please keep in mind that my brothers did not have very pleasant experiences of me. You're afflicted with a cough. Why don't you get it treated?'

'Treated? Doctors are donkeys. Three years ago they had predicted that I would die of tuberculosis within a year. You can see that I didn't oblige them. Now I consider all doctors stupid. The magicians and mesmerists are better than they!'

'I've heard the same statement from a gentleman before you.'

'Who's the gentleman?'

'My brother, Azim Beg. He's resting in his grave now.'

This led to a discussion on Azim Beg's art.

We had come to meet Manto just for a few minutes. But it was now eleven, and our discussion was not yet over. Shahid, who was sitting a little away and watching our verbal duel, was dying of hunger. It would be one o'clock by the time we reached Malad. So we decided to have dinner right there. Manto asked me to take out plates and spoons from the cupboard and went out to bring roti from the hotel.

The heated discussion even went on during the meal. Manto singled out 'Lihaaf', the story that had become a source of torment for me, and dissected it. I wanted to change the subject, but he stuck to it stubbornly and pulled apart each one of its strands. I was not prepared to accept that 'Lihaaf' was my masterpiece. Manto insisted on it. In a little while, we went far beyond 'Lihaaf' and began to discuss things quite openly. I was surprised at the way he could so innocently say the most vulgar or obscene things without the slightest self-consciousness. One did not feel ill at ease. Rather, he did not let one feel so. He made one laugh. One didn't feel angry or outraged.

Manto mentioned his wife quite a few times during the evening: 'Safiya is a nice girl.' 'Safiya cooks good curry.'

'You think of her a lot. Why don't you ask her to come?' I said.

'Arré . . . do you think I can't sleep without her?' He assumed his usual tone.

'One can sleep even on the gallows.' I changed the topic and we laughed.

'Do you love Safiya deeply?' I asked him conspiratorially.

'Love!' he screamed out as though I had called him names. 'I don't love her at all. I don't believe in love.' He frowned, his large eyeballs rolled around.

'Do you mean that you've never fallen in love with anyone?' I asked in fake surprise.

'No.'

'And you never had pustules on your neck or measles, but you certainly had whooping cough, I think.'

He burst out laughing.

'What do you mean by love? Love is something profound and all-embracing. We love our mothers, brothers and sisters . . . Wives, too. We also love our sandals and shoes. I've a friend who loves his bitch. Of course, I loved my son.' At the thought of his son, he leapt up in his chair. 'He used to toddle nimbly on his tiny feet. Full of mischief. When he crawled on the floor, he would pick up mud and put it in his mouth. He was deeply attached to me.' Like any other father, Manto began to convince us of his son's uniqueness.

'Believe me – he was just six or seven days old when I began to lay him down beside me to sleep. I would give him an oil massage before bathing him. He was barely three months old when his tinkling laughter reverberated in the house. Safiya didn't have to do a thing for him except feed him milk. At night, she would sleep soundly when I fed him quietly. Before feeding the child, it is necessary that he should be cleaned with eau de cologne or spirit; otherwise he may have pimples all over,' he said in a serious vein and I stared at him in surprise. What kind of a man was he who specialized in childcare!

'But he died,' he said with mock cheerfulness. 'Good that he has died. He had reduced me to an ayah. Had he been alive, I would have spent my time washing his dirty nappies. I would have been useless for the world, of no worth at all! Really, Sister Ismat, I loved him deeply.'

Before we left, he mentioned that Safiya was to join him shortly and that I would enjoy meeting her.

This prediction turned out to be true. I was delighted to meet Safiya. In a few minutes we grew so intimate that we began to discuss even forbidden things – things which only women discuss, not meant for men's ears.

When Manto saw that putting our heads together, we were talking in a hushed tone, he lost his temper and began to mock us. He had pressed his ears to the wooden partition and eavesdropped on our whispering. He chirruped like a mischievous boy, 'Tauba! Tauba! I couldn't have imagined that women can talk about such filthy things.'

Safiya's ears turned red with shame.

'And you, Sister Ismat, I certainly didn't expect you to indulge in small talk like the illiterate, stupid women of the mohalla – "When did you marry?", "How did you spend the wedding night?", "When and how was the baby born?" Shame on you!'

I immediately reined him in. 'Manto Saheb, this is the limit! I didn't think that you were so narrow-minded. You also think that these things are filthy? What's filthy about it? The birth of a baby is one of the most beautiful phenomena in the world. And these whispering sessions are our training school. Do you think that in college I was taught how to give birth to a baby? . . . I've learnt the most important secrets of life from the women of the mohalla.'

'Safiya is absolutely stupid! She doesn't understand art and literature. She has a very didactic outlook. She's angered by your writings. Don't you feel bored talking to her for hours about how much turmeric is to be put in korma, about dahi vadas made of urhad ki daal and so on?'

'Arré Manto Saheb! Who puts turmeric in korma?' Safiya asked, horrified.

If Manto and I made an appointment for five minutes, it would stretch to five hours. Debating with Manto was like sharpening one's cerebral tools. The cobwebs were cleared, and the brain was swept clean . . . But often the discussion would tend to get acrimonious. I knew how to accept defeat, but Manto would get maudlin, and his eyes would dilate like peacock wings. His nostrils would flare up, his face would wear a scowl and, getting provoked, he would call Shahid to his support. And then the battle would shift from the realms of literature and philosophy to the domestic realm. Manto would leave our house in a huff. Shahid would chide me. 'Why are you so rude to my friends? Manto left in such anger today that he won't come here again. And I do not have enough courage to go to his place. He's brutally outspoken. If he says something hurtful, our friendship will be spoilt.'

And I also felt that I had really been harsh on him. If he got himself into a rage, my friendship with Safiya which was now more intense than my friendship with Manto, would be at peril . . .

But often it so happened that we quarrelled with each other in the morning, and if we met the same evening, Manto would greet me with such enthusiasm and talk so cordially it was as though we had not quarrelled at all! For a little while our talk would be 'refined' and 'genteel', without any disagreement. But soon we'd get tired of this pretence. And then firecrackers would begin to spark from both sides. Sometimes people would provoke us, on purpose, to have some fun. We'd fight, but remain friends. We engaged ourselves in debates because we loved it, not to entertain others. Manto also felt that however much we fought between ourselves, at public gatherings we should present a united front. And our team would be so strong that no one would be able to beat it. But usually I'd forget about my loyalty to our team, and the team would itself turn into a hornet's nest.

I could never make out whether Manto drank to lose his senses or lost his senses after drinking. I never saw him unsteady on his feet, neither did his tongue lose its sharpness. I never saw any difference. I knew only this, that when he drank too much, he would try hard to convince me that he was not drunk, and get on my nerves.

'Truly, Sister Ismat, I'm not drunk at all. And I can give up drinking right today. I can give up drinking any moment – you can bet on it.'

'I won't put a wager because you're sure to lose . . . And you're drunk.'

How he would try to convince me that he was not drunk, that he could give up drinking any moment only if someone put a wager on it!

Manto loved self-praise. But if I was part of the company, he would also include me with him and would not be ready to concede that any other writer could be as great as us. He would especially turn against Krishan Chander and Devender Satyarti. If anyone praised them, he would flare up. If I told him that he was no critic and so his judgement could not be accepted as valid, he would begin to rail against critics.

'They write nonsense,' he would scream. 'Do exactly the opposite of what they say. These fellows object to my stories but read them secretly. Instead of learning anything from them they seek sensual pleasure and then develop a guilty conscience. They write gibberish in order to clear their guilty conscience.' He would continue to fume. To pacify him I'd say, 'If you know that they're writing gibberish, why respond to them? If you don't like their criticism, so be it. But why decry common people's judgement?' But he would not be pacified.

Away from self-praise, Manto would talk proudly about his friends with me. He had a strange attachment with Rafiq Ghaznavi that I failed to understand. Whenever he referred to him he'd say, 'He's a perfect lout, a loafer. He has got married to four sisters one after the other. There's not a single courtesan in Lahore whom he has not exploited.' He'd refer to Rafiq in the same way as a child refers to his elder brother. He would describe to me his amorous exploits in great detail. One day he said that he'd like me to meet him. I said, 'What's the point of meeting him? You say that he's a loafer.' Pat came his reply: 'That's why I want you to meet him. Who told you that a loafer or a lout must be a bad human being? Rafiq is a thorough gentleman.'

I said, 'Manto Saheb! I just don't understand what you mean. Maybe I'm not as intelligent as you take me to be.'

'This is your pretension,' said Manto with displeasure. 'That's why I'm arranging this meeting. He's a very interesting person. No woman can help falling in love with him.'

'I'm also a woman,' I said anxiously, and he felt awkward.

'I regard you as my own sister.'

'But your sister, too, *can* be a woman!'

'*Can* be a woman! Well said.' Manto liked my reply, but he was insistent all the same. 'You'll have to meet him. Just you wait.'

'I've already seen him – at the station. You had prejudiced me so much against him that I just ran away from there so that I didn't have to fall in love with him!' After meeting Rafiq I realized how deep was Manto's study of his character. Despite his blemishes, Rafiq was endowed with all the qualities that make one a gentleman. He could be a loafer, but at the same time, he was an absolutely honest fellow. How was it and why? I didn't try to understand. It was to Manto's credit. He could track down pearls among the socially discarded, and in dirt. He liked scratching filth.

As I said, he would often hold forth on the exploits of his 'loafer' friends. One day, to provoke him, I said that all their braggadocio was a mere lie. As a matter of fact, they never did have truck with so many courtesans, nor did they ever violate the chastity of any woman. Manto tried to convince me with all his skill that these fellows did really commit those acts. In fact, their crookedness went much beyond what he had described.

'All lies!' I asserted.

'Why don't you believe me? Anybody who wants, can go to the marketplace.'

'These people just don't have courage enough to go to a courtesan's kotha. The most they can do is to listen to the music there and then return.'

'I myself have visited the kotha of prostitutes.'

'To listen to music,' I teased.

'No, madam. To get what I paid for. And I always got it.'

'I don't believe it,' I persisted.

'Why so?' He got up and sat haunched up on the carpet before me.

'That is what I think. You want to impress me.'

'I swear by God that I have gone there.'

'You don't believe in God. Don't drag Him in.'

'I swear by my dead child that not once but . . .'

'The poor child is dead. What harm can you do by swearing on his name?'

And Manto kept sitting there right before me. He was determined to convince me that he was a womanizer. He asked Safiya to bear witness to his claim. I disabused her in two minutes.

'He would've told you that he was going to a courtesan's and gone somewhere else! And even if he had gone there, he must have returned after exchanging greetings with her!'

Safiya became silent. 'How can I say whether he returned after exchanging greetings or . . .'

She looked strangely out of her depth.

I don't know whether Manto had had first-hand experience of what he used to write about or whether it was a reflection of his principles and beliefs. Even if he had visited a courtesan's kotha, what must have been revealed to him was the heart of a woman. She may have been the worm of a drain but still loved human values. Manto did not abide by the conventional concepts of good and evil but had his own set of values. Even in a shameless and stupid fellow like Khushia, one can see the flicker of humanity. A lecherous fellow like Gopinath can be seen to achieve godly status. Saintly and noble persons may have feet of clay, national volunteers may be criminals, and a person who copulates with a corpse can turn into a corpse himself.

Sometimes our tiffs would get particulary nasty, and it would seem that the thread of friendship would snap. One day he got so angry that his eyes became bloodshot and he ground his teeth.

'Had you not been a woman, I'd use such words as would make you wince!'

'Do fulfil your heart's desire. There's no need to make concessions,' I teased.

'Let it be. If you were a man . . .'

'Come off it. Let us see what other darts you have in your scabbard.'

'You'll be embarrassed.'

'By God, I won't.'

'Then you're not a woman.'

'Why? Why is it necessary for women to show embarrassment even when they don't feel it? Manto Saheb, it is regrettable that you also have separate values for men and women. I had thought you were above "ordinary" people and their prejudices,' I said with implied flattery.

'Absolutely not . . . I don't discriminate between men and women.'

'Then why don't you say it – that embarrassing thing.'

'No. My anger has subsided now.' He broke into a smile.

Another day, it was too hot in my office, so I thought I would go over to Manto's flat, rest for a while and then return to Malad. The door, as usual, was open. I went in to see that Safiya was lying down on the bed, sulking. Manto had a broom in his hand. He had shielded his nose with the corner of his kurta and was sweeping the floor under the table.

'What're you doing?' I asked as I peeped under the table.

'Playing cricket,' Manto replied, rolling his peacock eyeballs.

'I had thought that I'd rest in your flat for a while, and there you are, angry and sulking.' I threatened to leave immediately.

'Arré . . .' Safiya got up. 'Please sit down.'

'What is the tiff about?' I asked.

'Nothing. I had just said that cooking and household chores are not for men. At this he flared up, as he does with you. He took up the broom and began sweeping. When I tried to stop him, he said, "If you feel that way, why don't you divorce me?"' Safiya sobbed.

To get the broom out of Manto's hands, I faked a cough. 'At dawn, while sweeping the courtyard, the municipal sweeper made me inhale dust. Now you also fulfil your heart's desire. I'm going to die of heatstroke.'

Manto flung the broom and ran down to the hotel to bring ice. Safiya left for the kitchen. Manto wrapped the ice slab in a towel and broke it into pieces by hitting it against the wall. Then he put the ice pieces on a plate before me and sat down once again.

'And, how's life?' he asked, as usual. The smell from the kitchen made me almost throw up. 'Oho, I don't know what kind of a corpse Safiya is burning in the kitchen!' I exclaimed as I pinched my nostrils. Manto looked at me with a start from top to toe, rolled his large eyeballs and leapt to the kitchen. Safiya kept on screaming while he emptied the entire water tumbler into the pan. I stared at him stupidly as he returned from the kitchen with a bashful smile on his lips and sat on the edge of the chair.

As Safiya came from the kitchen muttering to herself, Manto chided her and then said to me bashfully, 'Are you pregnant? I understood immediately, because when Safiya was pregnant, the smell of seasoning would nauseate her.'

'Manto Saheb, for God's sake don't talk like midwives,' I said, incensed. He laughed heartily.

'Come on, what's so objectionable about it? I'm sure you'd love to eat something sour. I'll get some raw mangoes right away.' He raced down and brought some raw mangoes tucked in the hollow of his kurta, like children do. He then peeled them, sprinkled them with salt and pepper and handed the plate over to me. He shouted out for Safiya, who came hurriedly.

'Manto Saheb, why are you shouting like this?'

'Stupid! She's in the family way,' he said, as he put his arms around her waist.

'Oh, this is the limit! That's why people call you a pornographer.' Manto just laughed off my anger and began to advise me like old women: 'An olive-oil massage will prevent stretch marks.'

'If you eat apple jam first thing in the morning, you won't feel nauseated.'

'Don't chew ice during pregnancy. It'll make the shins swell, won't it, Safiya?'

'Manto Saheb, be quiet. What is all this?' Safiya was feeling embarrassed.

When Seema was born, Safiya was sitting by me, scared and shivering. Seeing the baby, Manto was reminded of his son, and for a long time he continued to tell me about his little antics. Safiya was deeply moved. Within a year, Manto's elder daughter Nighat was born. When I heard about it on my return from Pune, I immediately went to visit him, but they had moved house. When I reached his new flat, after a great search, I found him in the drawing room engaged in wringing nappies and hanging them on the clothes line to dry. The new flat was quite small and not properly ventilated. Manto left the old flat because its floors were dirty, the child could not crawl on it freely and would often pick up the dirt and put it in her mouth. In the new flat, Nighat could move about freely.

When we were living in Malad, one night, at about twelve-thirty, there was knocking on the door. It was Safiya, and she was panting for breath. When I asked what the matter was, she said, 'I asked him not to bother you in such a condition, but he didn't listen.' Manto entered the next moment with Nandaji and Khurshid Anwar in tow.

'Who is she to stop me?' said Manto, pointing to Safiya. The three had liquor bottles and glasses in their hands.

Shahid gave the green signal to the party. They were all hungry. The hotels had put down their shutters. The last train had left. They said they would cook themselves – they only needed atta and daal.

Safiya did not like the idea of the men making rotis, but they wouldn't listen to her and raided the kitchen. Manto began to knead dough, Nandaji got busy preparing the stove and Khurshid Anwar was asked to peel potatoes, though he insisted on eating them raw rather than taking all that trouble. The bottles were also brought into the kitchen. They settled down comfortably in the kitchen, continued to prepare half-baked rotis and gobble them up. Manto had kneaded the dough nicely and prepared the rotis rather well. In addition, he also prepared some pudina ki chatni. After the meal they would have lain down to sleep right there if we had not pushed them out onto the veranda.

That is the kind of life Manto liked. A comfortable income that ensured a carefree existence enlivened by plentiful drink and the laughter of friends . . .

We had so many stormy discussions on love but could not reach any conclusion. He'd say, 'What do you mean by love? I love my gold-embroidered shoes, Rafiq loves his fifth wife . . .'

'By love, I mean the passion that grows between a young man and a nubile girl.'

'Okay. Now, I understand . . .' Manto had a faraway look in his eyes as though he was groping for something.

'In Kashmir, there was a girl who grazed goats.'

'Then?' I was consumed with curiosity.

'Then – nothing.' He became alert in self-defence.

'You discuss even the most vulgar things with me. But today you're being bashful.'

Manto protested vehemently, saying he was not at all embarrassed. After a good deal of coaxing, he began. 'When she lifted her hand to shoo the herd, I got a glimpse of her fair elbow. I had been unwell. Everyday I would wrap a blanket around myself and lie down on the hillock. I would hold my breath and wait for the moment when she would lift her hand and I could have a glimpse of her elbow.'

'Elbow?' I asked in surprise.

'Yes . . . I never saw any other part of her body. She wore a baggy dress so one could have no idea about the contours of her body.'

'Then?'

'One day I was lying on the hillock when she came and sat a little away from me. She began to hide something in her pocket, and I felt curious. I threatened her that as long as she did not show me what it was, I wouldn't allow her to go. She was in tears, but I remained stubborn. After a great deal of coaxing, she opened her palm and held it towards me and hid her face coyly between her knees.'

'What was there on her palm?' I asked impatiently.

'A piece of sugar-candy. It was glinting like an ice cube on her roseate palm.'

'What did you do after that?'

'I stared at it.' He was lost in thought.

'Then?'

'Then she got up to go. But after a few steps she turned back, came over to me, threw the candy into my lap and went away. That piece of candy stayed in my pocket for a long time. Then I put it inside a drawer, and ants ate it up.'

'And the girl?'

'Which girl?'

'The sugar-candy girl.'

'I haven't seen her since.'

'How funny your love is!' I was greatly disappointed. 'I expected a tumultuous love story from you.'

'It's not at all funny,' Manto challenged me.

'It's an absolutely rotten, third-class, stale love story. You left with the sugar-candy in your pocket, as though you'd done a heroic deed!'

'What else should I have done? Should I have slept with her and given her the gift of an illegitimate child? And then showed it off as a trophy and a sign of manhood?' he said belligerently.

It was the same Manto – the 'pornographer' with an 'obscene' mind who wrote 'Bu' and 'Thanda Gosht'.

Riots had broken out in the country. After the partition, people left their home and hearth and went over to the other side. At that time, Manto was working regularly with Filmistan. He looked perfectly contented. He received appreciation in ample measure, which spurred him on. However, when his film *Aath Din* failed at the box office, he left Filmistan and joined Bombay Talkies to work with Ashok Kumar. I do not know what it was that Mukherjee told him that turned Manto totally against him. 'Mukherjee is a fraud,' Manto would say bitterly.

After joining Bombay Talkies, Manto also got me a job there

for a year in the Scenario Department. He looked very happy. 'Now we'll write stories together. It'll create a stir. The story by us and Ashok Kumar the hero. Just wait and see!'

Manto wanted it to be a story that Ashok also liked. He liked my story 'Ziddi'. Manto was not displeased. Ashok Kumar suggested that I work on Manto's story and Manto on mine. The result was that we grew suspicious of each other. In the meantime, Kamal Amrohi came along with his story, 'Mahal'. Ashok Kumar took a fancy to his story, and ours were put in cold storage. It was not simply a question of honour. The impression was that if your story was not selected for the film, you were of no worth at all. However, we were told not to worry because we would be drawing the salary according to the contract that had been already signed. But no film would be made on our stories. After that, Shahid and I concentrated all our efforts on making our film *Ziddi*, without Ashok Kumar, under a banner that was considered second in film hierarchy.

But Manto's story was not being used. He would remain cooped up in his room for the whole day and work on it. He would try out all kinds of combinations – sometimes he would put the beginning in the end, sometimes the end in the beginning; sometimes he would start in the middle, then go to the beginning and put the middle at the end. In spite of a thousand surgical operations, Ashok Kumar did not like the story in any form. But Manto would say, 'You don't know Ganguly (Ashok Kumar) as well as I do. He'll definitely choose my story for one of his films.'

'In your story, his role is that of a father, not a romantic one. He'll never do the film.' And we would begin to fight. It happened exactly as I said it would. *Ziddi* and *Mahal* were completed while Manto's story remained untouched. Manto didn't expect that, and he felt humiliated. He could put up with everything except lack of appreciation.

The condition of the country went from bad to worse. His wife and relatives asked him to go over to Pakistan. Manto asked me to migrate along with him. He made it out that a glorious future awaited us in Pakistan. We would be allotted the mansions left by the refugees who had migrated to India. We would prosper quickly.

And I realized then what a coward Manto was! He was willing to save his life at any cost. He wanted to get rich by grabbing the wealth earned by people for generations. And I began to hate him. Then one day, he left for Pakistan, without meeting me, without so much as even a word.

Then I received a letter from him. He was very happy there. Theirs was a large house, furnished with expensive goods. He invited me again to go over to Pakistan. After *Ziddi*, we had started making *Arzoo*. Bad days came and went. Two more letters arrived. He repeated his invitation and held out the hope that a cinema hall would be allotted to us. I was sure of his love before; now I was utterly convinced. But I tore up his letters in anger because he did not live up to my ideals. I continued to receive snippets of information about him:

He had lost his old house, but the new one was also quite good.

He had had a second daughter.

Another year passed. Another daughter was born.

A letter came from Manto: 'Call me over to India by any means.'

I learnt that a lawsuit had been filed against him and he had been thrown in jail. All sat idle and impassive. No one protested against it. In fact, the general feeling was, 'Good that he has been thrown in jail. Now he'll come to his senses.' There was no conference, no meeting; no resolution was passed.

Then came the news that his brain was giving trouble and that his relatives had put him into an asylum. But one day there came a letter from Manto, a perfectly sensible one. 'I'm absolutely fine. It'll be great if you can call me to Bombay using the good offices of Mukherjee.' After that, there was silence for a long period . . . I got scared of any news from Manto. Visitors from Pakistan did not carry any good news about him. He had become a confirmed alcoholic and borrowed money from everyone. Newspaper owners got him to write articles in their presence and then paid him. If anyone paid him in advance, he just blew up the money.

In his last letter to me, Manto had asked me to write an article on him. 'I'll write the article only after your death.' I had blurted out the inauspicious words involuntarily.

And now I'm writing after his death. Not only Manto but also a lot that had grown between us had died a long time ago. Now there's just this heartache. I don't know why I feel this ache. Is it because Manto is dead and I'm still alive? . . .

There is a voice in my heart that says that I have a hand in Manto's premature death. The invisible bloodstains that smear my conscience can be seen only by my heart. The world that drove him to death is my world as well. It was his turn today. Tomorrow it will be mine. Then people will mourn my death. They will worry no end about my children. They will collect money for a gathering to commemorate me and fail to turn up for the meeting for lack of time. Time will pass, the burden of sorrow will gradually lighten, and then they will forget everything.

In the Name of Those Married Women . . .

It was about four or half past four in the afternoon when the doorbell rang loudly. The servant opened the door, then drew back in fear.

'Who's there?'

'Police!' Whenever a theft took place in the mohalla, all the servants were interrogated.

'Police?' Shahid got up in a huff.

'Yes, sir.' The servant was shaking with fear. 'I haven't done anything, Saab. I swear by God.'

'What's the matter?' Shahid went up to the door and asked.

'Summons.'

'Summons? But . . . well, where is it?'

'Sorry. I can't give it to you.'

'Summons for what? . . . For whom?'

'For Ismat Chughtai. Please call her.' The servant heaved a sigh of relief.

'But tell me this . . .'

'Please call her. The summons is from Lahore.'

I had prepared milk for my two-month-old daughter, Seema, and was waiting for it to cool. 'Summons from Lahore?' I asked as I held the feeding bottle in cold water.

'Yes, from Lahore.' Shahid had lost his cool by then. Holding the bottle in my hand, I came out barefoot.

'What is the summons about?'

'Read it out,' said the police inspector dourly.

As I read the heading – Ismat Chughtai vs. The Crown – I broke into laughter. 'Good God, what complaint does the exalted king have against me that he has filed the suit?'

'It's no joke,' the inspector said severely. 'Read it first, and sign it.' I read through the summons but could barely make out the sense. My story 'Lihaaf' had been accused of obscenity. The government had brought a suit against me, and I had to appear before the Lahore High Court in January. Otherwise the government would penalize me severely.

'Well, I won't take the summons.'

'You have to.'

'Why?' I began to argue, as usual.

'What's up?' This was Mohsin Abdullah sprinting up the stairs. He was returning from some unknown destination, and his whole body was covered with dust.

'Just see, these people want to inflict this summons on me. Why should I take it?' Mohsin had already passed his law exams and obtained a first class.

'I see, which story is this?' he asked after reading the summons.

'It's an ill-fated story that has become a source of torment for me.'

'You'll have to take the summons.'

'Why?'

'Don't be stubborn,' Shahid flared up.

'I won't take it.'

'If you don't, you'll be arrested,' Mohsin growled.

'Let them arrest me. I won't take the summons.'

'You'll be put in prison.'

'In prison? Good. I've a great desire to see a prison house. I've urged Yusuf umpteen times to take me to a prison, but he just smiles. Inspector Saheb, please take me to the jail. Have you brought handcuffs?' I asked him endearingly.

The inspector was flustered. Barely restraining his anger he said, 'Don't joke. Just sign it.'

Shahid and Mohsin railed at me. I was chattering merrily. 'When my father was a judge in Sambhar, the court used to be held in the mardana, the part of the house meant for menfolk. We would watch through the window thieves and robbers being brought in handcuffs and chains. Once a band of fearsome robbers was brought in. They had a beautiful woman among them. A stately figure in coat and breeches, she had the eyes of an eagle, her waist was supple as a leopard's, and she had a luxuriant crop of long, black hair on her head. I was greatly impressed by her . . .'

Shahid and Mohsin made me thoroughly confused. I wanted the inspector to hold the feeding bottle so that I could sign, but he retreated with shock as though I had held a gun at him. Mohsin quickly snatched away the bottle from me, and I signed.

'Come down to the police station to sign the surety document. The surety is for five hundred rupees.'

'I don't have five hundred rupees with me now.'

'Not you. Someone else must stand surety for you.'

'I don't want to implicate anyone. If I don't present myself in court, the money will be lost.' I tried to show off my knowledge of the law. 'Please arrest me.'

The inspector didn't get angry this time. He smiled and looked at Shahid, who was sitting on the sofa holding his head in his hands. Then he said to me gently, 'Please come along. It'll take a couple of minutes.'

'But the surety?' I asked, pacified. I was ashamed of my stupid behaviour.

'I'll stand surety for you,' said Mohsin.

'But my child is hungry. Her ayah is young and inexperienced.'

'Feed the child,' said the inspector.

'Then please come in,' Mohsin invited the policeman. The inspector turned out to be one of Shahid's fans and flattered him so much that he forgot his irritation and began to talk pleasantly.

Mohsin, Shahid and I went to the Mahim police station. Having completed the formalities, I asked, 'Where are the prisoners?'

'Want to see them?'

'Of course.'

There were ten or twelve men lying in a huddle behind the railings.

'These are the accused, not prisoners,' said the inspector.

'What crime have they committed?'

'Brawls, violence, pickpocketing, drunken fights . . .'

'What will be the punishment for them?'

'They'll be fined or imprisoned for a few days.' I felt sorry that I got to see only petty thieves. A couple of murderers or highwaymen would have made the visit more exciting.

'Where would you have put me up?'

'We do not have arrangements to house women prisoners here. They are taken either to Grant Road or Matunga.'

After returning from the police station, Shahid and Mohsin chided me severely. In fact, Shahid fought with me the whole night, even threatened to divorce me. I silenced Mohsin by saying that if he made too much fuss I would disappear and he would lose his five hundred rupees. Shahid could not bear the disgrace and humiliation of a public suit. His parents and elder brother would be terribly upset if they heard of it.

When newspapers published the news, Shahid received a touching letter from my father-in-law, which ran thus: 'Try to reason with Dulhan. Tell her to chant the names of Allah and the Prophet. A lawsuit is bad enough. That, too, on obscenity. We are very worried. May God help you.'

Manto phoned us to say that a suit had been filed against him, too. He had to appear in the same court on the same day. He and Safiya landed up at our place. Manto was looking very happy, as though he had been awarded the Victoria Cross. Though I put up a courageous front, I felt quite embarrassed . . . I was quite nervous, but Manto encouraged me so much that I forgot all my qualms.

'Come on, it's the only great story you've written. Shahid, be a man and come to Lahore with us . . . The winter in Lahore is very severe. Aha! Fried fish with whisky . . . fire in the fireplace like the burning flame in a lover's heart . . . the blood-red maltas are like a lover's kiss.'

'Be quiet, Manto Saheb,' Safiya reprimanded him.

Then, filthy letters began to arrive. They were filled with such inventive and convoluted obscenities that had they been uttered before a corpse, it would have got up and run for cover. Not only me, but my whole family including Shahid and my two-month-old child were dragged in the muck . . .

I am scared of mud, muck and lizards. Many people pretend to be courageous, but they are scared of dead mice. I got scared of my mail as though the envelopes contained snakes, scorpions and dragons. I would read the first few words and then burn the letters. However, if they fell into Shahid's hands, he would repeat his threat of divorce.

Besides these letters, there were articles published in newspapers and debates in literary and cultural gatherings. Only a hard-hearted person like me could put up with them. I never retaliated, nor did I refuse to admit my mistake. I was aware of my fault. Manto was the only person who would get furious at my cowardice. I was against my own self, and he supported me. None of my friends or Shahid's friends attached much importance to it. I am quite sure, but probably Abbas got the English translation of 'Lihaaf' published somewhere. The Progressives neither appreciated nor found fault with me. This suited me well.

I was staying with my brother when I wrote 'Lihaaf'. I had completed the story at night. In the morning I read it out to my sister-in-law. She didn't think it was vulgar, though she recognized the characters portrayed in it. Then I read it out to my aunt's daughter, who was fourteen years old. She didn't understand what the story was about. I sent it to *Adab-e-Lateef*, where it was published immediately. Shahid Ahmad Dehlavi was getting a collection of my short stories published and included it in the volume. The story was published in 1942 when Shahid and I were fast friends and were thinking of marriage. Shahid didn't like the story, and we had a fight. But the controversies surrounding 'Lihaaf' had not reached Bombay yet. Among journals, I subscribed only to *Saaqi* and *Adab-e-Lateef*. Shahid was not too angry, and we got married.

We received the summons in December 1944 to appear before the court in January. Everyone said that we would just be fined, not imprisoned. So we were quite excited and began to get warm clothes stitched for our stay in Lahore.

Seema was a small baby. She was weak and whimpered in a shrill voice. We showed her to a child specialist who declared that she was in good health. Nevertheless, it was not wise to expose her to the severe cold in Lahore. So I left her with Sultana Jafri's mother at Aligarh and set out for Lahore. From Delhi, Shahid Ahmad Dehlavi and the calligrapher who 'copied' the manuscript joined me. The Crown had made him one of the accused as well. The suit was brought not against *Adab-e-Lateef* but against the book published by Shahid Ahmad Dehlavi.

Sultana had come to the station to pick us up. She worked in the Lahore radio station and was staying at Luqman Saheb's place. It was a gorgeous mansion. Luqman Saheb's wife had gone to visit her parents along with her children. Thus the entire place was at our disposal.

Manto had also reached Lahore, and soon we were flooded with invitations. Most of the callers were Manto's friends, but many also wanted to have a look at a strange creature like me. We appeared before the court one day. The judge only asked my name and wanted to know if I had written the story. I admitted to the crime. That was all! . . .

We were greatly disappointed. Our lawyer kept on talking all the time. We couldn't make much of it as we were whispering among ourselves. Then the date for the next hearing was announced, and we were free to freak out. Manto, Shahid and I roamed around in a tonga, shopping. We bought Kashmiri shawls and shoes. When we were buying shoes, the sight of Manto's delicate feet filled me with envy. I almost broke into tears looking at my rough and graceless feet.

'I hate my feet,' said Manto.

'Why? They're so graceful.'

'They are absolutely womanly.'

'So? I thought you have an abiding interest in women.'

'You always argue from the wrong angle. I love women as a man. This does not mean that I want to be a woman myself.'

'Come on, forget this man–woman controversy. Let's talk

about human beings. But, do you know, people with delicate feet are very sensitive and intelligent. My brother Azim Beg Chughtai, too, had very delicate feet. But . . .'

And I was reminded of how his feet had swelled up before he died and become a detestable sight. And Lahore, decked like a newly wedded bride with apples and flowers, was transformed into the sandy graveyard in Jodhpur where my brother was sleeping in his grave under tons of earth. Thorny bushes were planted on his grave so that hyenas did not dig out the corpse. Those thorns began to stab me, and I left the fine pashmina shawl on the counter.

Lahore was beautiful, lush and lively. It greeted everyone with open arms. It was a city of people who were amiable and who loved life. It was the heart of Punjab.

We wandered about the streets of Lahore, our pockets stuffed with pistachios. We popped them into our mouths one after another as we walked along, deep in conversation. Standing in a lane we gorged on fried fish. My appetite was wonderful. In the salubrious climate of Lahore, whatever one ate was digested easily. We entered a hotel. My mouth began to water at the sight of hot dogs and hamburgers.

'Hamburgers contain "ham", that is, pig meat. We can have hot dog,' Shahid said, and we, like good Muslims, stuck to the religious prohibition and abstained from eating hamburgers. We stuffed ourselves with hot dogs, washing them down with the juice of Qandhari pomegranate.

However, we soon realized how crafty the white race is. If hamburgers contain pork, hot dogs contain pork sausages. When he heard this, Shahid felt like vomiting although it was two days since we had eaten the hot dog. It was only when a Maulvi Saheb expressed the view that if one ate it unwittingly one may be forgiven, that Shahid felt somewhat relieved of his emetic fits.

In the evening when Shahid and Manto got themselves drunk, the hamburger–hot dog controversy was revived and raged on for some time. Eventually, it was decided that one should abstain from both because it was impossible to prove conclusively which was halal and which was haram. Under the circumstances, they settled for chicken tikka.

We made the rounds of Anarkali and Shalimar, and saw Noor Jahan's mausoleum. Then followed endless rounds of invitations, mushairas and gossip.

And suddenly, my heart sent up a thanksgiving prayer to the Crown of England for providing us this unique opportunity of enjoying ourselves in Lahore. I began to look forward eagerly to the second hearing. I did not even care if the verdict was that I be hanged. If it occurred in Lahore, I would certainly achieve the status of a martyr. The people of Lahore would give me a befitting funeral.

The second hearing was scheduled for November 1946. The weather was very pleasant. Shahid was preoccupied with his film. Seema was now a healthy child, and her ayah was quite competent, so I left her in Bombay and flew to Delhi. Shahid Ahmad Dehlavi and the calligrapher joined me from there, and we went by train. I used to feel sorry for the calligrapher. He was dragged in for no fault of his own. He was a harmless and quiet sort of fellow with a permanent frown on his face. I used to feel guilty at the very sight of him. Copying the manuscript of my book had brought on all this trouble for him. I asked him, 'What do you think? Shall we win the case?'

'I can't say anything. I haven't read the story.'

'But . . . you've copied it.'

'I see each word separately and do not ponder over its meaning.'

'Strange! And don't you read them after they are printed?'

'I do, to see if there are mistakes.'

'Each word separately?'

'Yes.' He looked down in embarrassment. A few moments later he said, 'I hope you don't mind if I say something?'

'Not at all.'

'Your writings contain many orthographic mistakes.'

'I know. I always confuse siin, swaad and the, zwai, zwaad, zey and zaal. The same happens with the aspirates.'

'Didn't you practise spelling on the slate?'

'I did and always got punished for these mistakes.'

'The fact is, just as I concentrate on words but not on their meaning, you get so impatient to put across your point of view, that you can't pay attention to the letters.'

I prayed for the long life and prosperity of calligraphers. They would rectify my mistakes, and I'd be spared embarrassment.

I went to stay at Mr Aslam's house along with Shahid Saheb. Hardly had we exchanged greetings than he began to blow his top about the alleged obscenity in my writings. I was also like a woman possessed. Shahid Saheb tried to restrain me, but in vain.

'And you've used such vulgar words in your *Gunah ki Ratein*! You've even described the details of the sex act merely for the sake of titillation,' I said.

'My case is different. I'm a man.'

'Am I to blame for that?'

'What do you mean?' His face was flushed with anger.

'What I mean is – God has made you a man, I had no hand in it, and He has made me a woman, you had no hand in it. You have the freedom to write whatever you want, you don't need my permission. Similarly, I don't feel any need to seek your permission for writing the way I want to.'

'You're an educated girl from a decent Muslim family.'

'You're also educated. And from a decent Muslim family.'

'Do you want to compete with men?'

'Certainly not. I always endeavoured to obtain higher marks than the boys in the class and often succeeded.'

I knew that I was being pig-headed as usual. Aslam Saheb's face was red-hot with anger. I was afraid that he would hit me or that his jugular vein would burst. Shahid Saheb was aghast, almost in tears. I assumed a softer tone and said humbly, 'Aslam Saheb, actually no one has told me that it was a sin to write on the subject with which "Lihaaf" is concerned. Nor had I read in any book that such a disease . . . such aberrations should not be written about. Perhaps my mind is not an artist's brush like Abdur Rahman Chughtai's but an ordinary camera that records reality as it is. The pen becomes helpless in my hand because my mind overwhelms it. Nothing can interfere with this traffic between the mind and the pen.'

'Wasn't any religious education imparted to you?'

'Aslam Saheb, I've read *Behishti Zevar.* Such revealing things are written there . . .' I said innocently. Aslam Saheb looked upset. I continued, 'When I had read it in my childhood, I was shocked. Those things seemed vulgar to me. But when I read it again after my B.A. I realized that they were not vulgar but important facts of life about which every sensible person should be aware. Well, people can brand the books prescribed in the courses of psychology and medicine vulgar if they so want.'

The storm subsided, and we began to talk in normal tones. Aslam Saheb had cooled down quite a bit. Meanwhile, breakfast was served. We were four, but the elaborate arrangement would have been enough for fifteen people. There were three or four kinds of eggs – plain, fried, scrambled, boiled. Shami kabab, keema, parantha, poori, toast with white and yellow butter, yoghurt, milk, honey, dry fruits, egg halwa, carrot halwa and sohan halwa.

'By God, do you want to kill us?'

I had teased him enough. To make up for it I now began to praise his writings. I had read his *Nargis* and *Gunah ki Ratein* and began to praise them in superlative terms. Eventually he came round to the view that a deliberately stark style of narration made for both clarity and instruction. Then he began to enumerate the merits of all the books that he had written. Now he was in a genial mood.

'Tender an apology to the judge,' Aslam Saheb advised gently.

'Why? Our lawyer says that we'll win the case.'

'Nonsense! If you and Manto tender your apologies, the case can be wound up in five minutes.'

'Many respectable people here have put pressure on the government to bring the suit against us.'

'Nonsense!' Aslam Saheb said but could not look me in the eye.

'Do you mean the king of England or the people in the government have actually read the stories and thought about filing this suit?'

'Aslam Saheb, some writers, critics and people in high positions have drawn the attention of the government to the books as being detrimental to morality and urged that they be banned,' said Shahid Saheb in a subdued tone.

'If morally detrimental writings are not to be banned, should we offer homage to them?' Aslam Saheb growled and Shahid Saheb cowered in embarrassment.

'Then we deserve punishment,' I said.

'Being pig-headed again!'

'No, Aslam Saheb, I really meant it. If I've committed a crime and innocent people have been led astray, why should I escape punishment merely by tendering an apology? If I've committed the crime and if it is proved, only punishment can bring peace to my conscience then,' I said sincerely, without any trace of irony.

'Don't be obstinate. Tender the apology.'

'What will the punishment be after all? I'll be fined?'

'It'll bring you disgrace.'

'Arré, I've suffered enough disgrace. It can't be worse. This lawsuit is nothing compared to that.' Then I asked, 'How much will they fine me?'

'Two or three hundred, I suppose,' said Shahid Saheb.

'That's all?'

'Maybe five hundred,' threatened Aslam Saheb.

'That's *all*?'

'Have you come into piles of money?' Aslam Saheb was incensed.

'With your blessings. Even if I don't have money, won't you pay up five hundred rupees to save me from going to jail? You are counted among the aristocrats of Lahore.'

'You have a glib tongue.'

'My mother had the same complaint. She used to say, "A glib tongue invites misfortune."'

Everyone laughed, and the tension in the atmosphere dissolved. However, a few moments later he began to repeat his plea for an apology. I felt like smashing his head and mine as well.

Then he changed the topic all of a sudden and asked me, 'Why did you write "Duzakhi"?'

There was an explosion in my head.

'What kind of a sister are you to characterize your own brother as being hell-bound?'

'He might be hell-bound or heaven-bound, what's that to you?'

'He was my friend.'

'He was my brother!'

'Curse on a sister like you!'

I haven't told anyone till today what anguish I went through while writing 'Duzakhi', what fires of hell I traversed and how much of me was burnt in that fire. It was late in the night. The clock had struck two when I finished writing the sketch. What a terrible night it was! The sea had risen up to the steps of our house. The boundary wall had not been erected till then. A storm was raging in my breast. Whatever I had written seemed to roll around me like a cinema reel. As I put out the lamp I felt suffocated. Afraid, I lit the lamp again. I was afraid of the dark. I was reminded vividly of the grave in which the body of my brother was lowered by the pall bearers. After seeing his grave I could not sleep alone in my room for months. My aunt's daughter, much younger to me, would sleep beside me and keep me company. I felt suffocated in Jodhpur and ran away to Bombay. Out of ten pillars one had caved in. Who could have fathomed the gulf it had created?

Without giving any reply to Aslam Saheb, I quietly went to my room and started packing my suitcase. I phoned Sultana and asked her to come immediately and take me away. 'If Aslam Saheb tries to stop me, just blow him up,' I told her.

'What's wrong? . . . I'll be there as soon as the office shuts at 5 p.m.'

'Oh no! By then there will be a murder or two. Come right away.'

Sultana arrived in a few minutes. Aslam Saheb refused to let me go, but Sultana, as instructed, would not give in. As the tug of war between them went on, I split my sides with laughter. Eventually, I left with Sultana.

We appeared before the court on the day of the hearing. The witnesses who had to prove that Manto's story 'Bu' and my story 'Lihaaf' were obscene, were all present. My lawyer instructed me not to open my mouth till the interrogation began. He would answer the queries as he deemed fit.

'Bu' was taken up first.

'Is this story obscene?' Manto's lawyer asked.

'Yes,' answered the witness.

'Can you put your finger on a word which is obscene?'

Witness: 'The word "chest".'

Lawyer: 'My lord, the word "chest" is not obscene.'

Witness: 'No. But here the writer means a woman's breasts.'

Manto was on his feet instantly and blurted out: 'A woman's chest must be called breasts and not groundnuts.'

The court reverberated with loud guffaws. Manto also began to laugh.

'If the accused shows his frivolity a second time, he will be turned out or severely punished for contempt of court.'

Manto's lawyers whispered into his ear, and he understood the situation. The debate went on. The witnesses could find no other words except 'chest', and it could not be proved obscene.

'If the word "chest" is obscene, why not "knee" or "elbow"?' I asked Manto.

'Nonsense!' Manto growled.

The arguments continued. We went out and sat on the benches. Ahmad Nadeem Qasmi had brought a basketful of maltas. He also taught us a fine way of savouring them. 'Squeeze the malta to make it soft, like one does a mango. Then pierce a hole in it and go on sucking the juice merrily.' Sitting there, we sucked up the whole basket.

The maltas only whetted our appetite, and we stormed into a hotel during the lunch break. Because I had been very sick when Seema was born and lost a lot of weight, I was not allowed any fatty food. However, the chicken served to us was as tough as an eagle. We garnished it with large black peppers and ate it with kulchas. And in place of water, there was Qandhari pomegranate juice. Involuntarily a prayer came out from my heart for the people who had filed the lawsuit.

In the evening, Luqman had invited a few writers and poets. There, for the first time in my life, I met Hijab Imtiaz Ali. She was heavily made up, a thick lining of kajal in her eyes. She looked somewhat angry, somewhat melancholic. Whenever anyone asked her a question, she would start gazing into space.

'A fraud,' Manto whispered into my ears, dilating his large eyes.

'No, she is lost in the world of dreams created by her pen and prefers to stay in that multicoloured shell.'

Hijab Imtiaz Ali kept on looking into space while I hunted out Imtiaz Ali and started talking to him. What a world of difference there was in the temperaments of husband and wife. Imtiaz Saheb was garrulous, open-hearted and full of laughter. The assembly was at its glorious best. It seemed to me that I had known him for years. His talk was even more lively than his writings. Recently when I went to Pakistan, I met Hijab Imtiaz Ali again. She wore light makeup and looked younger and lively. She was absolutely informal and friendly. It was as though she had been born again!

I had a great desire to see an aarghanoon, allusions to which were too frequent in Hijab's stories. When I went to her house I asked her, 'Do you really have an aarghanoon?'

'Yes. Do you want to have a look at it?'

'Of course. This word in your stories had an intoxicating effect on me.' I also told her that at one time I had written some prose verse in imitation of hers, which I had burnt later.

At the sight of the aarghanoon all my zest and romance fizzled out. It was the same sort of baby piano that de Melo played in film songs! It was used as background music to produce tunes to suggest the heroine's mental state when she was angry! The word 'organ' is so dull, the addition of 'ghain' made it sound like a lilting tune of Asavari.

The court was crowded the next day. Several persons had advised us to tender an apology. They were ready to pay the fine on our behalf. The excitement surrounding the lawsuits was waning. The witnesses who had turned up to prove 'Lihaaf' obscene were thrown into confusion by my lawyer. They were not able to put their finger on any word in the story that would prove their point. After a good deal of reflection, one of them said: 'This phrase " . . . collecting lovers" is obscene.'

'Which word is obscene – "collect" or "lover"?' the lawyer asked.

' "Lover",' replied the witness a little hesitantly.

'My lord, the word "lover" has been used by great poets most liberally. It is also used in naats, that is, poems written in praise of the Prophet. God-fearing people have accorded it a very high status.'

'But it is objectionable for girls to collect lovers,' said the witness.

'Why?'

'Because . . . because it is objectionable for good girls to do so.'

'And if the girls are not good, then it is not objectionable?'

'Mmm . . . no.'

'My client must have referred to the girls who were not good. Yes, madam, do you mean here that bad girls collect lovers?'

'Yes.'

'Well, this may not be obscene. But it is reprehensible for an educated lady from a decent family to write about it,' the witness thundered.

'Censure it as much as you want. But it does not come within the purview of law.' The issue lost much of its steam.

'If you agree to apologize, we'll pay up the entire expense incurred by you . . .' someone I didn't know whispered into my ear.

'Should we apologize, Manto Saheb? We can buy a lot of goodies with the money we'll get,' I suggested to Manto.

'Nonsense!' growled Manto as his peacock eyes bulged out.

'I'm sorry. This madcap Manto doesn't agree.'

'But you . . . why don't you . . . ?'

'No. You don't know what a quarrelsome fellow he is! He'll make my life miserable in Bombay. I'd rather undergo the punishment than risk his wrath.' The gentleman was disappointed that we were not penalized.

The judge called me into the anteroom attached to the court and said quite informally, 'I've read most of your stories. They aren't obscene. Neither is "Lihaaf". But Manto's writings are often littered with filth.'

'The world is also littered with filth,' I said in a feeble voice.

'Is it necessary to rake it up, then?'

'If it is raked up it becomes visible, and people feel the need to clean it up.'

The judge laughed.

I was not terribly worried when the suit was filed, neither did I feel elated now that I had won it. Rather I felt sad at the thought that it might be a long while before I would get a chance to visit Lahore again.

Lahore! How beautiful the word sounds! Lahori salt crystals are like gems – white and pink. I felt like getting them chiselled and fixed in my chandan haar and then draping the garland around the swan-like neck of some fair tribal woman.

'Nammi nammi tariyan di lau' – Surinder Kaur's lilting voice was enchanting. The accompanying voice of Sodhi, her husband, was like the rustle of fine silk. The city of Lahore reminded one of the music of Surinder and Sodhi. One felt a tumult in one's heart, and a great sense of contentment. The memory of the unknown, ethereal lover invaded one's being with the force of an anguished ache.

The air of Lahore is shot through with a special light. The bells tinkle in silence and one almost feels the fragrant ambience created by the writings of Hijab Imtiaz Ali. And one is immediately taken back to that phase of life when one got so lost in the twilight world of her stories.

Then it all changed.

I read Charles Dickens – *David Copperfield*, *Oliver Twist*, *Tono Bungay*. And Gorky's *Mother* – all of which brought me back from the world of romance to the world of reality. Chekhov, Émile Zola, Gogol, Tolstoy, Dostoevsky, Maupassant . . .

All the castles of my dreams came crashing down! And I was thrown back, as it were, into the thatched bungalow near Lai Diggi in Aligarh where we lived. This bungalow was made of raw bricks, and if one hit a nail in the wall, the clay came down in a deluge of sand. The floor was littered with the droppings of pigeons who made their nests in the house. Bats hung from the beams. The bungalow had an earthen floor, and whenever there was a duststorm, a whirlwind would rage inside the house. There was neither electricity nor tap water. The bhishti would carry water to the house in his camelskin bag. There were string cots on which would be laid durries and dirty khaddar sheets. The pillows were sticky with oil. Amma had given up wearing her baggy farshi pyjamas that required twelve yards of cloth and had started wearing a dhoti.

There was a time when we had had a horde of servants in the house. Amma would provide shelter to the needy who came begging for alms. After Abba Mian retired, she had to exercise economy. Only Ali Bakhsh and his wife Shekhani Bua, who did the cooking, remained. In addition to them we had to retain the kochwan and his wife because we still owned two horses and a buffalo.

I was probably jealous of the poetic aura created by Imtiaz Ali. Our family atmosphere was not at all conducive to romance. I had written my first story, 'Bachpan', after a good deal of reflection. The only journal our family subscribed to was *Tehzeeb-e-Niswaan*, to which I sent this story. It came back along with a letter of reprimand from the editor, Mumtaz Ali Saheb, the father of Imtiaz

Ali Taj. In the story I had compared my childhood with that of Hijab Imtiaz Ali. The point of his objection was that I had described in the story how I was beaten by the Maulvi Saheb for my inability to recite verses from the Quran correctly. I could never produce the sound of 'ain'; if I tried hard, it would be 'qaaf'. He wrote that by making fun of the Quran I had been irreverent and blasphemous.

Later, when my writings began to appear in journals, this story was published in *Saaqi*, and people liked it a lot. I also got fed up with Azim Bhai's stories and their stilted romantic ambience. They were false, and didn't contain any inkling of the anguish of his own life. He wrote about the mischief and antics of his brothers as though they were his own.

I was a spoilt brat and used to get bashed up often for telling the truth. But when the disputes were taken to Abba Mian, he would decide in my favour. My elder sister, who had become a widow at nineteen, was extremely bitter about life. She was greatly impressed with the high society at Aligarh, particularly the Khwaja family. I couldn't get along with the begums of that family even for a moment. I was a madcap – outspoken and ill-mannered. Purdah had already been imposed on me, but my tongue was an unsheathed sword. No one could restrain it.

The world around me seemed like a delusion. The apparently shy and respectable girls of these families allowed themselves to be grabbed and kissed in bathrooms and in dark corners by their young male relatives. Such girls were considered modest. Which boy would have taken interest in a plain Jane like me? I had studied so much that whenever there was a debate, I would beat to a pulp all the young men who were scared of the sight of books. They considered themselves superior to women merely because they were men!

Then I read *Angare* on the sly. Rasheed Aapa was the only person who instilled a sense of confidence in me. I accepted her as my mentor. In the hypocritical, vicious atmosphere of Aligarh, she was a much-maligned lady. She appreciated my outspokenness, and I quickly read up all the books recommended by her.

Then I started writing. My play *Fasaadi* was published in *Saaqi*. After that I wrote several stories. None of them was ever rejected. Suddenly some people began to object to them, but the demand from journals went on increasing. I didn't care much for the objections.

But when I wrote 'Lihaaf', there was a veritable explosion. I was torn to shreds in the literary arena. Some people also wielded their pens in my support.

Since then I have been branded an obscene writer. No one bothered about what I had written before or after 'Lihaaf'. I was put down as a purveyor of sex. It is only in the last couple of years that the younger generation has recognized that I am a realist and not an obscene writer.

I am fortunate that I have been appreciated in my lifetime. Manto was driven mad to the extent that he became a wreck. The Progressives did not come to his rescue. In my case, they didn't write me off, nor did they offer me great accolades. Manto became a pauper in Pakistan. My circumstances were quite comfortable – the income from my career in films was substantial, and I didn't care much for a literary death or life. I continued to remain a follower of the Progressives and endeavoured to bring about a revolution!

I am still labelled as the writer of 'Lihaaf'. The story brought me so much notoriety that I got sick of life. It became the proverbial stick to beat me with and whatever I wrote afterwards got crushed under its weight.

When I wrote *Terhi Lakeer* and sent it to Shahid Ahmad Dehlavi, he gave it to Muhammad Hasan Askari for his opinion. After reading it, Askari advised me to make my heroine a lesbian like the protagonist in 'Lihaaf'. I was furious. I got the novel back even though the calligrapher had started working on it, and handed it over to Nazir Ahmad in Lahore. Lahore was then a part of India.

'Lihaaf' had made my life miserable. Shahid and I had so many fights over the story that life became a battlefield.

I went to Aligarh after many years. The thought of the begum who was the subject of my story made my hair stand on end. She had already been told that 'Lihaaf' was based on her life.

We stood face to face during a dinner. I felt the ground under my feet receding. She looked at me with her big eyes that conveyed excitement and joy. Then she cruised through the crowd, leapt at me and took me in her arms. Drawing me to one side she said, 'Do you know, I divorced the nawab and married a second time? I've got a pearl of a son, by God's grace.'

I felt like throwing myself into someone's arms and crying my heart out. I couldn't restrain my tears, though, in fact, I was laughing loudly. She invited me to a fabulous dinner. I felt fully rewarded when I saw her flower-like boy. I felt he was mine as well. A part of my mind, a living product of my brain. An offspring of my pen.

And I realized at that moment that flowers can be made to bloom in rocks. The only condition is that one has to water the plant with one's heart's blood.

Just one thing more.

I had asked a gentleman, 'Do you think "Lihaaf" is morally subversive?'

'Undoubtedly.'

'Why do you think so?'

'When one reads the story, one feels sexually aroused.'

'I see. And you want to snuggle into a lihaaf?'

'Oh no. Actually, Begum Jaan is very sexy. She's ravishingly beautiful, endowed with sap and sweetness. A well-proportioned body, warm lips, intoxicating eyes. She's a burning flame, a cup overflowing with wine.'

'So?'

'The devil tempts one.'

'What does she say?'

'To — her.'

'The devil is wise. My objective was just that. How I wanted that some brave fellow should release her from Rabbu's clutches, encircle her within his strong arms and slake her life's thirst. It's a virtuous act to provide water to a thirsty creature.'

'May I have her address?'

'You've been born rather late in the day. By God's grace, she's now a grandmother. Many years ago a prince released her from the magic castle of the Black Giant and transported her to the spring-garden of life.'

From a nearby apartment, the voice of Naiyera Noor came floating across. She was singing Faiz's verse:

In the name of those married women
whose decked-up bodies
atrophied on loveless,
deceitful beds . . .

And I wondered, Where is the Ideal Indian Woman?

Sita, the embodiment of purity, whose lotus-like feet cooled the flames on which she had to walk.

Mira Bai, who put her arms around God himself.

Savitri, who snatched away her husband's life from the Angel of Death.

And Razia Sultana, who spurned great emperors and joined her destiny with that of a Moorish slave.

Is she getting suffocated today under the lihaaf?

Or, is she playing Holi with her own blood in Faras Road?

PENGUIN WOMEN WRITERS

BIRDS OF AMERICA BY MARY McCARTHY
With an introduction by Penelope Lively

Peter Levi, a shy and sensitive American teenager, moves to Paris to avoid being drafted into the Vietnam War, where he is determined to live a life in harmony with his own idealistic views. But the world is changing at breakneck pace, with nuclear war looming abroad and racial tensions simmering at home. Before long, Peter's naïve illusions are shattered, as he finds himself an unwilling participant in an era of extraordinary change.

Birds of America is an unforgettable and deeply moving story of personal and political turmoil; of the strange and surprising nature of growing up; and of the questions we face when we examine who we really are.

'Fiercely intelligent, insatiably combative, McCarthy's novels invite controversy' Penelope Lively, from the introduction

'A writer known for her immaculate prose, her wit, her glamour' *New Yorker*

THE LARK BY E NESBIT
With an introduction by Penelope Lively

"When did two girls of our age have such a chance as we've got-to have a lark entirely on our own? No chaperone, no rules, no..."
"No present income or future prospects," said Lucilla.

It's 1919 and Jane and her cousin Lucilla leave school to find that their guardian has gambled away their money, leaving them with only a small cottage in the English countryside. In an attempt to earn their living, the orphaned cousins embark on a series of misadventures – cutting flowers from their front garden and selling them to passers-by, inviting paying guests who disappear without paying – all the while endeavouring to stave off the attentions of male admirers, in a bid to secure their independence.

'A charming and brilliantly entertaining novel… shot through with the light-hearted Nesbit touch' Penelope Lively, from the introduction

'An unparalleled talent for evoking hot summer days in the English countryside' Noel Streatfield